Praise for

SOMEONE KNOWS

"*Someone Knows* is a compulsive read that has it all: remarkable writing, gut-wrenching suspense, and a jaw-dropping ending."

—Holly Kammier
Bestselling author of *Lost Girl, A Shelby Day Novel*

"*Someone Knows* is an unrelenting thriller, deliciously written, with twists that come faster than you can turn the pages."

—Lacey Impellizeri-Papenhausen
Bestselling author of *Your Words Count*

"'Oh, what a wicked web we weave' has never been truer. *Someone Knows* is a nail-biting murder mystery that keeps you guessing all the way to the big surprise at the end."

—Pam McCord
Award-winning, bestselling author of *Under the Willows*

SOMEONE KNOWS

by

MARK ATTEBERRY

FROM THE TINY ACORN...
GROWS THE MIGHTY OAK

www.acornpublishingllc.com
For information, address:
Acorn Publishing, LLC
3943 Irvine Blvd. Ste. 218
Irvine, CA 92602

Someone Knows

Cover design by Damonza.com
Interior design by Lacey Impellizeri-Papenhausen
Interior formatting by Debra Cranfield Kennedy

Printed in the United States of America

ISBN-13: 979-8-88528-008-2 (hardcover)
ISBN-13: 979-8-88528-007-5 (paperback)
Library of Congress Control Number: 2021924793

PART 1

*"Everything can change at any moment,
suddenly and forever."*

—Paul Auster

- 1 -

Why did I do it?

Why did I have an affair?

Six months ago, if you had asked what the chances were of me ever cheating on Mary Beth, I would have laughed and said, "None." I would have argued that, while I find women as attractive as the next guy, what I *don't* find attractive is the idea of destroying my marriage and ruining my reputation. Anyone who knows me will tell you I am, at heart, a guy who prefers not to take big risks, and other than skydiving without a parachute, there is no bigger risk than cheating on your wife. There are so many things that can go wrong. So many ways your best laid plans can implode. If your own missteps don't do you in, some random, quirky, impossible-to-anticipate coincidence will blow in like the first wind of winter and expose everything. The smartest, most accomplished men in the world have learned that their brilliant plotting and scheming and playacting produced nothing but a house of cards.

To further mark the absurdity of your question, I would have had you get to know Mary Beth and tell me one thing about her a man—*any* man—wouldn't love. Her sparkling intelligence, character, and sense of humor—traits I have cherished since the moment I met her—

1

set her apart. And yes, she is physically attractive. Not movie star beautiful, but girl-next-door pretty, which, to my way of thinking, is the best kind of attractive a woman can be.

And then I would've pointed to my faith. I'm a guy who believes in God, who has actually read the Bible, who goes to church, who believes in right and wrong. I realize that might sound lame to you, considering that history is saturated with nefarious acts committed by religious people. Still, my faith has been a primary driver of my thoughts and decisions for virtually all of my thirty-seven years. I would have counted it as a trustworthy defense against the kind of turbo-charged temptation that is required to make a man throw his life away.

And yet, there I was, locked in our guest bathroom, hands on the counter, staring with contempt at my own face in the mirror. It's tempting to say I didn't recognize that face, that I had become a stranger to myself. And maybe there was a time early on when that was true. But after three months of lying and sneaking and pretending and stomping underfoot every one of my most cherished values, not to mention my marriage vows, I had come to know myself sickeningly well.

I was not the man I'd always believed I was.

I remember thinking as I stood before the mirror that I had aged dramatically since venturing off the straight and narrow. The lines in my face were deeper and the gray at my temples more pronounced, or so it appeared to me. I felt like a former U.S. president must feel when he looks at his pre-term and post-term photos. Wear and tear, they call it. Only mine came not from running a country but from running a scam. Who's to say which is more stressful?

All I had going for me at that moment was the determination to set things right. But it wasn't a decision I had come to easily. For months, my emotions had been running the gamut from shame to excitement, from wanting to drive off a bridge and kill myself out of guilt to fantasizing about running away with Faith to start a new life. I'd like to tell you some long-dormant virtue had risen within me, like a phoenix from the ashes, to restore my sanity. But in order for that to be true I would've needed to have some shred of virtue left, and I'm not sure I did. The one thing I do know is I was tired—tired of the lies, tired of the guilt, tired of the feeling I was one quirky coincidence away from being exposed and having my life blown apart. Most of all, I was tired of seeing the look of unfettered love in Mary Beth's eyes when she kissed my cheek as I left for work or when she blinked sleep from her eyes and told me good morning. Yes, I think that's what sickened me most . . . knowing I was so unworthy of my loving wife.

From the family room, Mary Beth muted the TV and called out: "Are you okay in there?"

"Fine. Be right out." I said it with as chipper a voice as I could muster. Then I flushed the unused toilet and ran some water in the sink as if to wash my hands in yet another tiny deception in a parade of lies that had been marching through our house for months. There would be more to come, at least for the next hour or so. By then I hoped to have taken the first step back to being the man I used to be, the man I truly, desperately wanted to be once again.

With one final glance in the mirror, I opened the bathroom door and walked into the family room where I found Mary Beth watching one of her Food Network programs. As far as I knew, she had never made a single recipe they ever demonstrated. She did, however, keep up a running commentary on the personal lives and foibles of the program hosts. How anyone could find people who cook for a living so interesting, I had not the first clue. Nor did I know where she got her information about their dark secrets. But she spoke about them with the authority of an Ivy League professor, which was good enough for me.

"I need to run to the office for a bit," I said, pretend-texting on my phone to help sell the lie. "I shouldn't be gone more than an hour."

Mary Beth glanced at her watch and said, "At eight-thirty in the evening? Why?"

"Mike needs the faculty's design ideas for the new multi-purpose building, and they're on my office computer." Mike Waterson was our district superintendent and a close friend.

"Can't he wait until morning?"

"Nope. He was meeting with the architects tomorrow afternoon, but he just found out the meeting got moved up to eight in the morning. One of them apparently had a family emergency and is flying out around noon. Mike wants a chance to look the list over tonight. I just need to check it and make sure we didn't forget to include something, then send it to him. I won't be gone long."

It was all true, every word of it. What I failed to mention was that, while the document in question was indeed on my computer at the school, it was also on a thumb drive in my briefcase not five feet from where I was standing. I could've gone into my home office right down the hall, reviewed it, and sent it to Mike.

I leaned over the back of the couch and kissed Mary Beth on the cheek as she made some comment about Bobby Flay's less than enviable record as a husband, something about three ex-wives and a girlfriend. "What is it with guys like that?" she muttered.

Sometimes life's ironies are just too much.

I grabbed my keys and was out the door before she had a chance to turn around and see shame written all over my face.

- 2 -

I hired Faith Connelly to teach second grade at Lake Arbor Elementary in South Orlando shortly before school started. The position opened midsummer, so I had to move the process along quickly. I interviewed three people for the position, all women. Of the two I didn't choose, one was fresh out of college and the other was returning to teaching after a several-year layoff because she'd grown weary of sitting home every day with her much older, retired, and very curmudgeonly husband. It would be easy to accuse me of hiring Faith because she was attractive, personable, and about my age, but I can honestly say those factors had nothing to do with my decision.

I never would have chosen her if I'd thought her qualifications were weak or that she might not be able to handle the job. Such a decision would have only made my life more difficult because, as principal, I would've been the one tasked with cleaning up her messes and working around her weaknesses. Who in his right mind would choose to make a hard job harder by adding someone he thinks will be a headache?

Any concerns I had about Faith's competence were laid to rest when I learned she had teaching experience and great references. In my mind, the factor that moved her to the front of the line was that she desperately needed a job. Her husband, Brian, who made a decent living remodeling kitchens and bathrooms, had sold drugs to an undercover police officer and then assaulted him for good measure. What might have been a one-year sentence was multiplied several times over when his fist connected with the officer's jaw. Faith, who'd gotten out of teaching when their daughter had come along, essentially became a single mom because of her husband's incarceration. She had been working part time on weekends as a cashier at Publix, but when her husband's sentence was announced, she immediately started looking for a job with benefits and insurance.

For all my faults, I've at least always had a heart for the underdog. It was true when I was a kid and would find a bird with a broken wing, and when I was in high school and would step up to protect the geeky kid everyone was picking on. In this case, I figured the applicant who was the recent college graduate had her whole life in front of her and the bored older lady with the cranky husband didn't need the job as much as she needed something to do, which she could find someplace other than in a classroom. Hiring Faith was, to my way of thinking, a win-win situation. She would get the job she desperately needed and our school would get a well-recommended, highly motivated teacher.

I'll never forget the day I told her she got the job. I'd called her in for a second interview, pretty sure I was going to hire her but still needing to tie up a couple of loose ends. I could tell she was nervously optimistic. She sat across from my desk, perched on the edge of the chair, clutching her purse in her lap. I could see the tendons working in the backs of her hands as she kneaded the leather.

After a few follow-up questions to clarify a couple of small matters, I said, "Well, Faith, you've answered everything to my satisfaction, so I'd like to make it official and offer you the job."

Her right hand flew up to cover her mouth and her eyes squeezed shut. I thought she was going to burst into tears, but after a few seconds she gathered herself and simply smiled. "Thank you so much, Mr. Vincent. I promise you won't regret this."

Again, life's ironies.

So yes, I can see where her general attractiveness, age, and the precarious state of her marriage might make one wonder about my motives, especially in light of what eventually happened. But with God as my witness, I didn't have a single illicit thought at the time. It was a solid, professional decision I believe most principals in my position would have made.

- 3 -

I was always nervous when I was on my way to meet Faith. We were careful, of course. We planned every rendezvous down to the tiniest detail. And we had a standing rule that if either of us caught even a whiff of danger, we would abort immediately and explain later. It didn't happen often, but there had indeed been a couple of instances when one or the other of us didn't show due to an unexpected development. I prayed this would not be one of those times. I was finally ready to clean up the mess I had made and set things right. If something prevented us from meeting, who knew when we'd have another chance? The longer things dragged on, the harder it would be for me to hide the stress of my growing guilt from Mary Beth.

The one thing I refused to do was end our relationship with a phone call. Though our behavior well surpassed the bounds of propriety, we were friends before we were anything else and had been through a lot together. I felt a phone call would seem callous or, even worse, cowardly. Plus, there were specific things I wanted to say to her face. I wanted to confess my sin and apologize for my behavior. Most of all, I wanted to ask her to forgive me. Somewhere in the back of my mind, I might also have been worried about how she would react and wanted to be there to reason with her if anger got the best of her. One thing I learned about Faith early on was that she had a fiery temper.

As I drove through the quiet streets, I wondered what Faith was thinking. I'd asked for the meeting on short notice, which was not our normal routine (as if anything about our routine could be called normal). I always respected the fact that she had Zoey, who is only six years old, to think about. She couldn't just run off and leave her because I decided I wanted to meet. Often, our get-togethers were planned at least a day or two in advance so she could make arrangements for Zoey to be taken care of, either by a sitter or a family member.

Naturally, the short notice request prompted Faith to ask me if everything was okay. I wanted to tell her no, everything was not okay, that nothing would ever be okay again as long as we were leading double lives, as long as hypocrisy was the defining essence of our relationship. Instead, I told her everything was fine and I just wanted to see her. She didn't question me further, but something in her tone told me she was suspicious.

It was dark when I arrived at the spot where I intended to leave my car. We'd learned, as I suppose all cheaters do, where we could meet and remain unseen. There were no guarantees, of course. When the majority of the earth's surface is under video surveillance, you don't ever get cocky about your ability to hide. But we were thoughtful about it and had discovered a place that worked well: a half-mile-long hiking trail that wound through a thickly wooded section of Belle Isle Park.

There were a few vapor lights along the trail and, at the halfway point, a bench with a water fountain for those pitifully out of shape people who found their endurance tested by such a short distance. After dark, the park was mostly deserted and the bench became the perfect out-of-the-way place to sit and talk. We'd been there several times and had never seen a soul. The trick was to leave our cars in different places outside the park so no one who knew us would see us enter the park together and draw the obvious conclusion.

I drove past one of the places Faith liked to leave her car and saw it sitting there empty. She'd apparently arrived a little early and had already made her way into the park. Feeling a sense of urgency, I stepped on the gas and quickly made my way to one of my own parking spots a couple of streets away. Before getting out, I looked around carefully. Even though the kids in this neighborhood were not zoned for our school, I was always afraid the parent of some kid I used to have in school might be out walking the family dog. *Oh, hi, Mr. Vincent. What are you doing here?* Many a cheater has been exposed by such quirky coincidences.

When I was certain the coast was clear, I jumped out of the car and took off into the park. Faith and I would be approaching from opposite directions. We usually met at the trail entrance and walked to the bench together, arm in arm. Tonight, I would not be putting my arm around her, which would tell her everything she needed to know about why I'd asked her to meet me. It occurred to me that we might not make it as far as the bench. Things might come to a head well before we got there, which would be okay. I just wanted to get this over with and get back home to Mary Beth.

My head was on a swivel as I approached the trail entrance. On a prior occasion, Faith had been standing well back among the trees, virtually invisible until she jumped out and scared me half to death. She had laughed so hard. Tonight, however, I saw her standing underneath one of the vapor lights in yoga pants and sneakers, with her hands jammed into the pockets of a short jacket. As I approached, she looked around to make sure no one was about.

Adulterers spend a lot of time looking around.

Ordinarily, I would have embraced her, and we would have kissed. That night I stopped a few feet short and said, "Thanks for coming."

She noticed the difference, which seemed to confirm her suspicions. She said, "What's going on?"

I nodded toward the trail. "Can we walk?"

She shrugged and fell in beside me. We hadn't gone ten feet when she said, "We're breaking up, aren't we?"

The last thing I'd expected was for her to tee it up for me with such a simple question. Even if she suspected I wanted to end our affair, I thought she would put me through the agony of trying to find the words.

"Don't you agree it would be the right thing to do?"

She scoffed. "What . . . you can't just answer my question? You have to ask one instead to somehow put this on me?"

She was right. I needed to be a man and say what was on my mind.

"Yes," I said. "I asked you to meet me so I could tell you I think we need to end it."

"You *think?*"

I sighed. "I *know.*"

We walked on for a while in silence, which was making me even more uncomfortable than I already was. Finally, I said as tenderly as I could, "Faith, you know it's the right thing to do."

"Oh, I know it is. I'd never argue that point. But you know what? It was the right thing to do one minute after we started. It's been the right thing to do every minute of every day for the last three months. I'm just wondering why you're getting so righteous all of a sudden."

Any hope I might've had that she would make this easy officially expired with those words. I said, "That's a fair question. I guess I've come to my senses."

She threw her head back and laughed. "Oh, thank you. Only a crazy person would be attracted to me, is that it?"

"That's not what I meant," I said lamely.

By then we had reached the bench. She sat down on one end and I sat on the other, leaving a good three feet between us. Always before, we'd sat in the middle, pressed up against each other.

"So what do we do now?" she said. "Go back to work and pretend nothing ever happened?"

"That shouldn't be too hard, should it? Seems to me we've become experts at pretending nothing was happening."

Just then we heard a twig snap as if someone had taken a step in the dark shadows surrounding us. It was hard to tell where the sound had come from, causing both Faith and I to look around in all directions. The vapor light above us cast a faint glow about twenty feet in diameter. Beyond, it was complete darkness.

"What was that?" Faith said.

"Probably a rabbit or something."

"Must've been a big rabbit."

"Do you want to go?" I said, hoping she'd say yes. The conversation wasn't going well, and I didn't see it turning around. The sooner we wrapped things up, the better.

Then we heard what sounded like another step, and another, this time clearly coming from the darkness across the path directly in front of us. And Faith was right: No rabbit I'd ever seen would make such a sound. Never before had I felt uneasy sitting on that bench at night. As I said, we'd never seen a soul. But now, suddenly, I felt very uneasy. Someone was out there.

She stood up and said, "Yes, I want to go."

I stood, too, just as a voice came out of the darkness: "What's your hurry?"

It was a rich, baritone voice and not at all unfriendly. The words were spoken like a gracious host might say them to dinner guests who'd just announced it was time for them to get going. Faith stepped closer to me and took my arm as a man stepped to the edge of the vapor light's glow. He was taller than me and broad-shouldered. He was also wearing a ski mask and holding a machete.

- 4 -

My first impulse was to grab Faith's hand and beat a hasty retreat back the way we had come. The impulse had a short life, however, for when we turned to leave, we saw another man, smaller and somewhat less imposing but also wearing a ski mask, blocking our way. He was holding a crowbar, which, while it couldn't hack off our heads like a machete could, still didn't feel like good news.

I've never been one to believe in luck, good or bad, but that moment tempted me to change my mind. What were the odds of this happening on the very night I decided to set things right in my life after months of shameful dishonesty? These two nutcases must have spotted one of us entering the park and decided to follow. Maybe they had some other nefarious act planned but thought we'd be a couple of pushovers for a quick robbery and changed their plan. They'd surely factored in the possibility that either Faith or I might be armed, but if one of us pulled a gun, they could simply disappear into the darkness, knowing we'd never be able to identify them because of the masks.

And speaking of identifying them, if they heard any of our conversation, they knew we were ending a secret, illicit relationship and would therefore be disinclined to talk about this rendezvous with anyone we knew. How elated they must've been as they stood in the shadows and listened to us, knowing they could take every dime we had without worrying about us reporting the incident to the police. It was the opportunity every criminal dreams of.

And since neither Faith nor I had pulled a gun when they appeared, they knew they had nothing to fear from us.

"Are you two having a nice time this evening?" Machete said.

His manner of speech threw me. I would have expected a machete-wielding terrorist/robber to offer little more than monosyllabic grunts, but this guy sounded like he'd just stepped out of a board of directors meeting at some Fortune 500 company.

When neither Faith nor I responded, he answered his own question. "No, I don't think you're having a nice time. I think you're a couple of lovers out sneaking around, coming to the bitter end of an illicit relationship. Don't you just love that word *illicit*? It speaks of dishonesty and darkness, which happen to be areas of expertise for my partner and me."

I glanced at Crowbar and noticed that he, too, had advanced toward us. They were roughly ten feet in front of us then, positioned at ten o'clock and two o'clock so the only sure-fire escape route was directly behind us. But we would have had to get over or around the bench we'd been sitting on and then crash into the almost complete darkness of the woods. I had no idea how dense it was and therefore no idea how far we'd be able to get before we got hung up. There was little doubt we'd be caught quickly, especially since Machete would be able to hack his way through the underbrush.

Trying to seem more courageous than I felt, I stepped in front of Faith and said, "You can have all the cash we have on us. We just want to go home and forget this night ever happened."

When I started to reach for my wallet, Machete said, "Whoa, whoa, whoa . . . keep those hands where I can see them!" and brandished the blade.

I froze and withdrew my hand slowly with my fingers spread so he could see it was empty. "I'm not armed. I was just getting my wallet."

"You won't do anything unless I tell you to. Got it?"

"Yes."

"And besides, who says we want your money?" Machete said with the good cheer suddenly back in his voice. I could see he had his eyes on Faith, and I felt a sickness rising in my gut. What I think we both assumed would be a robbery now suddenly held the potential of becoming something much worse.

Faith must have sensed this too because that's when she bolted.

Knowing she was fit and athletic with at least some of the quickness remaining that had served her well as a college basketball player, I can only assume she felt she could use the element of surprise to blow past Crowbar and then outrun him to the safety of a nearby neighborhood. The plan, of course, left me behind to face a machete-wielding psycho, but I didn't take offense then, and I don't now in retrospect. Considering the way Machete was leering at her, I assumed Faith was the one he was more interested in. I couldn't blame her for trying to escape before it was too late.

Unfortunately, she didn't make it.

Yes, Crowbar was indeed caught off-guard by her sudden burst. He'd been holding the weapon in his right hand, across his chest, resting the business end in his left hand. When Faith flashed by his right side, he reacted by taking a backhanded swing at her. I have to believe he only intended to clip her on the shoulder, maybe knock her down and then subdue her. Instead, the curved end of the crowbar crashed into the back of her head, making a sickening crunching sound and causing Faith to sprawl forward and land on her face on the pavement. She seemed to bounce once and then lay perfectly still, her arms and legs outstretched like a skydiver.

Without asking permission to move—without even thinking

about it—I screamed Faith's name and ran to her. I thought she was simply knocked out cold, but when I knelt over her, I saw blood on the back of her head. I put my face close to hers and saw that her eyes were closed. I said, "Faith? Faith, can you hear me?" but got no reaction. Then I touched the back of her head and realized the bleeding was too heavy for a simple laceration. I was no expert, but it sure looked like her skull had been crushed.

More urgently now, I tried to get a response. I took her hand and said, "Faith, can you hear me? Squeeze my hand if you can." But there was no response. Her eyelids didn't flutter, and her hand applied no pressure. It wasn't until I felt for her pulse and found nothing that I realized she was dead.

Horrified and enraged, I turned to face her masked assailant and realized both men were gone.

- 5 -

I stood and whipped my head around, looking in every direction. I'd been so concerned about Faith, about trying to get a response from her that I didn't notice the men running away. I assumed they disappeared into the same woods from which they had emerged, but I couldn't be sure. They might've run farther down the trail before ducking into the trees. The only thing I was sure of was that they hadn't run back toward the trail entrance because they would've had to practically jump over Faith's sprawled body in order to do so.

Not that it mattered where they went. I certainly wasn't going to chase them. What would I do if I caught up with them? One had a machete and the other had a crowbar. I had a set of car keys and a cellphone. Even more important, they now had tremendous incentive to remain anonymous. Any attempt I made to stop them or expose them would no doubt be met with extreme prejudice. Though they couldn't have known Faith was actually dead, Crowbar must have known he'd connected with the back of her head and done serious damage. Hurting one more person wouldn't seem like a big deal if it meant they could keep from getting caught.

Once again, I knelt over Faith's body and felt for a pulse, hoping I had somehow missed it the first time. I hadn't. The blow to the back of her head with a hard metal bar, coupled with the slamming of her face into the hard ground, must have caused a fatal head or neck injury.

At that instant, in the eerie lamplight with a light breeze rustling the leaves, reality hit me. The shot of adrenaline my rage had powered through my system moments ago drained out of me as I looked down at the attractively contoured face of what had moments ago been a woman brimming with life. Her hair and the skin of her neck were soaked with blood.

I broke down.

At the place the two of us had spent many intimate moments, I held Faith's hand and cried. As wrong as our behavior was, and as anxious as I'd been to untangle my life from hers, I did have feelings for her, vivid memories of the times we'd spent together, and until just now, an admittedly foolish hope that we could somehow put our transgressions behind us and go back to just being friends. It was those feelings, however tangled and illicit and naïve they may have been, that I knew I'd spend a lifetime trying to process.

The sound of a siren snapped me back to the moment.

How could the police have been called so quickly? Faith had only been dead two or three minutes, and I was sure Machete and Crowbar hadn't called them. Suddenly, it dawned on me that someone whose presence we weren't aware of might have been watching from the trees. We'd never seen anyone on the trail this late, but it was possible someone—perhaps another couple having an affair—had beaten us to the bench and heard us coming, then slipped into the trees to watch and listen. Still kneeling by Faith's body, I looked around, but of course I could see nothing beyond the small pale circle of light.

Soon the siren started to fade, and I realized it had passed by the park on its way to a different emergency. Still, the sound had been a wakeup call, a reminder that I needed to get my head together and think about what I should do.

Unquestionably, the moral response to what had just happened would have been to pull out my phone and dial 911, then stay by the body until the police arrived. I alone would be able to tell the police what had happened and give a description of the thugs who confronted us. The problem, of course, was that such a course of action would mean disaster for me. My affair with Faith would be exposed, both of our reputations would be ruined, my marriage would likely be irreparably damaged, and I would certainly lose my job. And if none of that was bad enough, I would also find myself in the middle of a three-ring media circus. I imagined the sensational headline that would be broadcast from coast to coast: *"Illicit affair with principal leads to teacher's violent death!"*

And that's *if* the police believed my story that Faith was killed by a masked assailant.

What if they didn't?

After all, I couldn't prove anyone else had been there. Yes, Faith's skull had been bashed in, but it wouldn't be unreasonable to suggest that I had done it and disposed of the weapon. Because I did have a motive, they would say. I had come to the park to tell Faith our affair was over and she, in her anger, was threatening to get back at me by telling the world what we'd been up to. Fearing the ruination of my life, I had panicked and struck her. Surely, such crimes of passion were not uncommon. The storyline sounded reasonable even to me.

The question was, would my telling the truth and facing the implosion of my life, not to mention a possible prison sentence for a crime I didn't commit, bring Faith back to life? The answer was no. As cold as it may sound, what was done was done. She was gone forever.

Some might say what I did next was smart. Others would surely call it cowardly. Perhaps it was a little—or a lot—of both.

I ran.

- 6 -

Men in street clothes, running in residential areas at night, inspire suspicion and phone calls to the police, so when I reached the end of the tunnel of trees at the trail entrance and exited the park, I slowed to a walk. I didn't see anyone around, which was encouraging. When I reached my car and got inside, the temptation to get out of there as quickly as possible was overwhelming. I knew, however, that squealing tires and a speeding car would also attract attention, which would surely be remembered when the police showed up and started asking questions of the folks in the neighborhoods surrounding the park.

I had no idea how long it would take for someone to discover Faith's body. Whoever was taking care of her daughter would probably grow antsy, especially as midnight approached and Faith hadn't returned and wasn't answering her phone. It wasn't like Faith to be out late. Even when we met, we would often make it a point to be home before ten so as not to arouse any suspicion with Mary Beth or Faith's babysitters. I wondered how quickly the police would be called and what their policy was on such matters. I assumed a person would have to be missing for a certain amount of time before they would start investigating, but I had no idea what it was.

My best guess was that Faith's body would be found sometime after dawn the next morning. An ear-budded jogger would surely come trotting along the trail and get the shock of his or her life. A quick 911 call could bring the authorities, and then the game would be on. As Faith's boss, I would likely be one of the first people they would call. I would also be one of the first people they would question.

I started the car and glanced at my watch. I'd only been gone from home for thirty-five minutes. I'd told Mary Beth I was going to the office to email a document to Mike Waterson, and now it was even more important than ever that I get it done as quickly as possible. I needed an alibi, and if I could point to a time stamp on a business email sent from my office IP address that coincided with Faith's approximate time of death, I'd have one. It might not be airtight, but it would be better than nothing. I started the car and pulled out of my parking spot with all the caution of a first-year driver's education student. The last thing I wanted was to attract the attention of a cop.

While on my way to the school, I took deep breaths and tried to think through what I was facing. Like most people's, my knowledge of criminal investigations came primarily from TV shows, movies, and crime novels, which I assumed couldn't always be trusted as accurate. I assumed also the first thing the authorities would do would be to call in the forensics professionals and go over every inch of Faith's body. I was thankful we hadn't walked arm in arm or snuggled on the bench like on previous occasions. The only time I had touched her was when I felt for a pulse and held her hand.

That's when a thought hit me like a piece of debris in a gale force wind. I reached up and flipped on the dome light.

I had Faith's blood on my left hand.

Which meant it could also be on my clothes, on my keys, on the door handle of the car, and possibly on the steering wheel. Of all the things that could get me sent to prison, only a video of me actually killing Faith would be more damning than her blood on my person and property.

I cringed when I thought about how easy it would have been to walk over to the water fountain and rinse my hands. It would have taken no more than ten seconds to eliminate what was now a potentially devastating development. Would I end up spending the next twenty-five years in prison because of such a stupid oversight?

Suddenly, my decision to leave the scene of the crime wasn't looking so smart. At the time, I'd been thinking only about the catastrophic consequences of my affair with Faith being exposed. But if that happened, I would at least be a free man. Broken and humiliated, for sure, but at least free. This way, I ran the risk of *both* having the affair exposed and spending my life in prison. *An innocent man wouldn't run*, they would say. *And he certainly wouldn't have the victim's blood on his hands and in his car.*

I felt physically sick as I pulled into the school parking lot. Regardless of the thoughts torturing me, I had to get into my office and send that email. But not before I washed my hands. In the restroom, I lathered and rinsed them twice and checked my clothing for any signs of blood. I didn't see any, but I knew that didn't mean anything. Forensics experts can find evidence that is invisible to the naked eye.

Once my hands were as clean as I could get them, I hustled to my office and fired up the computer. I should have reviewed the document before sending it, but there was no time. I needed the time stamp on the email to be as early as possible. It went out at 9:15, forty-five minutes after I left the house. I knew if I left the school right then, I would be home to Mary Beth well within the one-hour time frame I had suggested I would be gone.

On the way, I decided to take five minutes and run the car through an all-night car wash, the kind where you wash the car yourself with a hand-held spray gun. Even if it made me a couple of minutes late getting home, I had to get rid of any possible blood stains. And there would be no way I could do it in the garage without the risk of being caught by Mary Beth and having to answer questions.

I blasted the car all over with hot water but spent extra time on the driver's side door. Then I found a rag in the trunk and wet it with the sprayer. I was feverishly wiping the steering wheel when a car pulled up in front of me, blocking my exit from the bay.

It was a police car.

- 7 -

I had gotten acquainted with a few of the cops in our area, mostly the ones whose children were students at our school. However, I couldn't see into the car well enough to tell if this was one I knew. He didn't jump out of the car immediately and seemed to be doing something on his computer. I chose simply to continue wiping down surfaces inside the car—anything I might have touched—while trying to look like I wasn't terrified.

Eventually, the door swung open and officer Dan Ryland twisted and raised his considerable bulk out of the car. By no means a small man to start with, he looked positively bear-like with the bullet-proof vest underneath his dark blue uniform shirt. I'd known him for a few years. His son and daughter both went through our school. They were good kids, and my conversations with Dan and his wife were always pleasant.

Approaching my car, he squinted through the windshield glare caused by the overhead fluorescent lights and said, "That you, Mr. Vincent?" I am convinced the sun will rise in the west and set in the east before a school principal is ever called by his first name by anyone other than his family members.

I stepped out of the car, rag in hand, and smiled. "Hey, Dan. What's up?"

"Little late to be out washing your car, isn't it?"

I noticed he didn't bother to tell me what was up. Mustering my most innocent look in complete defiance of the maelstrom that was under way in my chest cavity, I glanced at my watch and said, "It's only nine twenty-five. Is that late?"

"You tell me. Do you usually wash your car at this hour?"

Normally, Dan was a friendly sort, but he was clearly all business tonight, which I assumed had something to do with why he didn't answer me when I asked what was up. Something *was* up. I just didn't know if it had anything to do with Faith's body being found.

"I've been at the office, working," I said. "I spilled a Coke inside the car and decided to stop here and clean it up on the way home so Mary Beth wouldn't find everything all sticky in the morning." The lies were coming fast and furious now. It was scary how good I was getting at conjuring a falsehood out of thin air.

Looking at the wet concrete at our feet and the drops glistening on the car, Officer Ryland said, "But you washed your whole car."

"Yes. It needed it and I was here, so why not?" Then I decided to push back a little. "Dan, what's wrong? Is there something I can do for you?"

He ignored the question and said, "Where have you been for the last hour?"

"I told you. In my office at the school."

"Was anyone there with you? I mean, like, was it a meeting or something?"

"No. I was at home when the superintendent called and told me he needed a document for a meeting that got moved up to eight o'clock tomorrow morning. The document was on my office computer, so I came over to review it one last time and send it to him. I did that, and now here I am cleaning up the car on my way home to keep from getting in trouble with my wife. For crying out loud, Dan, what's going on?"

"Something happened over in Belle Isle Park."

I almost blurted out, *I didn't do it!* My mouth actually opened to form the words, but I caught myself at the last instant. Instead, I said, "A mugging?"

"No, a murder."

"A murder? Are you serious? Who?"

Again, he ignored my question. "Let me ask you this: Do you have security footage at the school that would prove you were there within the last forty-five minutes or so?"

"I absolutely do, Dan. And I'd love to show it to you if you have any thought that I might have had something to do with a murder in the park."

"Okay then. Let's go."

And with that, we got into our cars. He followed me to the school, where I took him to the CCTV equipment in the office and ran the video back to show him my arrival and departure. As soon as he saw it and checked the time stamp, he loosened up and became the good-natured guy I'd known him to be on previous occasions.

"I'm sorry to trouble you like this, Mr. Vincent. It's just that we got a report of a suspicious vehicle the same color as yours parked just outside the park shortly after dark, which appears to have been about the time the murder occurred."

"My make and model too?"

"The witness wasn't sure of the make and model, only the color. You can see why I had to stop when I saw you in the car wash. I didn't know it was you, just that it was the right color of vehicle. And it's not uncommon for people to try to wash away evidence after committing a crime."

"Oh, yes, absolutely. You were just doing your job."

"Yes, sir."

"Are you at liberty to tell me who was killed? Was it a homeless person or a jogger?" Even though I knew, I felt like I had to ask to keep the charade believable. Not one person in a thousand would fail to ask that question.

Officer Ryland, who'd completely bought my email alibi, was now suddenly my confidant. He leaned closer in the conspiratorial manner of gossips the world over, and said, "Don't say anything, but at this point, we don't know who it is. We just know he was hacked up pretty good, like with a machete or something."

- 8 -

My brain was scrambled as I drove home.

Officer Ryland had used a masculine pronoun when describing the murder victim—*he* rather than *she*. Plus, he said the victim had been hacked up with a machete. The only way his comment made any sense was if there had been a second murder. Perhaps Machete and Crowbar ran into someone while making their way out of the park and decided to leave no more witnesses. They'd already killed one person—what was one more if it meant they could get away clean?

But if Faith's body wasn't the one Officer Ryland was referring to—if it hadn't yet been found when he approached me at the car wash—it likely had been found by the time we left the school and I started home. After finding a hacked-up body, the cops surely would have canvassed the surrounding area. Faith's body wasn't exactly hidden. I could imagine a couple of officers slowly walking the hiking trail, swishing their flashlight beams from one side to the other, eventually converging on Faith's bloody corpse.

I felt lightheaded as I imagined the officers standing around Faith's body, waiting for forensics to arrive. Would any of them have known her? It's doubtful in a city this size. But when they confirmed her identity, her occupation, and the fact that she was married to a violent drug offender who was currently incarcerated, they would have all kinds of questions. I tightened my grip on the wheel and took deep breaths, wondering what the forensics people would be able to discern. Would they know someone had touched the body? Would they have any way of knowing it was me? I'd read somewhere that we leave tiny traces of ourselves wherever we go. And everyone knows forensics professionals now have amazing tools at their disposal that allow them to find and identify those traces. Perhaps I'd just seen too many *CSI* episodes, but I didn't think so. Those people were good.

But they weren't my only worry.

I also wondered how on earth I was going to walk into our house in a few minutes without looking guilty. I hoped telling Mary Beth a slightly edited version of my encounter with Officer Ryland would help justify the anxiety I knew she would see in me. After all, it's not every day the police ask you for an alibi because someone has been chopped to pieces in your local park. Who wouldn't have an emotional reaction to news like that?

I pulled into the garage, shut off the car, and punched the remote to lower the door. As it slowly descended behind me, boxing me in, I thought about what an appropriate metaphor it was. I had begun the evening just trying to do the right thing. Now, it seemed that with every passing minute, I felt a little more trapped.

When I got inside, I saw that Mary Beth had turned off the TV in the family room and retreated to the bedroom, where the absence of any TV noise told me she was reading. She was addicted to epic, sprawling, multi-generational novels. She once told me that if a book didn't have at least seven hundred pages she wasn't going to waste her time on it. Sure enough, I found her in bed with Ken Follett. (That's how she would always say it: "I'm going to bed with Ken Follett tonight." Or whatever author she happened to be reading at the moment. Mary Beth had a great sense of humor, one of her many charms.)

When I walked in, I did so with what I thought would be an appropriate amount of seriousness and enough panic to seem reasonable in light of my encounter with Officer Ryland. Mary Beth glanced at the clock and said exactly what I expected her to say: "It takes over an hour to send an email?"

"Nope, but it takes over an hour to send an email and then be interviewed by the police."

Mary Beth slammed her book shut and stared at me. "You were interviewed by the police?"

I told her a version of the events of the last hour that was close to the truth but not quite all the way there. I left out the trip to the car wash and just said I'd been on my way home from the office when Dan Ryland stopped me. There'd been a murder in the park and a car the same color as ours had been seen in the area. I was able to satisfy his concerns by taking him back to my office and showing him the email I had sent to Mike Waterson at the approximate time the murder had occurred.

"Someone was murdered in Belle Isle Park?"

"Apparently."

"Did he say who?"

"I don't think he knew. But he did say it was a guy."

"Some homeless person?"

"I have no idea."

"Wow. And someone saw a car like ours leaving the scene?"

"Whoa, I didn't say that. I said the car was the same *color* as ours; there was no confirmation of a make and model. And it wasn't leaving the scene, it was just in the area. So when Dan saw me driving along, he thought he ought to check me out. All I had to do was prove I'd been at the office, and everything was fine. But that's why I'm later getting home than I thought I would be."

Mary Beth placed her book on the nightstand and grabbed the TV remote. It was almost time for the news, and she was determined to get more information about the murder. Sure enough, it was the lead story. A young male reporter, looking appropriately appalled, stood in the glow of some makeshift lights and said two bodies had been found in the park—a male and a female—the investigation was just getting started, and there was nothing else to report at that time.

Two bodies.

So they had indeed found Faith.

It's hard to describe how I felt just then. There was some sense of relief that Faith's body wasn't lying out there in the dark where animals could desecrate it even further than the crowbar that killed her already had. And of course, there was grief. Someone I had known on an emotional level, someone who knew me in some ways better than my own wife, and for whom I had had strong feelings, was gone from this world forever. But most of all, I felt fear. I seemed to be safely off the police's radar, but I knew that could change. Some obscure finding at the crime scene or some witness that hadn't yet surfaced could put me in an orange jumpsuit and ankle shackles.

Mary Beth said, "They're talking about two bodies."

"Yeah, Dan only mentioned one. Maybe they hadn't found the second one yet."

We watched to the report's conclusion. Then, I stepped into the bathroom to ready myself for bed and try to pull myself together. When I came out, Mary Beth was still watching the news. "Maybe they'll give an update before they go off the air," she said.

I crawled into bed beside her, and we both sat there, propped up on pillows, watching the news with very different mindsets. She was hungry to get the information I already had, which is when I realized that, wherever this path I was on might lead, I would always know things no one else knew—things that could destroy me and therefore demand that I maintain a constant charade without ever making a single misstep.

Mary Beth turned off the bedside lamp and snuggled up next to me. I knew what she was feeling. When something shocking and terrible happens, she always wants to be held. To her, it's reassurance. It's her reminder that while other people's worlds may be falling apart, hers is still intact. It struck me that, right then, she was like the skater who thinks the ice on the lake is a couple of feet thick when in fact it is only a couple of inches.

- 9 -

The call came just after midnight.

It was Mike Waterson calling to tell me our second-grade teacher had been murdered and to discuss how the situation would be handled at school the next day. Securing a substitute for Faith was an obvious first step. We would also schedule grief counselors for students and staff. My main job would be to meet with the faculty and staff a few at a time, explain what was going on, and answer any questions, at least as far as the official information I had would allow. As for the unofficial information only I possessed, I would be keeping it to myself. It would be a bad day at school, probably the first of several. But it is at such times when leadership matters. I knew I had to somehow become a tower of strength for my team and our students. I couldn't let them see how fragile I really was.

Mary Beth had dropped off to sleep before the phone rang and was sitting up in bed when I ended the call. She'd heard enough to get the gist and was patiently awaiting details. When I didn't say anything immediately, she said, "Well?"

"One of the bodies they found in the park was Mrs. Connelly."

Mary Beth gasped. "Oh, no!"

Sitting on the edge of the bed, I leaned forward and put my head in my hands. "I can't imagine what she was doing in the park after dark. She has a little girl at home." I knew I had to be very careful. I was trying to think of what a person who didn't know what I knew would say. One misstatement . . . one blurting out of the wrong piece of information . . . would arouse suspicion. And Mary Beth was sharp. I knew nothing would slip past her.

"Isn't she the one whose husband is in prison?"

"Yes. He was caught selling drugs to an undercover officer. And then he hit the officer for good measure."

"I wonder if her being in the park had something to do with that."

I could have said no, she was in the park to meet her illicit lover, who just happened to be me. Instead, I said, "I have no idea."

I would find myself saying those four words a lot over the next few days even though I did indeed have quite an idea.

Mary Beth said, "Do they know how she was killed?"

"Mike didn't know. I'm sure we'll learn more tomorrow."

"I wonder if she was raped."

I was not surprised her mind went immediately there. Rape and murder often go hand in hand, and while no one wants to think about a murderer being loose in the community, a murderer who first rapes his victims would be even more terrifying, especially for a woman. It hurt me to think I had the ability to put my wife's mind at ease by assuring her that Faith wasn't raped but couldn't do it. It was the first of many moments to come when a statement on the tip of my tongue could have done me in.

I said, "I don't know, but let's not jump to conclusions."

"I'm not jumping to conclusions. I'm just wondering."

There was a little heat in her response, so I turned and took her hand. "I'm sorry, Babe. We'll know more tomorrow, I'm sure. I just didn't want you worrying about something like that. It's too awful to think about if you don't have to."

She, too, was apologetic and scooted over on the mattress so she could wrap her arms around me. With her head on my shoulder, she said, "Tomorrow's going to be bad day, isn't it?"

"Probably the next few are going to be rough."

"The school is lucky to have you at the helm."

Knowing I was ultimately the reason Faith Connelly was dead, I almost laughed out loud. No, the school was not at all lucky to have me at the helm. The school and almost everyone associated with it—most of all a little first-grader named Zoey—was going to suffer terribly because it had me at the helm.

It was in that moment, sitting there with my wife's arms around me that I thought, *I can't do this. I should get up right now and go straight to the police and tell them everything I know. If I don't, I'll eventually end up saying or doing the wrong thing and digging my own grave.*

I often wonder what kind of account I would be writing if I had done it. How many different turns would the story have taken? Perhaps things would have turned out all right for me in the end. Maybe Mary Beth would have forgiven my infidelity because I at least had tried to make things right. Maybe my eyewitness testimony would have helped move the investigation forward quickly, taking Machete and Crowbar off the streets. Maybe all the terrible things that were still to come never would have happened.

Maybe, maybe, maybe.

But we'll never know because I ignored the urge to go to the police and soldiered on with my secret, hoping and praying, but not really believing, that things would turn out okay.

- 10 -

I was on my way to the school about five sleepless hours later. When it came into view, I was relieved to see there were no television news trucks in the parking lot. I knew they would be coming as soon as Faith's name was released as one of the victims—probably at a news conference later that morning—but for the moment, thankfully, we were still off the media's radar.

It was just before sunup when I climbed out of my car and saw Mike Waterson pulling into the space beside mine. He'd said he was going to cancel his meeting with the architects and would meet with me in my office at 6:00 a.m. to finalize a strategy for handling the fallout of Faith's death. He was an active man of just over fifty, but that morning, he looked ten years older.

"Get any sleep?" he asked as he shook my hand.

"Nope."

He sighed and shook his head. "Me neither."

When we got into my office, Mike said, "I imagine the cops are going to want to question you."

"Or you. You're the superintendent."

"The media will probably want a piece of me, but the cops will want you. You saw Mrs. Connelly every day; I barely knew her. They'll be looking for human interest stuff. And for anything you can tell them that will help them figure out why she was in the park after dark and why someone would want to kill her."

"I can't wait."

Mike stopped and looked at me as if the question he was about to ask had just occurred to him. "*Do* you know of any reason she might have been in the park at that hour?"

Yes, I do.

"No, I don't."

"She had a kid, didn't she?"

"Yes, a first-grader named Zoey."

Mike swore softly, something he didn't do often.

We trudged into the building and went straight to my office, then spent the next thirty minutes outlining a plan for the day ahead. I would speak to every faculty and staff member. We'd gather them in the faculty lounge in groups of four or five while the others managed the classrooms. I would go over the facts as we knew them, express my deepest sorrow, and ask everyone to be patient with any disruptions to our normal routine. I would also talk about when and how to address the situation with the students and offer some cautions about talking to the media. Finally, I would urge everyone to be cooperative if the police asked any questions and by all means, to speak up if they had any information they thought might have a bearing on the investigation.

The final challenge was to assemble a team of grief counselors—some faith-based and others not—who would be available to talk to students or staff in the cafeteria during the last two periods of the school day and after school for as many days as people showed up to talk. I called the local mental health clinic and my pastor, Brian Russell, who was eager to assemble some of his colleagues to handle the faith-based side of things. I remember thinking I probably needed counseling more than anyone but wouldn't be getting it any time soon.

It was shortly after I'd finished talking to the third group of faculty and staffers that one of our kindergarten teachers asked if she could speak to me in private. Her name was Molly Thomas. People called her Jolly Molly because she had an infectious giggle and seemed to laugh at every joke she heard, no matter how lame. I knew she and Faith had been friends and that they occasionally did things together on weekends.

Faith once told me Molly's "jolly act," as she put it, was a way of hiding her pain. Molly wasn't exactly fat, but she struggled with her weight and was apparently troubled by the fact that she had never been able to make any headway toward losing the excess pounds. Her weight struggle was exacerbated in her mind by the fact that she'd never had a serious boyfriend even though she was pushing forty and had always talked about how she would love to have children of her own. Faith characterized her as "desperate" but didn't seem to think any less of her for having feelings that were as common to the human race as a runny nose.

There was also the fact that she still lived with her parents, both of whom were in bad health and required much of her time and attention. It was a lot to deal with, but to her credit, Molly never brought her heartaches to school—not that I knew of. By all accounts, she was a good teacher who loved her kids and went above and beyond what was required of her.

We stepped into my office, and I closed the door.

"Have a seat and tell me what's on your mind," I said as I circled my desk and sat down.

"Faith was having an affair."

Talk about getting right to the point. She couldn't have shocked me more if she'd pulled a snake out of her pocket and thrown it on my desk. I found it almost impossible to draw my next breath, and my face instantly felt hot. I knew it had to be turning red.

"An affair?" I said dumbly, like I'd never heard the term before.

"Yes."

"But Faith was married."

"Her husband is in prison. And even if he wasn't, people have affairs all the time. You know that."

"Yes I do, but . . . I just never thought . . . "

"She was that kind of person?"

I couldn't tell if Molly was toying with me, if she already knew I was Faith's paramour, or if she only knew Faith was seeing someone on the sly but didn't know who. I felt like I had no choice but to play along as if I was completely clueless until I could find out how much she knew.

"No, I never thought she seemed like the type of person to . . . to do something like that," I said. "How long have you known?"

"Not long. About a week."

I braced myself as I asked the most obvious question. "Do you know who she was seeing?"

Molly looked down at her hands and seemed to count to ten. I held my breath.

"I think so."

"You *think* so?"

"I mean, I have a pretty good idea."

It was maddening how she was making me drag it out of her. Why didn't she just say it?

I said, "Well, who?"

"Coach Brooks."

Adam Brooks ran our physical education program at the school. He was in his thirties and had a wife and child. I could definitely see him as a philanderer. He was a well-built, tanned, meticulous dresser with blond highlights in his sandy hair. But the main reason I could see him as a cheater is that Faith once told me he hit on her about once a month. I was alarmed. I tried to quiz her about it, but she laughed it off and said he'd be the last guy she'd ever be interested in and could handle him without any problem.

Breathing a little easier, I said to Molly, "Why do you think she was having an affair with Coach Brooks?"

"Because a week or so ago . . . one night . . . I saw them together."

- 11 -

The right thing to do would have been to stop the conversation right there and encourage Molly to speak to the police. But of course, I didn't do that. I was both relieved and troubled by this new piece of information—relieved because it cast suspicion on someone other than me and troubled because it seemed there were things going on in Faith's personal life I was unaware of and that didn't mesh with what she had led me to believe about our own relationship. I was desperate to know more, but I had to tread softly.

I said to Molly, "Two people can be together without having an affair, can't they?"

"Yes, of course. But . . . "

"But what?"

"They weren't just *together*, if you know what I mean." She did air quotes with her fingers.

By then, with my nerves already shot, I'd had all of her cat-and-mouse game I could take. I didn't know if she was being intentionally difficult or if it was just her normal way of handling a sensitive topic, but I was done with the little dance we were doing. With exaggerated calmness I knew would communicate my frustration, I said, "No, Molly, I really don't know what you mean. Why don't you just *say* what you mean?"

"I saw them kiss."

For the second time in two minutes Molly had caused the room to tilt. I felt like I was on the deck of a boat being tossed by a hurricane. I placed my hands on the arms of my chair as if to steady myself. "Are you sure?"

Molly acted hurt and opted for sarcasm. "I may be single, but I know what kissing is."

I sighed. "I know you know what kissing is, Molly. What I'm asking is if it's possible you could be mistaken."

"Nope."

"Where were they when you saw them?"

"By her car in the Florida Mall parking lot. I had just pulled in a couple of aisles over when I saw them."

"And they kissed?"

"Yes. It was like they had been together and were saying goodbye."

"Exactly how far away were you?"

"I was a couple of aisles over. Maybe fifty or sixty feet away."

"And you said it was nighttime."

"Yes."

"Is it possible you misidentified either one or both of them? Maybe it was someone who looked like Coach Brooks or Mrs. Connelly."

Molly bristled. "I know what I saw."

"I'm not questioning what you saw. I'm questioning your interpretation of what you saw. You said you were fifty feet away in the dark. I think it would be easy for anybody to misidentify someone."

Molly stiffened her spine. "Why are you defending them?"

"I'm not defending anybody. But you have to be really careful with an accusation like this. There's a lot at stake. Adam's marriage for one thing. And both Adam's and Faith's reputations. What if you're mistaken?"

She just stared at me, so I continued: "If you were subpoenaed to testify in court, would you be able to say under oath that it was the two of them you saw?"

She hesitated, then said, "Yes, I think so."

"Thinking so doesn't get it, Molly. A defense attorney would tear you apart if you even hinted you could be wrong."

"You don't believe me, do you?"

"Wrong. I *do* believe you. I believe you saw exactly *what* you saw. I'm just having trouble with the *who*."

Just then I realized my mistake. I was arguing with Molly out of some prideful need to defend what was left of my male ego. The thought that Faith was both cheating *with* me and *on* me was too humiliating to acknowledge. If she had seen Faith and Adam kissing, I'd been duped six ways to Sunday. But arguing with Molly wouldn't fix anything. What I needed to do was let that part of the equation go and encourage Molly to go to the cops with her story. While they were trying to figure out who was kissing whom in that parking lot, attention would be diverted away from me, which was the most important thing. I could lick my wounds in private.

Molly was glaring at me, so I held my hands up in a peace offering. "You know what, Molly? You're absolutely right. I guess I was trying to be charitable toward someone who's been murdered. But the fact is, if you saw something, you have to report it. You *have* to."

She looked surprised by my about-face. "You mean to the police?"

"Of course. If you saw what you believe you saw, you need to tell the police and let them check it out. I'm sure it's information they would like to have. It's like they say: if you see something, say something."

Molly suddenly seemed troubled. "What happens to me if it turns out I *was* mistaken?"

I found it fascinating that after being so adamant about what she saw, she was suddenly willing to entertain the possibility that she was wrong.

I shrugged. "I don't think you'd be in any trouble with the police, if that's what you mean. All you'd be doing is telling them what you think you saw. I'm sure they get leads all the time that don't pan out for one reason or another. On the other hand, I doubt you'll be Coach Brooks' favorite person if he finds out you accused him, which could create some interesting dynamics around here. But hey, if you're convinced you saw him and Faith kissing at the mall, none of that matters."

Molly stared at her hands, which were clasped in her lap, and said nothing. I could tell she was having second thoughts about her testimony. I had no idea why. She'd come into my office with quite a story to tell, but when I shifted and encouraged her to talk to the police, her entire demeanor changed. I decided to apply a little pressure.

"Do you want me to pull you out of class so you can talk to the police if they stop by this morning?"

Was that a little flash of fear I saw in her eyes?

Yes, I think it was.

"I'm not sure," she said. "You may be right. I don't know."

Something about this whole conversation was off, but I had neither the time nor the energy to think about it. I said, "Why don't you just call the police yourself if you feel like you need to talk to them about this. There's no reason I need to be involved."

She liked the idea, which I interpreted as an indication that she really didn't want to talk to the police at all. After apologizing for taking up my time, she stood and walked out of my office. I was left sitting there completely confused and with far more questions and concerns than I'd had when she walked in.

- 12 -

Of all people, Adam Brooks was in the next group of faculty and staff I was scheduled to meet with. Adam and I had always maintained a professional relationship that ended at the perimeter of the school property. I had always pegged Adam as the kind of guy who would cheat on his wife in a heartbeat. Even before Faith told me he had hit on her multiple times, I'd seen him chatting up the more attractive female teachers and support staff and never going near the less attractive ones. He was one of those guys who would blatantly stare when an attractive woman walked into the room. I'd seen him do it a hundred times. It was the reason Faith gave when she said she could never be interested in someone like him. "He's a drooler," she said. "I'm not into droolers."

Adam and four other individuals were in the faculty lounge when I walked in. They were talking softly the way people do in funeral homes and hospital emergency rooms. Their conversation ended the second I walked through the door.

As with the previous groups, I didn't bother asking them to sit. I knew they were keyed up, and besides, I didn't plan on keeping them very long. I did notice Adam stepped to the rear of the group where only I could see him. What it meant, if anything, I didn't know.

Slipping my hands into my pockets, I exhaled a deep breath and began.

"I know you've heard that Mrs. Connelly—Faith—was killed last night. Right now we don't know anything except that her body was found in Belle Isle Park. The police are supposed to hold a press conference later today. I'm sure they'll have more information by then.

"Several people have asked why we didn't cancel school today. It's not the policy of our district to do that. If it seems disrespectful to Faith, consider that, given the ages of our students, hundreds of parents would have been caught on short notice without anyone to care for their children while they go to work. So if anyone seems put off by the fact that we're here today, please try to help them understand. We're all just trying to do the best we can."

I noticed all eyes were on me except for the two in the very back that belonged to Coach Brooks. He was shifting his gaze back and forth from the ceiling to the floor. Maybe I was making too much of it, but I sensed he couldn't bring himself to look me in the eye.

I continued: "This afternoon, we will have grief counselors available for anyone—students or staff—to talk to. They'll be in the cafeteria during the last two periods and after school. They'll be there every day until it's clear the need has been met.

"As for the students, you'll probably get more comments or questions from the older ones. I would encourage you not to get into any philosophical discussions about life and death or theology. It's perfectly okay to say you don't know why such terrible things happen. Mostly, we just want to talk about what a nice person Mrs. Connelly was, and if any of the students feel like they need to talk to someone, encourage them to talk to their parents, their clergyman, or the grief counselors.

"The only other thing I have to say is that the police and the media may show up on campus. Actually, I expect them any time now. I would encourage you to answer any questions the police might ask you but to be very careful with the media. I'm not saying you can't talk. We're not doing an information blackout or anything like that. Just be careful. The media people are just doing their job, but they need ratings, and I would expect them to make anything they get sound as sensational as possible."

Marjorie Hollingsworth, one of our office secretaries, raised her hand.

"Yes, Marjorie?"

"Is it true Faith was beaten to death?"

I wish I'd been more careful and kept it from happening, but when those words were spoken Adam Brooks and I locked eyes. Suddenly, the ceiling and floor weren't half as interesting to him as I was. And there was something in his eyes. Not grief and sadness, which I would have expected, but . . . anger?

Now, Molly's assertion that he and Faith were having an affair seemed more than likely. As did the possibility that Faith had told him things about her relationship with me. I couldn't think of any other reason he would look at me like that.

Somehow, I collected myself and said, "Marjorie, I know rumors are going around. I don't know how much of what you're hearing is true. I think the best thing to do is just let the police release whatever information they have as they see fit." Then, because I didn't want Marjorie to feel chastised, I said, "But I know it's hard. We all have questions."

Coach Brooks was the only one of the five who didn't speak or look at me as the group left the room.

- 13 -

It was just after 9:00 a.m. when I finished meeting with the last group of teachers and support staff. I had just stepped into my office to decompress for a few moments when my secretary, Alice Carr, poked her head in and told me a Detective Maribel Johnson had called and wanted to talk to me face to face as soon as possible.

Alice was one of those secretaries that is part assistant, part mother, and part drill sergeant. She read every situation and either helped me, consoled me, or planted the toe of her shoe firmly in my backside, depending on what she thought would bring the best out of me. She was as sarcastic as the day is long, but she loved me. I knew because if anybody hassled me her fangs and claws came right out in my defense. The only annoying habit she had was singing Beatles songs while she was working. Only Beatles songs. And singing them off-key to boot. I asked her once if she knew any other songs besides Beatles songs, and she said, "There are other songs besides Beatles songs?" I never mentioned it again.

I told Alice to call Detective Johnson and have her stop by my office at 9:45. Might as well get it over with.

Putting my elbows on the desk, I buried my face in my hands and rubbed my eyes, which were already burning from a lack of sleep.

Never in my life had I felt so overwhelmed, so helpless in the face of trouble. I'd arrived at school thinking no one knew about my affair with Faith, which, I reasoned, would mean no one would have any reason to think I'd been at the scene when she'd been killed. Add to that my email alibi that Officer Ryland seemed to have swallowed whole, and there was a reasonably good chance I could fly through this thing under the radar and escape scrutiny. After that would come what I wanted more than anything in the world: an opportunity to get my act together and be a better man.

So much for that pipe dream.

It took only about three hours at school for me to realize there were things I didn't know. Important things. About Faith. About Adam Brooks. About the two of them together. And about what she may have told him about me.

That was the scariest thing of all. If I had misjudged Faith and she was seeing Adam Brooks while also seeing me, I would eventually process it, learn a lesson, and get past it. But if she had confided in him that she was seeing me, that she sometimes met me in the park at night, then it would surely arouse suspicion in him and explain his peculiar behavior in our meeting that morning. All it would take would be for him to mention to the police that Faith and I were having an affair, and the spotlight would swing my way. I'd read enough novels and seen enough movies to know that when police detectives uncovered an adulterous relationship hidden within the folds and layers of a murder, they knew they'd struck gold.

In this case, as guilty as I was of adultery, it would be fool's gold they struck because I didn't kill Faith. But would it matter if I was found to have fled the scene of the crime and systematically withheld information and obstructed justice? Would any jury ever conclude I was innocent?

And then there was the mysterious second murder. I had to

assume the perpetrator was Machete because of Officer Ryland's reference to the body being "hacked up." I also had to assume he and Crowbar got away clean; otherwise the news reports would have noted their arrests. And if they got away clean, I could just imagine my story about their involvement seeming like the pathetic fabrication of a man desperate to explain why his presence at the scene of a murder didn't mean he'd committed it.

I glanced at my watch and saw I still had a few minutes before Detective Johnson showed up. Once again, I was tempted to tell her everything. Yes, it would throw my life into chaos, the likes of which I'd never known. It would be a confession that would brand me forever. Even if Mary Beth and I were able to somehow save our marriage, she would never look at me the same way again. All of our friends would whisper their disgust behind my back and talk about what a hypocrite I am. I would almost certainly be fired, never to be hired again as a school administrator. And I would likely be tried for Faith's murder, which would be an uncertain situation at best. Still, the thought of getting out from under the weight I was carrying was almost too appealing to resist. It was like a siren song calling me to my death.

My cellphone rang.

It was Mary Beth. I thought about letting it go to voicemail. She probably wasn't expecting me to answer, knowing what a crazy day I would be having. I decided hearing her voice for real and not just on a voicemail was what I needed.

"Hey there."

She sounded startled. "Oh. Hi. I didn't expect you to answer. I was going to leave you a message."

"I was just taking a moment before the police arrive. A detective is supposed to be here soon."

"Will it be someone you know?"

"I don't think so. Alice said the name was . . . Maribel something. I don't know anybody by that name, let alone a cop."

"What do you think they'll ask you?"

"Probably just stuff about Faith. Am I aware of anything going on with her that would lead to her being murdered . . . stuff like that."

"Are you done meeting with all the staff and employees?"

"Yes."

"Did it go okay?"

"I think so, or at least as well as anyone could expect."

Mary Beth fell silent, and I sensed something was bothering her. I said, "How about you? Are you okay?"

She was silent for another beat or two and then said, "I don't know. I just feel like something terrible is about to happen."

"Babe, something terrible has already happened."

"I know. I mean something worse."

"Something worse than Faith being murdered?"

"I know it sounds silly, and I can't explain it, but I've been feeling it all morning. I thought maybe hearing your voice would calm me down a little."

"Did it?"

She hesitated. "Maybe, but I still have a bad feeling."

At that moment, Alice knocked on my door and opened it. "Detective Johnson is here," she said softly.

I nodded okay. She understood I would be right out and closed the door.

I said, "Honey, I have to go. The detective is here."

"Will you call me later and tell me how it went?"

"Sure, when I get a chance. But with the way things are around here, I'm not sure when it will be. Don't worry if it takes me a while."

"Okay. Be careful."

As I ended the call, I stared at my phone and wondered about

Mary Beth's last words: *Be careful.* They seemed odd. What, in her mind, did I have to be careful about? Wouldn't *Hang in there* or *I love you* or some other word of encouragement have been more appropriate?

But that wasn't my biggest concern. What really unsettled me was that Mary Beth had always had an uncanny ability to feel when something bad was about to happen. She never knew what exactly, only that "darkness was descending," as she put it. Once it turned out to be the death of one of her cousins. I also remember a terrorist attack and a horrific plane crash followed such a feeling. Most recently, it had been a monster storm that blew the roofs off of several homes in our neighborhood.

And now she had the feeling again.

- 14 -

Often, when you most need time to stop and carefully think things through, life demands an immediate response. Such was the case when I hung up the phone. I would've loved some time to consider my options going into what I knew could be the most important conversation of my life up to that point. But Detective Johnson was waiting, probably anxiously, outside my door. Keeping her waiting wouldn't be a good idea.

In the next sixty seconds I had to decide whether I was going to confess everything or continue tracking with my chosen course. In my admittedly cluttered mind, it boiled down to this: I felt reasonably sure no one knew or could prove I'd been in the park the night Faith was killed. I also knew the cops wouldn't find incriminating emails on either Faith's or my computers. (We were stupid, but not *that* stupid.) Nor would they find anything particularly damning in our text messages. Of course we texted from time to time, but we had reasons to as coworkers and friends, and we never texted anything intimate. Mostly it was school-related business or funny comments or memes we thought the other would enjoy. I did this with several people who worked at the school, including Alice, my secretary. From the very beginning, Faith and I agreed our private communications would be face to face or—very occasionally—over the phone. But even then, the calls would be short. We never wanted to have to explain frequent hour-long conversations that have so often spelled the doom of countless illicit lovers.

The biggest concern I had was Adam Brooks.

If Molly Thomas was right—and judging from Adam's behavior, it sure seemed she was—Adam had his own Faith-related secrets. He, like me, was married and had a lot to lose if his affair with Faith became known. Even if he didn't love his wife, he had a little girl he adored and would not want to lose custody of. If he told the police I was having an affair with Faith, I could plead innocent, knowing Faith and I were careful to leave no evidence, and then recommend that the police have a conversation with Molly about what she saw one night at the mall.

Looking back, I realize none of these thoughts and theories were airtight. If I'd had some time, I could have reasoned through them more carefully and might have come to a different conclusion. But I didn't have time. I had to go with my gut. I truly felt that, short of a one-in-a-million microscopic discovery by the forensics people, no one would be able to prove I was anywhere near Faith when she was killed. Adam Brooks might have had his suspicions, but I didn't think he could prove anything. And I doubted he would risk his own secrets by pointing a finger at me. He had to suspect that if Faith had told him about me, she had also told me about him.

After exhaling a deep breath and uttering a prayer I doubt made it past the ceiling, I opened the door, walked out of my office, and greeted Detective Maribel Johnson.

She was an attractive woman, probably in her mid-forties, possibly Hispanic. She was not wearing a police uniform but was dressed in dark gray slacks and a light blue button-up shirt. Anyone walking through the room might have thought she was one of our teachers . . .

until they spotted the badge and sidearm clipped to her belt.

Standing beside her was a younger man, probably her partner. He, too, looked sharp and appropriately serious. Judging from his physique and his military-style haircut and posture, I would have bet anything he'd done a tour or two in the Middle East before getting out and pursuing a career in law enforcement.

"Detective Johnson?" I said, extending my hand. "I'm Jason Vincent."

Her handshake was firm, her smile measured. She introduced her partner as Officer Dean. He nodded and almost crushed the bones in my hand when he shook it. I tried not to wince and resisted the temptation to shake and rub my hand when he finally released it. I've always detested guys who feel the need to do that. There's something of the bully in them, I'm sure. Making another man wince feeds something dark in their nature.

Once seated in my office, Detective Johnson got right to the point.

"First, let me express our condolences for your loss. I'm sure this must be a very difficult morning."

I nodded. "Yes, I think we're all still trying to wrap our heads around what happened."

"Well, thank you for seeing us. We'll try not to take up too much of your time."

"No problem. Whatever you need."

Detective Johnson opened a small notebook she'd been carrying and glanced at it. Then she looked at me and said, "Was Faith Connelly a good teacher?"

"Yes, she was. Excellent. The kids loved her."

"Did she get along well with other school personnel?"

"Yes. There were never any problems."

"And with you, personally, as her boss? Did you ever have

problems with her, have to discipline or suspend her, or anything like that?"

"Never. She was a delight to work with."

"Do you know if she ever had a run-in with a parent that was, let's say, more intense than usual? I ask because I assume all teachers have to deal with difficult parents from time to time."

"Yes, they do. My answer is I don't know for sure if she ever had an out-of-the-ordinary run-in with a parent, but I can tell you I never heard about it if she did."

"Do you think you would have heard about it?"

"Yes, because I've instructed the teachers here to let me know if a parent crosses the line or seems a little off in some way. In this day and age, you can't be too careful.

I could only watch him out of the corner of my eye, but it appeared Officer Dean hadn't twitched so much as an eyebrow since he'd sat down. I had the fleeting, nonsensical thought that he might be some sort of android . . . that if I tore off his face, I would find a complex system of mechanical parts and wires and flashing lights.

"Do you know much about her personal life away from the school?" Detective Johnson asked.

Refocusing, I realized the question I'd been dreading was now hanging in the air between us. It's funny how you can know something is coming and still feel thrown off when it arrives.

"Some, I guess. I know her husband is incarcerated, and she has a daughter who's in the first grade here at our school. When I hired her this past summer, she really needed a job. But it wasn't a pity-hiring because she'd been a teacher before and had excellent references. I spoke to a principal who had worked with her seven or eight years ago, and he had nothing but good things to say."

"Do you know if Mrs. Connelly was faithful to her marriage vows after her husband went to prison?"

I shook my head and smiled in a way I hoped would communicate my complete inability to believe Faith was capable of being unfaithful. "Since I mostly only saw her at school, and since I didn't keep tabs on her away from school, I guess I can't say definitively whether she was or wasn't faithful. But I can tell you she struck me as a woman of high morals."

"So your answer is that you don't know if she was faithful or not?"

"Yes, that is my answer."

I was thankful I wasn't hooked up to a polygraph. I'm sure I would have failed so spectacularly that a SWAT team would have been called to surround the building and drag me away in cuffs. My heart was slamming against my chest wall so hard I wouldn't have been surprised if either Detective Johnson or Officer Dean had looked toward the windows and said, "Is that thunder?" However, I must have done a decent job of maintaining my composure externally, because Detective Johnson moved right along.

"Do you know if Mrs. Connelly had a drinking problem or ever used drugs?"

"Again, I can't be one hundred percent sure, but I would be shocked if either one of those things was true."

What about run-ins with other teachers? Did you ever have to settle a dispute or deal with any kind of sexual harassment situation involving Mrs. Connelly?"

"Never."

"Do you know of any reason Mrs. Connelly would have been in Belle Isle Park after dark on a school night?"

"I don't."

Detective Johnson looked back at her notebook. What was probably only about ten seconds seemed like thirty. Finally, she looked up and said, "Yes or no . . . do you know of anyone who might have wanted to do Mrs. Connelly harm?"

"No, I don't."

"Is there anything you'd like to tell me that you think might have a bearing on our investigation? Anything at all you think I might need to know?"

I shook my head. "No. As far as I'm concerned, Faith's death makes no sense on any level. But I would like to ask you a question."

"Go right ahead."

"I saw on the news that there was a second body found in the park last night. Were the two deaths related?"

"I'm sorry. I can't talk about any of that. We will, however, make a statement very soon, and I'm sure your particular question will be answered."

It was the answer I'd been expecting, but I still had to ask. Not only because I wanted to know but also because I thought it was a question anybody would ask.

"I understand," I said.

And with that, Detective Johnson smiled, slapped her notebook shut, and said, "Once again, thank you for your time. We know this is not an easy day for you, but we really needed to get a handle on her professional life. I assume you won't mind if we talk to a few other people—teachers and staff?"

"Not at all, as long as you can be somewhat discreet. We don't want to scare the kids."

She knew I was referencing her badge and sidearm, and she nodded. "That's a fair request. Maybe we'll come back this afternoon when school lets out. Can you point us toward anyone in particular who knew Faith well?"

The last two people I wanted Detective Johnson to talk to were Adam Brooks and Molly Thomas, so I recommended a couple of Faith's other coworkers whom I was pretty sure would have nothing particularly enlightening to share.

When they were gone, I closed the door to my office and collapsed into my chair. I felt exhausted, both physically and emotionally, but I also felt somewhat reassured. I had a good feeling about how the conversation went and how it ended. Yes, I'd had to lie through my teeth, but after so many lies, what were a couple more if it meant I could finally get this thing behind me and start putting my life back together?

I stood up and stretched, then walked over to my office window. What I saw outside was the last thing I wanted to see.

Adam Brooks was standing on the sidewalk, talking to Detective Johnson.

- 15 -

I stepped back from the window so they wouldn't see me if they glanced toward the building. The only thing I could read from their body language was that they didn't appear to be old friends or prior acquaintances. There were none of the smiling head nods you give to someone who's catching you up on their recent history. In fact, there were no smiles whatsoever, suggesting this conversation was all business. Adam was doing most of the talking. Detective Johnson was listening attentively but not writing anything down in her notebook. Officer Dean stood as still as—and with the same amount of emotion as—the light pole near which he was planted.

The conversation ended with a handshake and a parting of the ways after only a couple of minutes. I half-expected the officers to march back into the building and head straight to my office demanding to know why I had lied to them. Instead, they got in their car and drove away. This made it seem likely that whatever Adam said had nothing to do with me. Surely, if it had, the conversation would have lasted longer. Detective Johnson would have been asking questions right and left and making notes in her book. And Officer Dean wouldn't have looked so bored.

Perhaps it was my own paranoia—and having just talked to

Molly—that caused me to misread Adam in our earlier meeting. He definitely was not himself, but why would he be if Molly was right and he was having an affair with someone who'd just been murdered? Maybe the anger I saw in his eyes wasn't anger. Or if it was, maybe it wasn't directed at me but at the situation. These thoughts, and the fact that I wasn't being ushered out of my office and pushed into the back of a police car, made me feel marginally better.

But if I was right that Adam was not talking to the police about me, then what *was* he talking to them about? He was supposed to be in class. Had he seen the police cars arrive from his vantage point on the athletic fields? Did he leave someone else in charge of his class so he could catch the officers as they left? And the most curious question of all: Why would he want to go anywhere near them if he'd been cheating with Faith? Could he possibly have been trying to point them in a different direction? I had no idea what to make of the situation. It was all very confusing. But I was at least reasonably sure he hadn't pointed them in my direction.

When I returned to my desk, I poured four Advil out of a bottle I kept in my drawer and swallowed them with a big gulp of Dasani. It wasn't even lunchtime yet, and already I felt spent. Of course, when I stopped to think about what I'd been through in the last fourteen hours, not to mention the fear I was harboring and the acting job I was attempting to pull off, I guess it's amazing I was able to function at all.

Suddenly, I remembered I was supposed to call Mary Beth and report on my interview with Detective Johnson, so I picked up my phone and speed-dialed her cell. It took a few rings for her to answer. When she did, I sensed her mind was elsewhere as if she had put someone on hold to talk to me and was having trouble switching gears. I'd expected her to be anxious and full of follow-up questions, but she listened to my brief account of my conversation with

Detective Johnson and seemed satisfied with it. There was none of the anxiety that had prompted her to call earlier and tell me to be careful.

I said, "Honey, are you all right?"

She said, "Yes, of course." Then, after a brief pause, almost as if she was scrambling to think of something to say, she added, "I'm worried about you."

"I'm fine. It's just a crazy day is all."

Another silence.

From the first day I met Mary Beth all the way back in college, I'd never known her to have trouble thinking of things to say. Our conversations just didn't have awkward silences. Ever. Now, all of a sudden, she was talking as if she thought the phone might be bugged. I almost asked her if there was someone in the room with her, listening to her half of the conversation, but decided the thought was just another manifestation of my paranoia. Frustrated and anxious to get off the phone, I asked her to back off dinner by an hour in case I got tied up with things at school. She said she would and we told each other goodbye.

Mary Beth hadn't worked outside the home in three years. She had a degree in social work and was running a non-profit outreach to the homeless when she was physically attacked by a mentally unbalanced man who was convinced she'd been counseling his estranged wife to run away with their child. She'd ended up with a concussion and two broken ribs.

After a few days of bedrest, she announced she was quitting her job. I was very supportive, certain she'd be able to find something safer. But she never looked for another job. She did a little volunteer work from time to time, but nothing steady. Fortunately, my salary was sufficient to meet our financial needs. Still, it troubled me that this woman who'd always been so effective in her service to those in need was no longer using her gift. Yes, she kept a spotless house and had dinner on the table every evening. She also took good care of herself by working out and eating healthy, so it's not like she had become a bum. But I felt she had so much more to offer the world than a vacuum cleaner, a spatula, and five miles a day on the treadmill. She'd proven she did.

When she still showed no interest in going back to work after six months, I suggested we step up our efforts to have a baby. She'd always expressed a desire to have one someday, and it seemed to me that with so much time on her hands, "someday" had arrived. She disagreed. It seems she had fallen in love with being a stay-at-home wife and didn't want to start adding 2:00 a.m. feedings and dirty diapers to the mix. It took a while, but I finally accepted that this was who Mary Beth was at this point in her life. It seemed a drastic change for someone who was once so driven, but I was at least glad she seemed happy and kept the machinery of our domestic life running on all cylinders.

I sat at my desk for a minute or two and tried to process the strangeness of the conversation we'd just had. I finally chalked it up to the situation. None of us could be expected to be ourselves on such a day. She might have been sitting at home, thinking I sounded strange too. Yes, that's what it had to be.

- 16 -

It was the media's turn to have a go at me.

I had informed Alice earlier that I would be available to answer questions at 1:00 p.m. in the cafeteria. This would be after the students were back in class from lunch. I also said I would not do any on-camera interviews but would answer questions and offer comments that could be used however the reporters saw fit.

I was hoping for no more than three or four reporters. When I walked into the cafeteria just after one o'clock, there were nine present. Alice had made it clear to them that I would not appear on camera, so there were no lights on tripods set up. However, there were a couple of handhelds sitting on the floor. I assumed they would record video of the campus and the sign out front to run with their reports. I had approved the taking of such generic shots as long as no faces, either of students or staff, could be seen.

The reporters, who'd been milling around, compressed themselves into a tight huddle when I approached and held out an array of microphones, some bearing the call letters of their stations. I stepped in close. Alice stood a few steps back and to my right.

"My name is Jason Vincent. I'm the principal here at Lake Arbor Elementary. As you know, we've suffered a terrible loss. Faith

Connelly was an outstanding teacher who'd only been here a short time but was dearly loved by her students, their parents, and her coworkers. There's not a lot I can say about what happened last night because I don't know anything about the investigation other than what I've seen on the news, but I'll try to answer whatever questions I can."

A young female reporter spoke right up. "Were the police here earlier today, and did you talk to them?"

"They were, and I did."

"What kinds of questions did they ask you?

"Just basic stuff. How long had Faith worked here? Did she get along well with people? That sort of thing."

"And did she get along well with people?"

"She did. Faith was a joy to be around. I'm quite confident you wouldn't be able to find anyone in this school who would say a negative word about her."

A balding, disheveled man who looked to be in his forties spoke next: "In doing some checking, I, and I'm sure most of my colleagues here, learned that Mrs. Connelly's husband is in prison. How would you say that situation was affecting her? Did it affect her job performance or her interactions with other people in any way?"

"You're right. It's no secret Faith's husband is presently incarcerated. I'm sure the situation had some struggle built into it for her, but I can assure you she did not bring it to work with her. If anything, I would say she enjoyed being here and embraced her work even more because it was something positive she could focus on."

There were a few other fairly generic questions, and then, just as it seemed things were winding down, an attractive redhead at the back of the huddle turned the session on its ear: "There's been a report that Mrs. Connelly was having an affair. Can you tell us anything about that?"

Once again, I was glad I wasn't hooked up to a polygraph. The non-threatening questions I'd been fielding had caused me to relax, and now, in the time it took the woman to speak two sentences, my heart rate had kicked into high gear. I could only assume my face had turned red too, judging from the heat I felt in my cheeks.

I almost asked the woman how she found out. Instead, I said, "Um, I don't know what report you're talking about. I haven't heard anything, and I've never seen anything out of Faith that would lead me to believe it was true."

Yet another lie. Maybe the most egregious yet. I once heard it said that the more you lie, the easier it is to keep lying, that you eventually become numb to what you're doing. I certainly wasn't finding it to be the case. Even as I stood there, the shame and guilt I felt was almost unbearable. I thought I might double over and vomit, but somehow managed to hold it together.

The question affected Alice, too. I could tell she took offense at it by the way she stepped up and announced that our little press conference was over. She said, "I'm sure you understand Mr. Vincent is extremely busy today."

I nodded in agreement and snuck a quick look at the woman who'd asked the last question. Though she was attractive enough to be an on-camera personality—perhaps even an anchorperson—I noticed she was using the kind of small, handheld recorder anyone can buy at Staples. The others in the huddle had lanyards and station logos on their polos and equipment bags, but there was nothing to indicate whom or what she represented.

A short time later, Alice knocked on my office door. I knew it was her because she always knocked in a rhythmic pattern that sounded like "a-chew, a-chew." I was kicked back with my feet up on my desk and made no effort to sit up as I invited her in. I wanted to look as relaxed as possible, like I was trying to find a moment's respite in the middle of a hellish day, even though on the inside I felt like screaming.

She was irate, as I knew she would be. "Can you believe what that woman said about Faith having an affair?"

As calmly as I could, I said, "You know the news media. They're after whatever will help them attract viewers or listeners, even if they have to invent something."

"But she said there was a report about it. *What* report?"

That, of course, was what worried me too. "I have no idea."

"Do you know who she was . . . who she was representing?"

"I don't know that either," I said.

But I intended to find out. It just so happened that shortly before one, right before I headed to the cafeteria for the interview, I was looking out my office window when that particular reporter pulled up in a black BMW with tinted windows and parked in a space near the front entrance designated for visitors. I noticed her because of her flaming red hair and movie-star good looks. So after I left the reporters to collect their gear and Alice shepherded me toward the front door, I walked quickly out to the parking lot—under the guise of needing some fresh air—and memorized her tag number.

- 17 -

There's been a report that Mrs. Connelly was having an affair.

The words played on a loop in my head like the ice cream truck calliope echoes in my brain for hours after it cruises through our neighborhood, the main difference being that the ice cream truck is annoying while the mysterious reporter's words were terrifying.

By two o'clock, I had finally met all my obligations and even managed to stamp out a couple of small administrative fires, so I told Alice I was going to take a few minutes for myself in my office. She'd worked with me long enough to know that was code for "Do not disturb."

With the door closed, I jumped on the Internet and searched every article I could find about Faith's murder. They were pretty much all the same, which is to say they contained very little new information, and none of them even hinted Faith had been having an affair.

There's been a report . . .

I racked my brain.

Where could such a report have come from? Was it possible there was no such report, that the redheaded mystery woman simply threw the notion out there to see what kind of reaction she might get? My impression of the modern news media led me to believe such a tactic was probably common. Throw something against the wall and see if it sticks. But why in this case? Wasn't the murder of a popular second-grade teacher tragic enough on its own? Was it really necessary to weave a thread of scandal through the story?

Then another idea struck me: If I couldn't track down the report, I'd try to find the reporter.

I did a search of news outlets in our area and came up with a list of links, everything from television stations to radio stations to newspapers to websites. I started with television stations, seeking pictures of reporters and anchor people. It took about ten minutes to get through them all. I found lots of attractive faces but none resembled the mysterious redhead. Next, I perused radio station websites and came away thinking the old adage "a face for radio" was apropos. There was no one even remotely as attractive as the woman I was looking for. It was the same with the newspaper sites.

Who *was* this woman, and who did she represent?

I picked up my cellphone and called an old high school buddy I'd stayed in touch with over the years. He was a state trooper named Ed Dickerson. We'd played a lot of golf together over the years and gone on a couple of fishing trips to Canada. I was pretty sure he would run the tag number I'd memorized if I could come up with a half-decent reason I needed him to.

He picked up on the second ring: "Jason! What's up, my man?"

"Hey, Eddie. Did I catch you at a bad time? You parked at a Dunkin' Donuts somewhere?" It was my standard opening anytime I called him.

"Just licking the powdered sugar off my fingers now. What's on your mind? "

"I was hoping you might be able to do me a favor."

"Let you beat me at golf for a change?"

"That, too. For now, though, I was hoping you could run a tag number for me. We had something a little unusual happen today, and I'm curious."

"Does it have anything to do with the teacher who was murdered? I heard about that."

"Indirectly, yes. I spoke with some reporters today at the school, but I think one of them might have been an imposter."

"Oh, really."

"Yes, she was asking some strange questions, and then, when I tried to find out who she was, nobody knew." It was a slight variation on the truth but nothing compared to the other lies I'd been spewing lately.

"And you got her tag number and want to know who she is."

"Exactly."

"It's not so you can ask her out on a date, is it? Because Mary Beth probably wouldn't approve."

"Nope. I'd just like to know who she is. My secretary and I both thought she gave off a weird vibe. Maybe we're all a little skittish right now, but I'd feel better if I could ID her."

"Sounds reasonable. Read me the number, and I'll get back to you as soon as I finish my donuts."

It was almost an hour before he called back.

I didn't bother to say hello. "What did you come up with?"

"The car is registered to one Angela Wells, of 2174 Palm Court, in your fair city."

"Angela Wells?" I said, quickly running the name through my mental database. When I got no hits I said, "The name means nothing to me, but at least now I can look around online and on social media and see what I can find."

I was just getting ready to thank Ed again and hang up when he stopped me with a question: "Aren't you going to ask?"

"Ask what?"

"Ask if the lovely Ms. Wells—and she *is* quite lovely, by the way—has ever had any skirmishes with the law."

"Um, yeah, sure. Has she?"

"Only a couple" was all he said.

"Are you going to make me beg?"

Ed snickered. "She's been picked up for criminal solicitation and misdemeanor assault."

I was stunned. "Has she done any jail time?"

"Nope. Fines and community service only. But she's certainly no Girl Scout."

I was having trouble processing what I was hearing. I had no idea what any of it meant, but I'd have to think about it later. It was almost time for school to let out, and I needed to get off the phone. I thanked Ed again and hung up.

As I walked out of my office and prepared to face the pandemonium the school day's final bell always produced, I knew one thing for certain: I was going to investigate Angela Wells.

- 18 -

For a woman who spent so many hours watching the Food Network, Mary Beth wasn't very "chef-ish." The dishes she typically made, while great-tasting, were nothing like what you'd see the celebrity chefs whipping up on their syndicated programs. I, however, preferred this. I've always been a nothing-fancy, meat-and-potatoes kind of guy. In fact, when I found Mary Beth locked into to a program where the host was demonstrating how to make some hifalutin dish that looked like weeds and gravel on a dinner plate, I often said, "Be careful now. Don't go getting all *chef-ish* on me."

That day when I got home from school, she wasn't getting chef-ish, but she was obviously going all-out to prepare a meal she knew I would like. Normally, our evening meals were simple: a salad, a meat, and a vegetable. That night she served a roast with carrots and potatoes (one of my favorite dishes) along with her homemade coleslaw. She'd also been a busy little baker, serving up a plate of hot yeast rolls and a chocolate cake for dessert.

I know she did it as an act of love, for the rough twenty-four hours I'd had. What she didn't realize was my last twenty-four hours had been far rougher than she knew and the wonderful meal she'd prepared only added to my guilt. I saw the love in her eyes and the food she prepared and started hating myself all over again for cheating on her.

Dinner time had always been talking time for us, so when we sat down to eat, she began her interrogation: "Was the day as bad as you thought it would be?"

No, it was a thousand times worse. "It was about what I was expecting."

"I saw on the news that they haven't come up with any clues to who might have killed Mrs. Connelly. They're asking for anybody who might have seen something to come forward."

I, of course, was already aware of this and considered it the one piece of good news I had received all day. There were plenty of other things for me to worry about, however.

Mary Beth said, "Did you speak with the media?"

"Yes, at one o'clock."

"How did it go?"

I didn't dare tell Mary Beth about the mysterious Angela Wells because that would have necessitated an explanation about her comment regarding a report Faith was having an affair. If such a report really was out there somewhere and surfaced in the news at some point, I would play it off as something I knew nothing about. But there was no way *I* was bringing up *anything* that had to do with adulterous affairs.

I said, "It was fine. We met in the cafeteria after the lunch periods were over. About nine reporters showed up. Their questions were very generic." *Well, all but one.*

"Did you recognize any of the reporters from TV?"

It was so like Mary Beth to ask a question like that, her interest in TV personalities being what it was.

"I thought one or two of them looked familiar, but that was about it."

"What about the students and faculty? Was everybody upset?"

"Early this morning, yes. But as the day wore on, things settled down. By this afternoon anybody who didn't know what had happened probably wouldn't have been able to detect anything unusual. They handled it like the professionals they are."

When dinner was over Mary Beth washed the dishes, and I dried them. We had a perfectly good dishwasher that ran like it had just rolled off the assembly line, yet we still did them by hand most of the time. I once asked Mary Beth why, and she said, "Does it bother you to help me with the dishes?"

I opened my mouth to answer and froze.

There are moments in a husband's life when the words *"you can't win"* flash across his mind. The sooner a man learns to heed that warning, the happier his marriage, and therefore his life, will be. I assured Mary Beth I loved doing dishes with her, and the subject hasn't been brought up since. I've concluded we only have a dishwasher because the cabinet maker left an opening for one.

When the dishes were done, Mary Beth asked if I wanted to rent a movie to take my mind off of things. I told her it would be fine, but before we could get settled in to watch it, my cellphone rang. It was Ed Dickerson. An alarm sounded in my mind as I stepped into my office to take the call.

"Hey, Ed."

"I didn't catch you in the middle of dinner, did I?"

"Nope. We finished a while ago. What's up?"

"I've been thinking about your situation with the tantalizing Ms. Wells."

"And?"

"Is she really somebody you're concerned about?"

I knew I had to be careful. I didn't want to draw too much attention to Angela Wells because I didn't want to explain why she unnerved me. On the other hand, I was curious to hear what Ed had to say. I knew he wouldn't have called me if he didn't have an idea percolating in his brain.

"I don't know if '*concerned*' is the right word. Let's just say I have a feeling she wasn't on the level. Something about her seemed off. Even more so when you found out what you did about her background."

"Well, if you want to have her checked out so you can put your mind at ease, I know just the guy who can do it for you."

"Oh yeah? Who?"

"Buddy of mine named Jake Dobbs. He was a cop up until two years ago. Got himself shot up and had to retire. Now he works as a PI because he can't stand sitting around the house, listening to his wife complain. Least that's what he says."

"Is he expensive?"

"Not if you mention my name. He told me if I sent any clients his way he'd treat them right. I'm sure he will, too. He's a good guy."

I wrote down his contact info even though I knew I wasn't going to hire Mr. Dobbs. Anything he might discover about Angela Wells he would almost certainly share with Ed. It sounded like the two of them were pretty tight, and Ed would be curious. The last thing I needed was for someone in my circle of friends to take an interest in what was happening in my life.

"I really appreciate the info, Ed. I'll think it over and see how I feel tomorrow."

"It's up to you. I just thought of Jake and figured he might be a good contact for you to have."

After promising each other we would get together for a round of golf soon, we hung up. I knew Mary Beth was waiting for me to watch a movie and I wasn't going to disappoint her. But I doubted I'd be able to keep my mind on it because, even though I had no intention of calling Jake Dobbs, Ed had given me an idea. There had to be other private investigators around. All I had to do was find one that had no connection to me. I could pay him out of the secret envelope of cash I kept hidden in my desk so nothing would show up on our credit cards. Mary Beth knew I had the envelope; she just didn't know how much was in it.

Buoyed by having an idea to pursue, I joined Mary Beth in the family room where she was already curled up in an afghan. We watched *La La Land*, which Mary Beth chose because she said we needed something light after a couple of days of darkness. She made her judgment based on the fanciful dance routines she'd seen in the previews. She didn't realize it was a movie about an ill-fated love affair. She was crying when it ended.

I knew what that meant.

Every time Mary Beth watched a sad movie about ill-fated lovers, she wanted to make love. I asked her about this once, and after first denying it was true, she finally admitted such movies made her want to reaffirm the loves in her own life. So after I was sufficiently reaffirmed, I lay on my back and stared at the ceiling, waiting for her to fall asleep so I could slip out of bed and go to my office to surf the net for private detectives.

- 19 -

By midnight I was in my office with the door closed, trying to decide what to type into the search engine. I thought about "private investigators in my area" but decided I needed a basic understanding of how private investigators do business before I started. So I typed in "how to hire a private investigator" and hit search. In the very first link I found the info I was looking for.

It looked like I could expect to pay about fifty dollars per hour, not counting mileage or other incidentals. I also needed to find out if the PI required a retainer. I had over three thousand dollars in what I called my "cash stash." It came from classes I'd taught, articles I'd written, and pieces of my deceased father's coin collection I'd sold off over the last several years. I'd made a habit of cashing the checks and stashing the cash in my not-so-secret envelope. Mary Beth once asked me why I did it, and I told her it was my rainy-day fund, that someday it would come in handy. The rainy day I'd been referring to, which turned out to be more of a stormy day, had arrived.

My preliminary research also helped me realize I needed to give my PI some specific instructions. Just handing him Angela Wells' name and asking him to follow her wasn't good enough. He needed to know what he was looking for. PIs have many investigative tools at their disposal, and they're going to charge the client at least fifty dollars an hour whether they use them or not. I decided to come up with a list of things I wanted to know to try to maximize my investment.

After about twenty minutes of this kind of research, I decided to start looking at some actual PIs. Naturally, it wasn't as easy as I thought it would be. What is?

Instead of finding a list of links to various PIs in my local area, I kept hitting sites for nation-wide companies with 1-800 numbers. They wanted me to begin the process by filling out and submitting an online form with my contact information and zip code, which I did not want to do. Finally, on the third page of my search results, I found a link for *Bloodhound Investigations*. When I clicked it I was greeted by a picture of a cartoon bloodhound with his nose to the ground and the words "Let me sniff out what you need." The sight was obviously not built by some high-priced web designer, but I felt inclined toward it anyway because it listed a local phone number and address and didn't ask me to submit anything online. Perhaps I also thought that if the guy was competing with the big boys, he might be a little cheaper.

I copied down the info I needed. Then I grabbed a notepad and pen and started thinking about exactly what it was I wanted the PI to do for me.

First, I wrote down "Employment Status." I wanted to know if Angela Wells really worked for a legitimate news outlet. The fact that I couldn't find her on the websites of any TV, radio stations, or newspapers was worrisome but not definitive. It was possible, for example, that she'd been hired only recently and her company's website hadn't yet been updated. But if she didn't work for a news outlet, then who *did* she work for?

Next, I wrote down "Connections." Somehow, someway, Angela

Wells knew Faith was having an affair. Or two, if Molly Thomas was correct. Or the person who was employing Angela knew. Or maybe not. Maybe Angela was a friend of Faith's whom Faith had never mentioned to me. Maybe they were college roommates way back when. Maybe Faith had confided in her about the affair but hadn't given her my name. Or Adam's name. That would leave Angela with a burning curiosity but nothing to take to the police, perhaps causing her to launch her own investigation. Was I being crazy, or were these things actually possible? I had no idea how a PI would find the answers to these questions, but it made me feel better to think through them and write them down.

Finally, I wrote down "Daily Routine." My gut told me Angela Wells was not a reporter and she was doing someone else's bidding. If that were the case, would she meet the person for lunch or maybe on a bench at Lake Eola? Would she go to their house? Would they go to hers? Did they perhaps live together? I wanted to know what a day in the life of Angela Wells was like. What did she do when she wasn't pretending to be a reporter?

When I glanced at my watch, it was 1:20 a.m. I needed to be back at the school in less than six hours. My neck and shoulders were tight and sore from hunching over my computer, but I knew if I went to bed I'd just lie there and stare into the darkness. I went to bed anyway. I felt like I'd done all I could do for the time being and needed to at least try to get some sleep. I tore my page of notes off the pad, folded it, and stuck it in my wallet.

That night I dreamed about an attractive redheaded woman who was walking around at an upscale party with blood stains on her dress.

- 20 -

The next morning was a Friday. I was in my office by 6:45 a.m.,
feeling like I usually did on the morning after a long, hard day.
I have a TV mounted on my office wall, so I tuned in to the local
newscast to catch the latest updates on the murders before students
and teachers started arriving. The lead story had to do with the other
murder victim, the one Officer Ryland had said was "hacked up pretty
good."

His name was Damien Robillard. He was 31 and had a colorful
past. "Colorful," as in "criminal." He was from Jacksonville and had
been in trouble with the law pretty much his whole life. From his
height and weight and the description of his clothing, plus the fact
that he was "hacked up" according to Officer Ryland (a bit of
information that was not being reported on the news), I knew he had
to be Crowbar, Faith's killer, though no mention was made of finding
a ski mask or a crowbar at the scene. I suspected Machete had removed
those items after killing Crowbar, or else the police did find them and
weren't releasing the information.

As horrifying as Faith's death was, I knew it was accidental. She'd
made a run for it, and Crowbar swung his weapon. He didn't have
time to think or aim. He just flung his right arm out in backhanded

fashion as she was flying by. I feel like it was a panic move on his part, that he and Machete didn't intend to kill anyone. Why else would they have been wearing masks if they'd planned to leave no witnesses? Unfortunately, Crowbar's shoulder was the same height as Faith's head, causing the curved iron bar to connect with the back of her skull.

Once the accident happened, everything changed for them. Machete and Crowbar took off, probably in a panic, while I was checking on Faith. I can see Machete, who seemed to be the one in charge, thinking his sidekick, who was now a murderer, had become a liability. He must have wondered how Crowbar would process what he had done? He may have committed crimes before, but had he ever killed anyone? Would he be able to keep his head together in the coming days? If the pressure mounted, would he break down and confess? Or would he go the other direction and brag about it sometime when he'd had one too many beers? If you're Machete, why not just kill him and eliminate the only person on earth who could place you at the scene of the crime? And it would be best to do it right there in the park instead of trying to work out a time and place to do it later.

It all made sense.

Or did it?

What if the victim was actually Machete? Maybe Crowbar suddenly feared Machete, seeing him as the only witness to his crime . . . at least the only one who could identify him. Maybe he conked Machete over the head with his crowbar as they were making their escape and then used the machete to chop him up. Witness eliminated. If he could get out of the park unseen, no one would ever know he was there. Yes, that made sense too.

I had to admit it could be either one of them lying in the morgue.

Or neither one.

Mr. Robillard's criminal record didn't automatically prove he was Machete or Crowbar. Maybe he was just a guy going for a late evening jog. Maybe Machete and Crowbar ran smack into him as they were running away and saw him as a threat. *Yes, officer, I saw two men running out of the park, one carrying a crowbar and the other a machete. I thought it was really strange, so I kept an eye on them to see where they would go. I saw them run down Clark Street and jump into a blue pickup with this tag number . . .*

There was no way Machete and Crowbar would let it happen.

The longer I thought about it, the more I realized I had no idea if Damien Robillard was Machete or Crowbar, or if he had anything whatsoever to do with them, other than being hacked up by one of them. That's the one thing I did think seemed likely. I had trouble believing there were other people running around in the park that night carrying machetes.

The newscaster went on to say police were assuming the two deaths—Faith's and Damien's—were connected and anyone with information should come forward. If Faith had a wealthy relative somewhere, I figured it wouldn't be long before they started offering a reward for information leading to an arrest.

When Alice arrived, I clicked off the TV. As usual, she popped her head in, said a cheery good morning, and started a pot of coffee. I usually didn't drink it, but that morning I made an exception. I desperately needed the caffeine.

Thankfully, as the day got going, things felt pretty normal. Everyone had had some time to process the news about Mrs. Connelly and an evening at home to have whatever conversations they needed to have with their loved ones or therapist or clergy. Plus, it was Friday. Everyone around a school feels a little more chipper with the weekend on the doorstep.

I was further encouraged when Adam Brooks stopped into the

office to ask Alice a question and seemed his old self. Never the warmest guy in the world (unless he was talking to an attractive female), he asked if I was hanging in there. He said he knew yesterday must have been a horrible day for me. I don't know if there was a hidden meaning to the comment, but I chose to think there wasn't because of the kindness in his voice. If he'd been sending some kind of subtle message, I doubt he would have been able to carry it off without showing some tension. I told him yesterday was a hard day for all of us and I was proud of how everyone was, to use his phrase, hanging in there.

Returning to my office, I breathed a sigh of relief though I knew I wasn't out of the woods. Angela Wells was a wild card I needed to know more about before I'd be able to truly relax. But overall, I was feeling optimistic. With an uneventful police interview behind me, with apparently no clues at the scene of the crime pointing to me, with Adam Brooks back to being his old self, and with Damien Robillard, whoever he was, getting all the attention in the press, I felt like I just might get through unscathed.

Then, at 9:30, Alice sent a call through to my desk.

A call that turned my day on its ear.

- 21 -

"This is Jason Vincent."

"Mr. Vincent, this is Dwayne Tucker. *Pastor* Dwayne Tucker over at Woodcrest Community Church. I was Faith Connelly's pastor."

For obvious reasons, Faith and I never talked much about our faith or our church lives. We knew each other went to church and maintained some level of involvement, but talking about it would have forced us to come up with some sort of lame rationalization for our affair. I'd heard of cheating couples trying to spiritualize what they were doing. *We know God wants us to be happy. He wouldn't have brought us together if he didn't know we were just what each other needed.* As terrible as our sin was, at least we didn't stoop so far as to try to drag God into it and make him a co-conspirator.

"Yes, pastor, what can I do for you?"

"I just had a meeting with Faith's parents to plan her memorial service. They said Faith always spoke so well of you. Apparently, you gave her a job when her back was to the wall and became a good friend to her and her daughter as she got back into teaching. Doris and Joe, Faith's mom and dad, would like to know if you'd share some personal reflections at the service. It's common to have someone from the family and then someone from the person's professional life to speak. Is that something you would be willing to do?"

Of all the things I thought I might face in the aftermath of Faith's death, this one hadn't even entered my mind. Naturally, I didn't want to do it. The thought of standing in front of a crowded auditorium and pretending Faith and I were nothing more than professional colleagues truly frightened me. Part of it was the hypocrisy thing again. I'd been doing so much lying and pretending the last few months, I was sick of it. But there was also the fear I might be too emotional. Unbeknownst to the people who would be listening to me, my life had been deeply, intimately tangled with Faith's. I even felt responsible for her death . . . at least responsible for her being in the park that night. Would I be able to stand up there and speak without breaking down?

"Um, well . . . I don't know."

"You do plan to be at the service, don't you?"

"Oh, yes, of course. I just . . . that sort of thing isn't in my wheelhouse."

"Well, if it makes you feel better, it isn't in anybody's wheelhouse. But you're a man who often speaks in front of people. When Faith's mother mentioned you, I just knew you were the perfect choice."

"Hmm, I don't know, Pastor. Maybe one of the other teachers would be better."

"Possibly, but the thing is, they asked for you."

Clearly, I was trapped. If I refused to grant this request, I would seem unsympathetic, which would probably draw as much, or more, attention than me just going ahead and muddling through. I asked the pastor how long I would be expected to speak.

"Oh, not long. I'd say five minutes would be enough."

Five minutes may have seemed short to the pastor, who was probably used to speaking from his pulpit for thirty minutes or more at a time. But to me it seemed like forever.

"Does it sound doable?"

"I guess so, though I've never done anything like this before, and it's way out of my comfort zone." I was starting to sound pathetic even to my own ears. I knew I needed to man-up and just do it. "But sure, for Faith, I can do it. She was a great person."

The pastor was delighted and filled me in on the details regarding the service. It would be on Sunday afternoon—just over forty-eight hours away—at his church. The mere thought of standing before a packed auditorium knowing what I knew scared me. I was afraid everyone there would be able to see guilt written all over my face. The only hope I had was that they would misinterpret what they were seeing . . . that they would see my guilt and shame and think it was grief.

The pastor thanked me for agreeing to help and ended the call. I sat at my desk and marveled at how the measured relief I was feeling before his call had completely vanished in less than five minutes. This was what people were talking about when they said they were on a rollercoaster. I hated to think it, but my gut told me there would be more loops and curves and drops to come before things finally evened out.

Later that afternoon, something strange happened that cranked up my anxiety even more. I had gone to the county superintendent's office to discuss plans for replacing Faith on a permanent basis and swung past my house on the way back to school. It was only a few blocks out of the way, and I wanted to change my shoes, of all things. I'd put on a pair of recently purchased dress shoes that morning and the right one was rubbing my heel raw.

Our development features a beautiful red brick entryway with landscaping that is meticulously maintained. It was the first thing the developer built, for obvious reasons. People saw how beautiful the entrance to the new community was and rushed to buy their homes because they assumed the building construction would meet the same standards. Unfortunately, the entryway turned out to be far and away the most attractive part of the development. Not that our neighborhood was a dump; it wasn't. We were happy living there. But the houses were strictly middle class.

I tell you that so you'll understand when I say we don't get many BMW's in our neighborhood. Lots of Fords, Chevys, Kias, and Hyundais, but hardly ever a BMW. I would have said *never* a BMW until, as I turned down the street I live on, I saw one coming my way. My mind had been wandering, but the similarity of the car to the one Angela Wells had driven to our school snapped me to attention. I tapped the brakes, hoping to get a glimpse of the driver, praying the windows weren't so deeply tinted I wouldn't be able to see through them.

It turned out I could see well enough to recognize the outline of a female head with long hair like Angela Wells had, but not well enough to positively identify her. I stomped on the brake and whipped my head around, but the glare of the sun off the back windshield of the BMW blinded me and kept me from reading the tag number. I watched helplessly as the car cruised to the end of the block and turned left.

- 22 -

I was a few hundred yards from our house, stopped in the middle of the street.

I eased off the brake and started rolling slowly forward as I tried to figure out why she would be on our street. For a terrifying instant, I wondered if Mary Beth was safe. Then I saw Mary Beth up ahead, walking down the driveway toward our mailbox. I had to get my head together and act like I hadn't just seen a mysterious person who might be trying to destroy me drive past our house.

Mary Beth, looking fine and patriotic in a red tank top, white shorts, and blue flip-flops, put her hands on her hips and gave me a surprised look as I rolled into the driveway. "What are you doing home?" she said as I opened the car door.

"I was on my way back from the county office and decided to stop by and change my shoes."

She looked at my feet. "What's wrong with them?"

"They're killing me. The right one's rubbing my heel."

"You just bought them." She said this as if I had no way of knowing.

"I know."

"You need to take them back."

"I know."

"They were expensive."

"I know."

Mary Beth often did this. No matter what topic we found ourselves discussing, she would state the obvious. Early in our marriage I would call her on it, gently, of course. I remember the time she said, "Cars don't run without gas." This was after I had forgotten to get gas and found myself stranded in the middle of nowhere. I said, very patiently, "Honey, I understand cars don't run without gas." She said, "So you need to stop and get some when you see the gas gauge pointing toward empty." I took a deep breath and agreed. Once, I couldn't stand it anymore and asked her why she always stated the obvious. She gave me a puzzled look as if she had no idea she did this. Then she said, "I'm not stating the obvious; I'm just thinking out loud. There's a difference." I opened my mouth to ask her to explain the difference, but decided to let it go. Her stating the obvious is something I've had to learn to live with.

The point is, Mary Beth stating the obvious about my shoes was what she would do under perfectly normal circumstances, which told me nothing abnormal had happened as far as she was concerned. She hadn't had a visitor, nor did she have any concerns about a mysterious black BMW cruising our neighborhood. She probably didn't see it if she stepped out of the house to get the mail after it had already passed by. Nevertheless, I decided to probe a little.

As I was putting on the old pair of dress shoes I thought I would never wear again, I said, "What have you been doing today?"

"I decided to tackle my closet. I pulled out two trash bags full of stuff to take to Goodwill."

Poking fun at her clothes-shopping addiction, I said, "Two trash bags full? Wow, you better be careful. You might end up having to wear the same outfit twice within the same calendar year."

"Hardy-har-har, you're so funny."

The way Mary Beth was acting, I could tell nothing out of the ordinary had happened, which was a relief. On the other hand, I now had something else to think about. What on earth was Angela Wells doing driving past my house? Was she casing the joint, as they used to say in the old cops and robbers movies I watched as a kid? I couldn't think of another reason she would be driving by, which led me to believe Angela Wells, whoever she was, wasn't done with me. She'd tried to embarrass me at my meeting with the media and now she was sniffing around my house.

I kissed Mary Beth and told her I needed to get back to the office. She asked if I wanted to go out to dinner after work. I said I thought that sounded good and she could pick the restaurant.

As I drove away, I made a decision. I didn't know how I was going to do it without Mary Beth finding out, but the next day, which was Saturday, I was going to find a way to contact the head bloodhound at Bloodhound Investigations.

- 23 -

It turned out to be easy. A friend of Mary Beth's called and asked her to go shopping and to lunch. It was such a fortuitous turn of events I almost wondered if God felt sorry for me and had decided to step up and turn a few circumstances in my favor. Then I remembered my affair with Faith and realized that probably wasn't the case. Sometimes even the worst person sees circumstances fall his way. It's the law of averages. Either way, I was grateful for the chance to be on my own for a few hours.

Mary Beth didn't ask what I planned to do while she was out shopping, which was unusual. I was prepared to tell her I wanted to get out and run a few errands. If she had pressed me to be more specific, I was going to tell her I wanted to go to Best Buy and checkout the new iPhone. It wouldn't be a lie because I actually did want to. It was a measure of how messed up my life was that I had to resort to parsing words and splitting hairs in such mundane conversations.

Mary Beth and her friend Laura rolled out of our driveway and turned left toward the parkway that would lead them to the area's biggest shopping and dining complex. I rolled out less than five minutes later and turned right toward the seedier part of town where the office of Bloodhound Investigations was located.

When my GPS informed me I had arrived at my destination, I whipped my head around, trying to locate it. There were two rundown strip malls sitting side by side that offered a collection of unimpressive storefronts: a thrift store, a laundromat, a nail salon, a Chinese takeout place, and a vinyl record store. Sprinkled among these were several dark places that appeared empty.

At the far end of the farthest strip mall, a storefront window had a sniffing bloodhound painted on it. The glass was tinted, so I couldn't tell if there were lights on inside, but I pulled in and parked in front of the door. For a moment, I sat there and wondered what I was doing. The sneaking, the general seediness of the neighborhood, and the nature of the work I was going to hire done made me feel dirty. Then I thought about the mysterious Angela Wells driving past my house, and all my misgivings vanished.

The front door was locked, but there was a button next to a small speaker. A sign above it read, "Ring Bell." I pressed the button and heard the ding. Immediately, the door clicked, and a voice from the speaker said, "Come on in."

What I saw when I stepped inside couldn't have been more surprising or more appropriate. Right in front of me, curled up on the floor, was a real, honest-to-goodness bloodhound. He was either old or lazy, or both, because all he did was raise his head slightly, give me the once over, and lay it back down.

Just beyond the dog was a desk with an old computer. I say "old" because it looked like the ones I had before laptops and flat screen monitors became the norm. There were also a few file cabinets and a small table with a coffee maker, cups, and packets of yellow and pink sweeteners. The room and its furnishings were not fancy or even up-to-date, but the place seemed clean enough and fairly well organized. The main thing I noticed was the absence of a human being. I was pretty sure the dog wasn't the one who'd invited me to "come on in" though, so I stood there and waited for someone to emerge from the back room.

Sure enough, a few seconds later, the door opened.

And my heart sank.

The person who stepped through the door was not the grizzled veteran gumshoe I had envisioned but a young Asian woman who looked like she should be grabbing her book bag and her Starbucks and heading off to class at the local community college. I thought, *Oh no, just my luck. On the day I really need to talk to the boss, only the secretary is here.*

But at least she was friendly. She stuck out her hand and said, "Hi. My name is Mia Li. It's a pleasure to meet you, Mr. Vincent. What took you so long to get here?"

- 24 -

I'd been reaching for her hand, but I froze when I heard what she said. If she'd walked out and slapped me hard across the face, I wouldn't have been more shocked. I stammered but finally got the words out: "How do you know who I am? And how could you have been expecting me?"

Mia giggled and said, "Was it your intention to remain anonymous?"

"Well, I . . ."

"If so, you should have rented a car or parked a block away and walked here."

So that was it. "You saw my plate and looked me up before I came in." I hesitated. "But . . . wait a minute . . . my tag is on the back of my car. You can't see it from here."

"No, but the tiny camera I have mounted on the light pole on the corner can."

I spun around and looked out at the pole but didn't see the camera. Turning back to her, I said, "Okay, but . . . how did you know I was coming?"

Mia giggled again. "I didn't. I just like to say that to mess with people."

I chuckled. "A secretary with a sense of humor. I like that."

This time Mia laughed full out. "Secretary? I'm the boss!"

For the second time in a minute, I was floored. "You're the *boss*?"

"Now, now, Mr. Vincent. You're not going to go all sexist on me and imply that a young woman can't run her own business, are you?"

"Uh, no . . . I just . . . didn't . . . "

Mia giggled again, and for the first time, I realized what a beautiful smile she had.

"Relax," she said. "I'm only teasing. I know I look like a college freshman, but I'm actually twenty-nine years old. I inherited the business from my father who started it when I was a baby. He died a couple of years ago, and I decided to keep it going. I've worked here, helping him out and learning the business since I was in high school. Did you notice his desk? It's exactly how he left it the day he died. It's my little tribute to him. All I do is dust it. It's a good reminder to me of where I came from."

"Wow, that's . . . "

"Weird, I know."

"No, no, I wasn't going to say that. I'm just surprised is all. But I think it's great. And please believe me. I'm not sexist."

She giggled again. "Oh, I believe you. You couldn't survive as a school principal if you were."

She got me again. Almost helplessly, I said, "Is there anything about me you *don't* know?"

"Oh, maybe a few things. Come on back to my office."

I followed her into the backroom where I found an office that looked much more in keeping with what I would expect from a person of her age. There was a large L-shaped desk with, not one, not two, but three flat screens and three keyboards. There was also a bookshelf mounted on the wall over her desk, holding a variety of reference books touching on topics ranging from medicine to law. Attached to the bottom of the shelf, which hung only a foot or so above her computer monitors, were a variety of clippings and handwritten sticky notes. On the wall to the left of the desk was a large map of the city with a red push pin stuck into the spot where we were. A few blue and yellow pins were stuck at other locations. I assumed the colors had some significance.

I said, "It's cool you have an actual bloodhound, given the name of your business."

Mia chuckled. "Yeah, that's Doctor Watson. He was my dad's dog. He sits there by the door every day. I honestly think he's waiting for my dad to come back from wherever he's been. He likes me okay, but he loved my dad." She motioned to a chair across from her desk. "Go ahead and have a seat."

As I settled in, I said, "Are you a one-person operation or do you have people who work for you?"

"Just me and Doctor Watson; although, I have some friends with, shall we say, some *special talents*, that I occasionally contract a little work out to."

"Special talents?"

Mia grinned. "Very special. Now, what can Doctor Watson and I do for you?"

The visit to Bloodhound Investigations was so far from what I'd been expecting and so laden with surprises I actually had to stop and think about why I was there. Mia was very impressive, but suddenly I was unsure how to begin. It was easy to think about hiring a PI to help me solve my problem when I was at home or at the office, but when the moment came to actually explain my problem, all I could think about were the things I didn't want to tell her. She read my hesitation correctly and said, "You're not so sure you want to tell me what's going on. Am I right?"

I shrugged and said, "You're good."

"Yes, I am, but not because I can read your mind right now. Actually, most of my clients feel exactly what you're feeling at the beginning. Whatever it is you're dealing with is of a very personal nature, and you don't know me. You aren't sure you can trust me. You have control of your situation right now, but if you let me in on it, you relinquish control. Suddenly, you're at my mercy. Am I right?"

I nodded. "Yes."

"Well, look at it this way, Mr. Vincent. You actually *don't* have control of your situation. If you did, you wouldn't be here. Whatever it is you're dealing with, there's something about it that is beyond your ability to manage. What I'd like for you to remember is that I am a *private* investigator. *Private*, as in *secret*. The moment I start betraying the confidence of my clients is the moment my business crashes and burns. Not only that, but it could put my life in danger. I'm not fool enough to believe everyone who walks into this office is a Sunday school teacher. I don't break the law, but I'm pretty sure some of my clients do, which is their business, not mine. But I certainly don't want to make them mad at me, and the fastest way I could do that would be to blab about their business."

Her little speech, which I was sure she'd made many times, won me over. I told her everything except what I had learned about Angela Wells from Ed Dickerson. Perhaps it was silly, but rather than helping her, I decided to see if she could come up with the same information about Wells' criminal past. If she did, it would verify Ed's information and make me feel good about Mia's investigative ability. If she didn't, I'd ask for my unused retainer back and try someone else.

- 25 -

Mia was not only a good talker but also a good listener. She stopped me at points along the way to ask a question or to get me to elaborate, but mostly she just listened and wrote some things down on a yellow legal pad. When I was finished, she said, "I've been reading about Mrs. Connelly's murder online and seeing the reports on the news. I'm sorry things turned out the way they did for her and also for you. You were just trying to do the right thing."

"I don't deserve any sympathy. None of it would have happened, and Faith would still be alive, if I had honored my marriage vows."

"Something else you don't deserve is to be harassed by Ms. Wells. I take it you want me to get the scoop on her? Find out who she is and what she might be up to?

"Yes. I'd like to know if she's really a reporter or if she's impersonating one. And if she *is* impersonating one, why? Who is she working for? And how did she know Faith and I were having an affair?"

Mia smiled sympathetically. "Mr. Vincent . . . "

"Please, call me Jason."

"Jason . . . I know you think you were careful. But the oldest story in the world is the one about the cheating couple that thinks they're getting away with something. I've seen situations where the spouses knew, the kids knew, the coworkers knew, and even the family pet knew. It's almost impossible to completely hide an affair, at least for very long."

"So what you're saying is . . . "

"What I'm saying is, yes, you may be among the ten percent who manage to get away with it, but more likely you're among the ninety percent who don't. My guess is somebody knew and didn't like it. Now that Mrs. Connelly is dead, they think you might've had something to do with it though they don't have proof. So they're trying to scare you or pressure you into giving yourself away."

I shook my head. "You really know how to cheer a guy up."

Mia smiled. "If I wanted to be in the cheering up business I would've become a clown and learned how to make balloon animals."

I nodded and gave a little smile that I knew didn't have a speck of mirth in it.

"Look, Jason, I think you're a good guy. A better guy than you realize. People make mistakes like this all the time. I'm no Bible scholar, but I seem to remember a certain king in the Old Testament had an affair and then had the woman's husband killed so he could have her as his own. The thing I like about you is that you didn't wait till you got caught to set things right. That tells me there is good in you—probably a lot more than you think."

I raised my head and looked Mia in the eyes. "Thank you. Maybe someday I'll be able to see it that way."

"In the meantime, I'll be happy to help you."

"I guess we better talk about your fee. I'd like to pay you in cash if it's okay."

She laughed. "Seventy-five percent of my clients want to pay cash. If I didn't accept cash I wouldn't have a business."

I reached into my pocket and pulled out a wad of bills. "How much do you need?"

"I ask for five hundred upfront. My fee is fifty dollars an hour and I refund what I don't earn. However, what you're asking me to do will likely involve some surveillance, which is more time consuming than simple research. In such cases, I ask for a thousand up front. I keep meticulous records, and again, I refund what I don't earn."

I peeled a thousand dollars off the wad of bills I was carrying, then leaned forward and laid it on her desk. She picked it up, counted it, said "Thank you," and wrote me a receipt. As she handed me the receipt, she said, "Oh, here. Let me give you my business card" and started reaching for one.

I said, "That's okay. I've got your number memorized. I don't want to take a chance on my wife or someone at the school finding a business card from a private investigator. I don't think I'd be able to explain it."

"What about the receipt?"

I looked at it and saw the very same information that was on the business card. I looked at Mia, back at the receipt, and then at Mia again. Then I tore up the receipt and handed it back to her. "Would you mind throwing it away for me?"

She smiled and said, "Sure."

"I'm completely at your mercy now. I can't even prove I gave you a thousand dollars."

Mia, who was one of those people who seems wired to smile at the slightest provocation, suddenly looked serious. "I don't take that kind of trust lightly, Jason. My Dad believed nothing was more important than a person's honor, and he instilled that same idea in me. I've never cheated anyone, and I'm not going to start with you. I promise you'll get your money's worth. And you'll get back whatever I don't earn."

I believed her.

We walked back into the outer office and toward the front door. Doctor Watson didn't bother to lift his head. When we reached the door, Mia stuck out her hand and said, "I won't be calling you because I'll never know where you are or if it's a good time to talk, and I don't want you to have to lie about who's calling you if someone, like your wife for example, asks. So you can feel free to call me on Monday afternoon. I'm sure I won't have anything to report before then."

I shook her hand and thanked her.

Once in the car, I backed out and drove away, feeling almost euphoric, not because I knew more than I did when I arrived but because I felt like I wasn't alone. I had an ally, and a formidable one, it seemed. There was always the chance Mia Li would turn out to be all surface and no substance, but I didn't think so. She struck me as a force to be reckoned with.

I slammed my fist against the steering wheel and felt a surge of adrenaline as I pulled out into the street. *Angela Wells, wherever you are, it's game on!*

- 26 -

When Mary Beth got home from her shopping trip, I was on the couch, taking a nap—not faking it but really sleeping. The stress of the last couple of days had robbed me of sleep and sapped my strength to the point I either had to lie down or fall down. And the comfort I felt after talking to Mia Li had made it easier for me to relax. I might have slept for a few hours if Mary Beth hadn't come through the door humming. It was a habit I'd had to get used to. Often the tune was unrecognizable. Always it was off key. But her musical limitations didn't hold her back. I'm confident that some days the notes she hummed were more numerous than the words she spoke.

When she saw me groggily trying to sit up, she froze and said, "Oh, I'm sorry. I didn't know you were sleeping."

I yawned. "It's okay. I need to get up or I won't sleep tonight."

She sat her purse and several shopping bags on the kitchen counter before walking over and dropping onto the sofa beside me. While untying her sneakers and kicking them off, she said, "My feet are killing me. Not to mention my ankles and knees and hips."

"Come on, you're not *that* old."

She gave me the evil eye and said, "What do you mean 'not *that* old'? I'm not old at all."

"Then why are you moaning about everything being sore?"

"Because Laura and I sat down in the food court for a grand total of ten minutes. Other than that, we were on our feet the whole time."

"You couldn't take a break?'

She sighed. "You see those bags over there?"

"I do."

"Do you understand that every one of them contains an article of clothing that will cause your heart to flutter and your pulse to race when you see it on me? And do you further realize that at the start of this day every one of those pulse-pounding articles of clothing was available for anyone—*anyone!*—to purchase? And that I would not be the owner of them right now if I had not gotten to them first? I ask you, do you understand what I'm telling you?"

"Uh . . ."

"I mean, really, I did it all for you. You should show a little appreciation."

"Sorry. I don't know what I was thinking."

She snaked her arm around my waist and pulled me close, planting a kiss on my cheek. "I'll let it go this time. Just don't let it happen again. Men who question their wife's shopping habits tend to meet with terrible fates."

It was all fun and games until that comment.

Both of our minds went straight to Faith, who met a terrible fate for real, and the joke fell flat. Mary Beth slumped back on the sofa and said, "Oh, man. I can't believe I said that. I'm sorry."

I sat back and put my arm around her. "It's okay."

She snuggled up to me and threw a leg over my thigh. After a moment of silence, she said, "How are you doing with everything?"

"Just getting past the funeral tomorrow will help. I'm dreading it."

"Do you know yet what you're going to say?"

"I've been mulling a few things over, but I need to sit down this evening and put some things on paper. I don't want to get up there and babble like an idiot."

"You know what Laura told me while we were shopping?"

"What?"

"She said she heard Faith had a reputation as a homewrecker."

"A what?"

"A homewrecker. You know, someone who breaks up a marriage by having an affair with the husband."

Mary Beth's head was resting on my chest, just over my heart. Terrified she would notice the sudden accelerated pounding, I sat up, causing her to pull away. I said, "That can't be true."

"Why not?"

"Because I know her. I mean I *knew* her. She wasn't that kind of person."

"How do you know?"

"Because I worked with her. I got to know her."

"Jason, you knew her for six months. You have no idea what her life was like before she walked into your office."

"But a homewrecker? That seems like a terrible thing to be telling people about someone who isn't able to defend herself. Did she tell you who said it?"

"No, I didn't ask."

"Why not?" It came out more passionately than I'd intended.

Mary Beth scrunched her eyebrows at me and said, "Boy, *you're* touchy."

She was right. I was overreacting to what she would probably have been willing to accept as a silly piece of gossip. I was almost forcing her to defend her friend Laura's assertion. I knew I had to dial it back.

I said, "Sorry. I don't mean to be touchy. I guess I just don't like hearing such a thing about one of my teachers."

But of course, the real reason I didn't like hearing it was because

I'd always told myself we truly cared about each other and on some level, we actually loved each other even though our actions were clearly wrong and we had no long-term future. I did not want to think of myself as just another notch on her headboard.

Mary Beth said, "I understand. The whole thing stinks."

"Yes, it does."

An hour later we had dinner. Afterward, I retired to my man cave to think about what I wanted to say to a chapel full of people about the woman whose death I felt responsible for.

PART 2

"Nothing makes us so lonely as our secrets."

—Paul Tournier

- 27 -

I've never been a particularly tenderhearted person. I'm not an ogre, mind you. But I'm definitely not the kind of guy who swoons at pictures of puppy dogs or mops tears from my cheeks as the credits are rolling in a movie theater. Nevertheless, there was something about Faith that touched me the first day I met her.

I've already said I thought she was pretty. I think most people would have agreed with me that she was above average but not a classic beauty. What ran through my mind the first time I saw her was that several nice little nuances I've seen in various women's facial features were blended together in hers: the hint of dimples when she smiled, the arched eyebrows that gave her every expression a little shot of surprise, and the asymmetrical smile that never quite seemed to leave her face. But I especially liked her eyes. All my life I've heard poets and troubadours wax eloquent about how eyes can twinkle or sparkle or shine, but I swear hers actually did. They were dark blue—indigo, she called them—and I do believe they had hypnotic powers. I remember a couple of occasions when I had to look away from them or risk completely losing my composure.

As for her body, I'll just say she had all the right stuff in all the right places. Lots of women do, of course. What lots of women *don't* have is the kind of physical grace that makes every movement of their bodies look carefully choreographed yet unpretentious. I've known women—attractive women—who lumbered or slumped or shuffled when they walked. Faith seemed to waft through a room like a gentle breeze through an open window. And her always-perfect posture gave her a regal bearing. I don't think any queen has ever carried herself with more dignity.

But her poise under pressure may have been what I found most impressive. When I met her, she had a lot of things to worry about. Her husband had committed multiple felonies and was going away for a while, leaving her in dire straits financially. She also had a young daughter, Zoey, who was trying to process her father's sudden absence and having a hard time of it. Normally a quiet child, she'd started breaking things and throwing screaming fits, which would put any parent on the verge of panic. On top of it all, Faith herself was feeling alone and scared. Yes, she had some family, but they were inclined more toward trying to control her than trying to encourage her. Her mother, in particular, had a way of insinuating things without actually saying them . . . things that made Faith feel like even more of a failure than her trying circumstances already did. When Faith would question her further, her mother would claim Faith had completely misinterpreted the comment, causing Faith to feel even more frustrated. Still, at least in my company, Faith never once lashed out at her mother or her husband, or even God, for allowing her to be dealt such a crummy hand.

The first time I interviewed her, I asked her why she was getting back into teaching after being out for a few years. It was a perfect opportunity for her to pour out her sob story to gain some pity points that might give her an advantage over her competition. She didn't. In fact, only by asking a series of follow-up questions did I finally realize how difficult her circumstances were. When I asked her why she didn't tell me everything up front, she said, "Mr. Vincent, everybody has problems. I don't consider myself special in that regard. And I was hoping to get this job on merit rather than pity. I haven't taught in a few years, but when I did I was good at it. There are plenty of people who will tell you that."

That was the moment I decided to hire her.

I've always loved strength in anyone but especially in women. When I was young I dated a few girls who were very nice looking but needy and whiny. My buddies called me crazy for walking away from them, but I had to. I'd jump off a cliff before I'd let myself get tied down to an emotional wimp.

So yes, Faith made a good first impression. That does not mean, however, that I saw her as someone I might someday have an intimate relationship with. As I've already said, it was completely out of character for me to think such thoughts about any woman other than Mary Beth. I know all males get lumped together as pigs, but there are a few of us who still take pride in defying the stereotype. Also, from a purely practical standpoint, how big of an idiot would a man have to be to fool around with a woman who has severe financial problems, a husband in prison, and a child with anger issues? Any guy with only a handful of functioning brain cells would have to see such a combination as the ultimate invitation to trouble. Because of all of these things, Faith, even with her attractiveness, brains, and bearing, did not stir anything primal in me.

Not at first.

- 28 -

I have a buddy who had an affair. It cost him his marriage, which at the time didn't bother him much because the girl he was cheating with was younger and sexier than his wife. It wasn't until he caught Ms. Younger and Sexier cheating on *him* that he came to his senses and realized what an idiot he'd been. Anyway, this friend had a name for the attraction he felt when the girl was around. He called it "The Tingle." He even stipulated that the first letters had to be capitalized to do justice to the sensation. He said, "Jason, my boy, if you ever meet a woman who gives you 'The Tingle,' run as fast as you can in the opposite direction."

I still remember the first day I felt "The Tingle" in Faith's presence.

The desk chair in my office looked and felt like it had been manufactured before World War II. I know it sounds like a joke, but I was actually watching a movie one time about what the Nazis did in Hungary and spotted a chair just like mine in a Gestapo officer's office. Whether it was authentic or the prop guys at the movie studio were desperate and borrowed it from the producer's office, I don't know. But that's when I decided it was time for a new one. Instead of submitting a request to the county office, I decided to spend my own money and get what I wanted. It was a brown leather La-Z-Boy I hauled to my office one Saturday morning to assemble.

I had parts laid out all over the carpet and was sitting in the middle of them reading the assembly instructions when I heard a knock on the outer office door. "Yoohoo! Anybody home?"

"Yeah, I'm back here. Come on in!"

I was scrambling to my feet when Faith appeared in the doorway wearing black spandex shorts, sneakers, and a fluorescent orange T-shirt. She looked good. "I saw your car and wanted to say hi," she said. Then, looking at the chair parts littering the floor, she added, "Did you get a new chair?"

"Nah. I just come in every couple of weeks and take it apart and put it back together to stay in practice."

Then we both said, simultaneously, "Here's your sign!" before breaking into full-scale hooting laughter. Turns out we were both fans of comedian Bill Engvall, whose best routine includes his assertion that people who ask dumb questions should have to wear a sign around their necks advertising to the world that they are idiots. "Here's your sign" is the punchline to all of his dumb question jokes.

And just like that Faith and I had a connection that made us smile. We spent the next five minutes quoting our favorite *Here's your sign* jokes and talking about our favorite comedians. I'd never heard her laugh before and was taken by how pleasant and infectious the sound was. Some people cackle, others giggle, and then there are those like Faith who land somewhere in the middle, managing to register high on the fun meter without being annoying. I found myself wanting to keep the conversation going so I could hear her laugh again and again.

Eventually, she asked if I needed help with the chair. I said I could handle it but thanks anyway. Her eyes did that twinkling thing as she said, "May I make a suggestion?"

I said, "Sure. What is it?"

"I think you should shut the door and close your blinds until you get the chair put together."

I had no idea what she was getting at, but her eyes told me I was about to be on the receiving end of a witty barb. "Why?"

"Because if people see you reading the assembly instructions, they might demand you turn in your man card. Don't you know real men don't read instructions? If you're not careful, you're going to single-handedly undermine the macho image of masculinity it's taken thousands of years to create."

I laughed. "Maybe it needs to be undermined."

She stuck her index finger in the air and said, "Ahhh. Now there's an idea I could get behind! On second thought, go ahead and leave the door and blinds open and let's hope this is the beginning of a revolution."

"Will do," I said. "By the way, what are you doing here on a Saturday morning?"

"I'm in search of a quiet place to work on lesson plans. Zoey's pretty high maintenance these days. If I'm at home, she demands my full attention, and I can't get any schoolwork done. I asked the neighbor girl who's in high school to hang out with her this morning while I do this. They're good buddies."

"She must really miss her father."

"She does, and I'm not sure why. He barely spent any time with her. Even when he was home, which wasn't often, he was always glued to the TV or playing his stupid video games."

Faith looked stricken.

"I am so sorry," she said. "I made a commitment to myself that I wasn't going to be the woman who always trashes her husband. I know women who do that, and all it does is make them even more bitter than they already are. I'm determined to do better."

It struck me again what an impressive woman she was.

I said, "Well, I asked the question. All you did was answer it honestly, which is something I appreciate."

"And I appreciate your concern, I really do." Then, after a slight pause that told me neither of us knew quite what to say next, she said, "Well, I guess I better get to work. I promised Zoey we'd go to the movies this afternoon."

"Thanks for stopping in. It's good to know there's someone around here who appreciates my sense of humor."

She did that thing with her eyes again and nodded toward the assembly instructions I still held in my hands. "And thank you for revolutionizing masculinity. It needs it."

And then she was gone.

Not one word spoken between us was inappropriate. There were no insinuations, no suggestive remarks, no flirtations whatsoever. Still, I sat there on the floor, strangely enchanted by the simple encounter.

It's called "The Tingle."

- 29 -

The problem with "The Tingle" is that you know when you feel it, but you don't know if the other person also feels it. As my buddy, the originator of the term, explained, "You know you're 'The Tinglee,' but you don't know if 'The Tingler' is also a 'Tinglee.'" Suffice to say, I understood after our Saturday morning encounter that I found Faith attractive, but I had not the slightest notion whether she felt the same about me. I'm embarrassed to admit it, but yes, I did wonder about it. Not because I had any thought of pursuing her, but probably because I'm approaching middle age. I've read it's true of both men and women; you get to about my age, and you can't help wondering if you've still got "It," or at least some semblance of "It." Whatever "It" is.

The next school week passed without any out-of-the-ordinary contact between us. I saw her several times, always within the context of a normal school day and always with other people around. We were both cordial and professional. I will confess I stole a few surreptitious looks at her, once as she shepherded her class to the cafeteria and another time when she was on car loop duty. Not once did I notice her looking at me. As far as I could tell, she didn't think of me any differently than she did anyone else on our campus.

Another week went by, again without any out-of-the-ordinary contact. By the end of the second week, I had gotten over "The Tingle" and its residual effects and was fully back to normal. I was no longer thinking about her or stealing looks at her. She was just another teacher. End of story.

And then one morning at the start of the third week of school, she caught me in the hall and asked if I might have a few minutes to talk after school. I said sure and suggested she stop by my office after she got her classroom buttoned up.

Of course, it's not unusual when a teacher wants to speak to her principal. There are a thousand legitimate topics to discuss. Whatever she had in mind, even if it was a problem that needed my attention, I found myself looking forward to the end of the day when I would once again have a conversation with her.

Alice was just gathering up her things when Faith arrived. I heard her say, "Go ahead on back, honey. He's in his office."

I was trying to act busy when she stepped into the doorway and knocked. I was writing something on a piece of paper. The only thing more meaningless than the piece of paper was what I was writing on it. It was just something to make me look busy. Why I felt like I needed to look busy I have no idea. When Faith said, "Is this a bad time?" I dropped the pen and said, "Of course not. Come on in and sit down."

When she got settled, I said, "How are things going?"

From the look on Faith's face, I could tell she didn't know if I was referring to her personal life or professional life. Honestly, I didn't know myself. I threw the question out there because, well, it's what you say to almost anybody you haven't talked to in a while. *Hey, howzit goin'?* I almost jumped in and said I meant with her class but decided to let the question sit there.

She shrugged and tilted her head. "It's going."

I scrunched my brow. "Hmmm, what that answer lacked in

enthusiasm it made up for in ambiguity."

She smiled at my feeble joke and looked at the floor.

I could tell something was up, so I said, "Talk to me, Faith. What's going on?"

"I don't want to get anybody in trouble."

When those words are spoken, it usually means someone is going to get in trouble. I waited for her to continue. When she didn't, I said, "The very fact you would say that tells me there's a problem. If it has anything to do with this school, I need to know what it is. If it's personal, I guess I don't *need* to know, but I'd like to help you if I can."

"It's coach Brooks."

"What about him?"

She sighed. "I don't know how to say it. There's something about him that makes me uncomfortable."

"What has he done?"

"That's just it. He hasn't done a thing. Every encounter I've had with him has been completely professional. The problem is, I've caught him staring at me several times. Last week, I was on playground duty with Mrs. Charles when I spotted him in his classroom, staring out at me through the window. I told her I was going to walk to the other side of the playground and stand. I asked her to watch him and see if his eyes followed me. She told me he never took his eyes off of me, that he stared at me for a good ten minutes before he turned and walked away from the window."

I shook my head. "That's . . . weird."

"Yes, it is. But like I said, every time I'm in the same room with him, every time we've had a conversation, he's been a perfect gentleman. I can't point to anything he's said or done, other than the staring, that has been inappropriate."

I got up from my desk and walked to my office door and closed it. School was out for the day, but I didn't know who might still be around, and I didn't want anyone to hear what I was about to say.

Once I was back behind my desk, I said, "Can we keep what I'm about to say between us?"

"Of course."

"Thank you. The fact is, you're not the first teacher to tell me this about Adam. Two years ago, I got the same complaint from a teacher who's no longer here. I don't think her transferring to another school over the summer had anything to do with him, but I'm not one hundred percent certain. Like you, she told me he had never said or done anything inappropriate, just that he stared at her."

"He's married, isn't he?"

"Yes and has a child. Anyway, after she spoke to me I started watching him, and sure enough, I found that he does have an eye for attractive women. It's like he has some kind of internal radar. If one walks into a room, his eyes are pulled to her like magnets. And they often don't let go very quickly. The thing is, you fit the profile perfectly."

"The profile?"

"I mean, you're attractive. Just the kind of woman he'd notice."

Faith's eyes lingered on mine as she processed those words. With God as my witness, I wasn't thinking beyond the problem with Adam Brooks when I told her she was attractive. I was *not* trying to send her a subtle message. I was simply making a point related to my assessment of the man she'd come to talk to me about. But once the words were out and I saw her reaction, the emotional trajectory of our conversation changed. And it wasn't a subtle change. When I saw the tiniest smile appear on Faith's face, I knew Adam Brooks' roving eye would no longer be the major takeaway for either of us.

I cleared my throat. "Anyway, I've never been able to do anything about him because, as you say, he's never said or done anything inappropriate."

Faith smiled and nodded. "I understand."

"But if he ever does step out of line, I want you to tell me. I promise you I'll handle it."

"Oh, I will. Don't worry."

And then, for about five seconds we just stared at each other. You couldn't see or hear electricity crackling in the air between us, but it was there.

Then she stood up and said, "Thank you for making time for me."

I stood and said, "No problem, Faith. Anytime."

She walked to the door and placed her hand on the knob. Before turning it, she looked back at me and smiled again. I can still see her smile in my mind. It was one I hadn't seen on her face before. I was pretty sure I knew what it meant.

And then she was gone.

The next morning, she caught me in the hall and invited Mary Beth and I to her house for dinner.

- 30 -

It wasn't unusual for Mary Beth and I to socialize with teachers and staff from the school. I am a big believer in relationship building. We've done team-building exercises, holiday parties, and yes, occasionally a few couples get together for dinner. Still, I felt a little uneasy with Faith's invitation, coming as it did on the heels of our conversation in my office. I'd told her I found her very attractive, and it was clear she was pleased. Less than twenty-four hours later I'm being invited to her home.

Or was I being ridiculous?

When she offered up the invitation, she told me she'd been wanting to have Mary Beth and me over as a way of thanking me for me giving her a chance to get back into teaching and that now, with a few weeks of teaching under her belt, she finally felt settled enough to do it. She also asked what Mary Beth liked to eat and drink. Not what *I* liked to eat and drink, just Mary Beth. And I did not get the twinkling eyes. Not at all. She was cordial, for sure, but also as professional as a nurse taking someone's medical history.

Yes, I was being ridiculous.

Still, I felt nervous as I prepared to broach the subject with Mary Beth: *Um, honey, remember Faith, the new teacher at school? The pretty one? Well, I told her I thought she was attractive, and guess what . . . she immediately invited us over for dinner. Can we go?* Somehow, I had to run the invitation past her without seeming overly enthused about it. Or Faith. *Especially* Faith.

I never got a chance to bring up the subject. Mary Beth was wound up about something as we ate dinner, so I was letting her talk, waiting for her to wind down so I could act like I'd just remembered to tell her we had an invitation. *Boy, I almost forgot. See how little it means to me? It almost slipped my mind.* But before I had a chance to mention it, Mary Beth's phone rang.

I've thought back through these events a thousand times. I've replayed every scene, rehashed every conversation, reevaluated every decision. What I've come to believe is this: everything turned on that phone call. I'm not blaming the phone call and I'm not trying to mitigate my guilt. I am still fully responsible for my actions. But if the call had never been made, Faith would probably be alive today. Why? Because it came from a hospital about forty miles east of Atlanta. Mary Beth's mother, who was sixty-seven, had suffered a massive heart attack and was in the ICU. Mary Beth was told that if she wanted to see her, she needed to come quickly.

After she hung up the phone, Mary Beth raced upstairs to pack. I trailed along behind her, listening as she spewed a flood of words I had trouble making sense of. In no time, she had the suitcase open on the bed and was dragging things out of closets and drawers like she'd only been given two minutes to pack and catch a cab at the curb. This seemed pointless since she didn't even have a plane ticket yet, not to mention the fact that it was so late in the day, she probably wouldn't be able to fly out until early the next morning.

I stepped in front of her and gently placed my hands on her upper arms. "Baby, stop for a minute."

"What?" She was almost hyperventilating.

"I think the best thing to do right now is get on the computer and see what kind of flight you can find. There probably won't be another one until tomorrow, which means you can slow down and take your time packing. There really isn't a rush."

She stared at me like I'd just spoken Japanese. Then what I said must have clicked because she agreed and headed off to find her iPad. Indeed, there was a flight out the next morning at 8:30. It was perfect timing because I would be able to take her to the airport on my way to school. At my suggestion, she purchased a one-way ticket. I knew she would not want to come home until her mother's health crisis was resolved one way or another. I told her not to worry about me; I would be fine.

Later that evening, Mary Beth got herself a little more under control. She was still agitated, but at least she wasn't bouncing off the walls. Her coping mechanism was to talk about her mother. She told story after story about things her mother said or did, all of them casting her mother in the best possible light. I'd heard most of the stories many times, but I listened to them all like it was the first time I was hearing them.

When we got into bed, we held each other. With her head on my chest, Mary Beth pulled even more stories out of her storehouse of memories. At one point, she caught me dozing and seemed hurt. "You weren't listening."

"I was. I just . . . it's been a long day."

She turned away from me with movements that told me she was upset. I admit I should have wooed her back with a soft touch and gentle, loving words. But honestly, I really was exhausted and didn't have the energy for it. I figured I'd give her some space and we'd make up in the morning.

We didn't.

I got the silent treatment while she was getting dressed and during the ride to the airport. In fairness, her mom was on her mind. At one point, she did open up and say she was afraid she would walk into her mom's hospital room five minutes after she'd died. I encouraged her to try to be more positive, which she took as a criticism, and then she lectured me for being so insensitive. I knew then that the sooner she got on the plane, the better off we both would be.

I'll admit I was disappointed when she didn't kiss me goodbye. I was ready for it, even leaning in a little bit because I assumed it was coming. For crying out loud, people were kissing hello and goodbye all around us, so much so that *not* kissing would have seemed weird. But when we reached the central atrium she simply gave me half a hug and took off, a woman on a mission, for the security line.

All the way back to the parking garage, I fought to suppress my frustration. I knew I was being petty. I knew I should have been more understanding. Finally, I took a deep breath and said out loud: "Just let it go." The last thing I wanted to do was show up at school with the stench of anger coming off me.

When I pulled into the parking lot it was 7:30, later than I usually arrived but about when most of the teachers arrived. I really had to wonder if I was being messed with by the Devil himself when I got out of my car and heard a car door slam behind me. I turned and saw Faith getting out of her car wearing a smile brighter than the morning sun.

- 31 -

"Good morning," she said and walked toward me.

"Hi."

I thought I had gotten my head straight, but she apparently saw something in my face that didn't look right. She said, "Are you okay?"

I didn't want to get into what was going on with so many students within earshot, so I asked Faith if she could spare a minute and step into my office. She said, "Sure." And then she hesitantly added, "Am I in trouble?"

"What? No, of course not. I just have something I need to tell you."

When we got there, Alice was settling in behind her desk. Both Faith and I said good morning to her as we passed through her office and into mine. I closed the door and asked Faith to take a seat.

"Jason, you're scaring me."

I noticed she called me Jason. If the door had been open and Alice had been able to hear us, I know she would have called me Mr. Vincent. It was a clear sign a more intimate side to our relationship was developing.

I gave her a look that reflected my surprise. "Why are you scared?"

"Um, who *doesn't* get scared when they get called into the

principal's office?"

"Relax. I just wanted to update you on some things. A lot has happened since we talked yesterday."

"Did Mary Beth have a problem with coming to my place for dinner?"

The question hinted that Faith had been a little nervous about the invitation too. I thought that was interesting but filed it away to think about later.

"No. I didn't even get to ask her."

"Why? What happened?"

"Before I had a chance to tell her, she got a call telling her that her mom had had a heart attack and was in the ICU up near Atlanta. I guess she's pretty bad. They aren't sure she's going to make it, so Mary Beth flew up there to be with her. I just got back from taking her to the airport."

"Oh, no. Jason, I'm so sorry to hear that."

There it was again. *Jason.*

"Thanks. There's no way she'll be back by the weekend. And if her mom doesn't make it, I'll be flying up there myself for the funeral. So maybe we can do the dinner some other time."

"Oh, absolutely. No problem at all."

"Thanks."

That was the moment I would have expected her excuse herself and head for her classroom, but she didn't. Instead, she tilted her head and gave me a sympathetic look. "Are *you* okay?"

"Me? Sure, I'm fine."

"You don't seem fine."

To this day, I don't know if she was truly reading something in my countenance or body language or whether she was just trying to prolong the conversation and steer it into deeper waters. If the latter was the case, I stupidly played along by admitting I was feeling a little frazzled from what had turned into a difficult evening and morning with Mary Beth. Of course, it went without saying that if the evening and morning were difficult, the night was too.

Faith said, "I'm sure she's just upset and worried."

I liked that she spoke up for Mary Beth, but the frustration that had built up in me overnight and at the airport hadn't completely drained out of my system. "Yeah, I know. I'll be fine once I get started working. It's just a little fresh at the moment."

She smiled. "Did you at least get a goodbye kiss?"

I chuckled. "Nope."

Even as I answered, I marveled at how personal the conversation had become. There was a tiny thrill in sharing something with Faith that I knew I wouldn't tell another soul.

She said, "Oh man. I hate it when that happens. And trust me, I know how it feels. It happened to me all the time."

"It did?"

"Let's just say, I am not married to the most romantic guy in the world."

You didn't have to possess the deductive powers of Sherlock Holmes to recognize there were two levels to the conversation. There was the surface level where we were talking about my morning. But there was also a deeper level where we were making statements that were carefully shaped to allow the other person to read between the lines and draw conclusions. Bluntly put, we were dropping hints about our marital unhappiness. Part of me felt bad about the implications of my words because Mary Beth and I were not unhappy. Sure, the prior evening and morning had been rough, but all married couples have those moments. Overall, we were doing fine. Still, I felt strangely excited by the intimate tone of our conversation and therefore did nothing to set the record straight.

Finally, Faith had no choice. She simply had to get to her

classroom. As she gathered up her things and walked to the door, she turned and said, "I hope your day gets better." Then she smiled softly and did that thing with her eyes before walking out of my office.

I sat at my desk for a moment, knowing what had just happened was far more significant than anyone reading a transcript of our conversation would ever be able to discern. There was a part of me—the better part—that knew the smart thing would be to pull back a little, to not be so transparent with Faith, to establish some healthier parameters for our relationship. The other part of me—the part I am not proud of—started thinking of her schedule and what time I needed to pass through the cafeteria in order to "accidentally" run into her.

As it turned out, I didn't have to wait until lunch.

Between first and second periods, my phone dinged. I looked at the screen and saw a message from her:

> Thinking of you and hoping you're feeling better.

And that's how we started texting.

- 32 -

What comes next are a lot of words and actions I'm not proud of. In fact, I feel a strong temptation to gloss over a few of the uglier and more embarrassing details in an effort to make myself look better. But the whole purpose of this exercise is to *exorcise* some of my lingering demons. I need to come clean here and now, or I'll never be able to look at myself in a mirror again. I'd rather you know the terrible truth about what I did and hope you'll remember that I did come to my senses eventually and do the right thing. My only other option is to stake out some morally ambiguous middle ground where I'm no angel, but not really a devil either. It was Jesus who said it's better to be hot or cold, but whatever you do, don't be lukewarm.

So here goes . . . the *cold*, hard truth.

I answered Faith's text immediately:

> Thank you!

Then I added a smiley emoji.

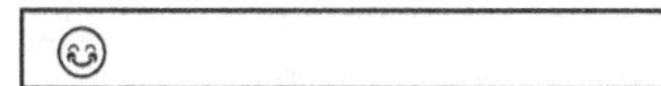

I am generally not one for emojis, but in this case it seemed like a way to communicate my pleasure with her concern for me without the risk of saying anything too forward.

For the rest of the morning she was on my mind. Whatever anger I felt toward Mary Beth was completely overshadowed by the positive energy I was getting from Faith. Only when Mary Beth texted me did I even think about her.

Arrived and picked up rental car

I texted her back.

Be careful

Not "*Love you*" or "*Call me when you can*" or "*Miss you*" or any of the things I normally would've said. I figured two could play the cold shoulder game.

At lunch time, I did make it into the cafeteria, which was not unusual. I try to be a presence throughout the school. It's important for any leader to keep his thumb on the pulse of the organization, and one way to do that is to get out of your office and rub shoulders with the people who are the machinery of the operation.

On that particular day, I managed a five-minute conversation with Faith. It pleased me to see the smile on her face as I approached.

"How has your morning been?" I asked.

"Wonderful. Matt Hurley only threw one temper tantrum, and Maddie Burress refused for the twelfth day in a row to participate in computer lab, but at least this time she didn't threaten to have me put in jail."

I chuckled. "They don't make seven-year-olds like they used to."

"Tell me about it. How was your morning?"

"Good."

"Did Mary Beth make it to Atlanta okay?"

"Yeah. I got a text from her."

"No call?"

"Nope. Just a text."

I sensed from her hesitation that Faith wanted to tread lightly.

"Well, she was probably picking up her car and didn't have a lot of time. I'm sure she'll call when she can."

"She already had the car."

"She did?"

"That's what she said."

"Hmm."

"Yeah, hmm. Got any words of wisdom for me?"

Faith thought for a moment. "Become a monk and move to a monastery in Tibet?"

I looked at her and we both laughed.

I said, "You should've been a marriage counselor."

"I was. I just couldn't get my husband to listen to me."

We chatted for another minute or two, and then I was on my way, feeling good. I didn't see Faith that afternoon, nor did I get a text from her. I did keep my eyes open for her in the after-school madhouse as I visited the car and bus loops, but again, there was no sign of her. I decided it was just as well. I didn't want people to get accustomed to seeing us together.

When I got home, I changed into some workout clothes. It had been a few days since I'd gone for a run, and I thought that would be as good a way as any to work out some stress and frustration. Then, as I was headed for the door, my conscience finally breached the wall of stubbornness I had erected after Mary Beth's perfunctory text that morning. Suddenly, I had an overpowering urge to call her. I figured she would've had plenty of time to get to the hospital and get settled in her mother's room.

When she answered, I said, "Hey there," in a soft, conciliatory voice.

She said, "Oh, hi." Like, *Oh, it's just you.* At least that's how it sounded to me.

I said, "I just wanted to see how you were."

"*I'm* fine. *Mom's* not so good." And then she launched into a full medical report, which boiled down to the fact that her mom was stable. There was some reason for optimism, but she definitely wasn't out of the woods.

I tried again for a personal connection. "I know you said you were fine, but are you, really? All of this came at you out of left field."

I wanted her to say, *I'm trying my best; thank you for asking. And by the way, I'm sorry about this morning.* Or even, *Look, I'm sorry I didn't kiss you goodbye this morning. I was being childish.* Yes, that's what I *really* wanted her to say.

Instead, she said, "I'm fine." Then she put me on hold: "Hang on a minute."

I had no idea what she was doing. Perhaps a nurse had come into her mom's room, though I didn't hear any voices in the background. I waited for a couple of minutes. Then, she came back on. "You still there?"

"Yeah, I'm here. What's going on?"

"Just stuff. You know how hospitals are: always people in and out."

Right then our doorbell rang. Mary Beth heard it through the phone and said, "Is someone at the door?"

As I made my way toward the front door, I said, "Yeah, let me see who it is."

I parted the blinds covering our front window and looked outside. When I saw who was there, I said to Mary Beth, "It's Joe." He was our neighbor from across the street. "Can I catch you later?"

She said, "Sure. I need to go get something to eat anyway."

After we hung up, I dropped my phone into my pocket and opened the front door.

I had lied to Mary Beth. It wasn't really Joe standing there; it was Faith.

- 33 -

"Pizza delivery!" she shouted and held up a 14-inch box from a mom-and-pop Italian place she knew I loved. A week or so earlier, several teachers and I were claiming our favorite restaurants in the area. Faith had been a part of the conversation and had obviously been paying attention.

Playing along, I said, "I don't remember ordering a pizza."

"I didn't say you *ordered* it. I said I'm *delivering* it."

I smiled and nodded. "True. Come on in."

I stepped back, and Faith waltzed through the door, looking very nice in jeans and sandals and a pink sleeveless top that accentuated her physical assets. The pizza smelled amazing, too, but at that moment, none of my other senses were reading data that could compete with what my eyes were drinking in.

I followed Faith into the kitchen, where she deposited the pizza box onto the counter and said, "We've never talked about your culinary skills, but I assumed from your aversion to cooking shows that you're probably helpless in the kitchen. So, to save you from yourself, I decided to step in and do my good deed for the day."

I, uhhh . . . wow. I wasn't expecting this."

"All the better. Surprises are good things."

"Yes they are. Can you stay and help me eat it?"

"Do you want me to?"

"Sure."

"Then yes, I can stay."

I didn't ask who was watching Zoey. I didn't want to know. Or rather, I didn't want to spoil the moment by reminding either of us of our lives outside of that room. Faith had been on my mind all day, and now, almost unbelievably, I had the opportunity to be alone with her without anyone knowing. The thought was very seductive. Not that I expected anything sexual to happen; I knew it wouldn't. It was just one of those moments in life that sets your blood pumping and makes you feel like a teenager again. For a middle-aged man, those moments come all too infrequently.

I had some Mountain Dew in the fridge, which Faith claimed was her favorite soft drink. It took us only a couple of minutes to pop the tops on the cans, grab some plates and napkins, and tear into the pizza at the kitchen table.

"Pepperoni and green peppers," I said. "My favorite."

"Of course. Why would I bring something you didn't like?"

"I'm just surprised you remembered. That conversation was what . . . a week ago?"

"At least."

"And do you remember the favorite kind of pizza of every person involved in that conversation?"

She scoffed. "Of course not."

"Why not?"

"None of them are my boss, silly."

"Ooooh, I get it. So this is just a way to butter up your boss and get on his good side."

Her eyes twinkled. "Is it working?"

I tore off a big bite and stuffed a long string of cheese into my mouth. "Ummm, yeah. I'd say it's working."

Faith chomped a big bite of her own and said, "I wasn't sure you'd be home. I figured you'd go out to dinner somewhere."

"That was my plan. If you'd gotten here after I went for my run, I might've been gone."

"I knew it! That's why I made it a point to get here early."

"You've thought of everything."

"Not quite."

"Oh yeah? What did you forget?"

"Dessert. I'd planned to stop and pick up some sherbet but didn't remember until I already had the pizza. I figured the pizza would get cold if I took the time."

I took a swig of Mountain Dew. "I don't have any sherbet, but I have something that might work."

"Oh yeah?"

I walked over, opened the freezer, and pulled out a box of chocolate-dipped vanilla ice cream cones sprinkled with nuts.

"Drumsticks!" Faith shouted. "Zoey loves those!"

"And you don't?"

"No, I do. I just . . . I don't know, they seem like something kids eat."

"And pizza doesn't?"

Faith laughed. "I guess you got me there, counselor."

"Well, I'm a kid at heart. I eat Drumsticks. Sherbet is too grown-up for me."

"Next you're going to tell me you have a toy train set up in your spare bedroom."

"I don't, but I wish I did."

For two full hours we bantered like this—laughing, poking fun at each other, throwing out one-liners. We even cleaned up the kitchen mess together after we polished off the pizza and ate our Drumsticks.

There wasn't a word spoken that carried any sexual overtones; though, I will admit there was sexual energy in the room. She looked really good, and I was not a big enough fool to believe it was an accident. Truth be told, it was a potent mixture in that kitchen: two people with an obvious attraction to each other, both of whom happened to have strangeness in their marriages at that moment. She much more than I, but still . . .

Finally, Faith looked at her watch and said, "I should get going."

I hated to see her go but knew it was time. "I really appreciate you coming by."

She grew a little serious and said, "I almost didn't. I thought maybe . . . I don't know, it might be a little forward."

It wasn't a little forward; it was a *lot* forward, and we both knew it. But I'd had such fun and was feeling such attraction that I suppressed any thoughts along those lines. I simply looked her in the eyes and said, "I'm really glad you came."

We stared at each other for a few seconds, seemingly frozen, the atmosphere crackling with emotion. Then she blinked herself back to reality and stood up. "I really do need to go," she said.

I followed her to the front door where she stopped and turned to face me. Again, we looked each other in the eyes. I wanted to kiss her, and I believe she wanted to kiss me. If we'd stood there another few seconds, there's no telling what might have happened. But we didn't. She broke the spell by saying, "Goodnight, Jason" and then walked out the door.

"Goodnight. And thank you again," I said as she walked away, and then I closed the door.

I stood with my back against it for a moment, feeling emotions I hadn't felt in a very long time.

- 34 -

I'd like to tell you she texted me later that night, but I was the one who texted her. I was lying in bed. It was after ten, and I couldn't have been more restless if my pillow case had been full of rocks. I'd thought Mary Beth might call, but she didn't. And of course, my thoughts were on Faith. In my mind, I kept seeing her looking beautiful and being funny and yes, with that look she had on her face when she left.

Suddenly, I had my phone in my hands and was tapping out a message:

> You awake?

Almost immediately, I saw the indicator that she was typing. Seconds later her response appeared:

> Yes. Can't sleep.

> Me neither.

> Too much pizza?

> Nope. Too much fun.

> It was fun, wasn't it?

> Indeed.

After a brief pause:

> Heard from Mary Beth?

I hated that she broke the spirit of our conversation by bringing up Mary Beth. But thinking about it later, I figured she probably thought she needed to in order to cling to some shred of decency. I typed,

> No.

> She's probably busy.

> I'm sure she is.

Another pause. Then this from Faith:

> You up or in bed?

Just the word *bed* did something to me. I answered:

> In bed. You?

> Same.

> Does this mean we're in bed together???? 😂

It was the first time either of us had made a blatant, sexually charged comment.

> I think it does! 😁

Another pause. My heart was pounding. I'd have bet everything I owned hers was too.

> This has been an amazing day.

> It has.

> When is she coming home?

Mary Beth had become *she*.

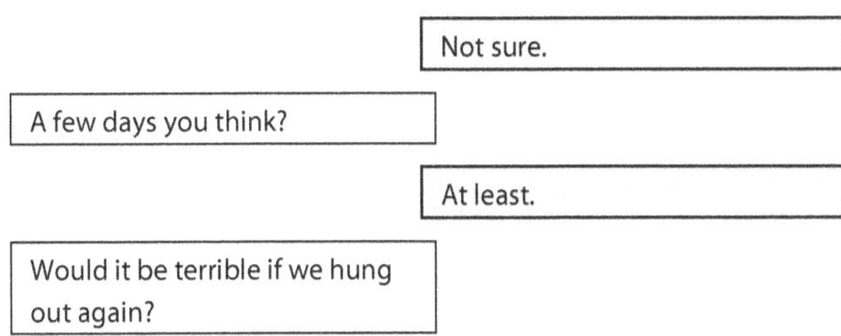

This was one of many points at which I could have slammed on the brakes. All I had to do was say I didn't think it would be a good idea. I'm confident Faith would have immediately agreed and never brought up the subject again. Probably, she would be alive today if I could have mustered the character to do the right thing. But I didn't. Instead, I typed:

Another pause. Then this from Faith:

I tingled when I read those words.

Now you're embarrassing me.

I doubt that, Mr. "He's Hot for a Principal."

What????

That's an exact quote from one of your teachers.

What are you talking about?

I'm talking about a direct quote I heard from one of your subordinates.

Stop it.

I kid you not.

Who? When?

A couple of weeks ago. Jolly Molly Thomas.

Oh brother.

Jolly Molly has a thing for you.

PUHLEEEEZE!

LOL I think you two would make a cute couple.

You're not funny.

She'd be so jealous if she knew I was texting you right now.

Will you stop!

Actually, you being uncomfortable with women being attracted to you is kind of adorable.

😐

It is! You're so unlike Coach Brooks who thinks he's God's gift to women.

Thank you for that. I would never want to be like him.

He is creepy. 🐯

You're not. 😍

Wow. That's one of the best compliments I've ever received: You're not creepy.

LOL

But I'll take what I can get. 🤓

Slight pause. Then from Faith:

Talking to you makes me feel so good. Makes me forget all the junk in my life.

I'm glad.

Me too. I'll sleep better tonight because of this conversation.

I'll probably have nightmares thinking about Jolly Molly.

LOLOL Funny man.

We should get some sleep.

Yes, we should.

Talk to you tomorrow.

You can count on it. 😉

It took me a while to drift off to sleep. Deep down, I knew that what had just happened was not good. But there was enough adrenaline sloshing through my system to suppress any feelings of remorse. That night I had a dream. Thankfully, Jolly Molly was not the leading lady. Sadly, Mary Beth wasn't either.

- 35 -

The next morning, I felt guilty.

The emotional high I'd been on after I texted with Faith subsided during the night, allowing me to think more clearly. There was a voice inside my head arguing vociferously that I had done nothing wrong: *You're friends. You texted. What's the big deal? It was all in good fun. Neither of you is taking anything seriously.*

But there was another voice asking the only question that really mattered: *How would you feel if Mary Beth read a transcript of that conversation?*

The conscience can be a ruthless prosecutor.

And so I headed off to school determined to be a better man. I would try to catch Faith alone at some point during the day and apologize to her for losing my head the night before. I never should have texted her. It was over the line. I would take full responsibility and ask her to forgive me. I told myself if I could get a handle on things now and keep them from progressing any further, it would be a "no harm, no foul" situation. I could come out of it with a lesson learned and be a better man.

To bolster my determination, I called Mary Beth on my way to school. Hearing her voice would be good for me. I would even apologize to her and get things between us back on the right track. I felt excited as I listened to her phone ring through the car speakers. It was only 7:00 a.m., but she was an early riser. I knew she would be up.

But she didn't answer.

Her phone kicked over to voicemail, leaving me dispirited.

Of course there were a dozen possible reasons to explain why she didn't answer. I pictured her talking to the doctor about her mom, buying an omelet in the hospital cafeteria, or even taking a walk around the block to get her circulation going after sleeping in a chair beside her mother's bed all night. No doubt she would see my missed call and call me back. In the meantime, I was determined to set things straight with Faith.

It never happened.

I thought it was strange when I didn't see Faith in the usual places around campus before school started. I soon discovered why. She had called in a sub at the last minute. What had happened in the last eight hours to keep her from coming to school?

Had she come down with some sort of sickness overnight?

Had Zoey?

Or was she feeling as guilty as I was? Did she also wake up with her internal prosecutor wagging a finger in her face? Was she feeling too ashamed to come to school and face me? Part of me found it hard to believe. She wasn't the type to let her conscience keep her home from work. She was more likely to do what I was planning to do: come to school, apologize for being stupid, forget the whole thing, and move on. I checked my phone to see if I had a text from her. Nothing. By 9:00 a.m. I had convinced myself I was the reason Faith wasn't at work. The thought of her at home feeling ashamed of what we had done the night before was tearing me up. To say I was feeling desperate to talk to her and apologize would be an understatement.

Finally, just after 9:00, I slipped into my office and closed the door. My heart was pounding as I brought up my speed dial list and tapped her number.

"Hey." Her voice was weak. She was either sick or she'd been crying.

"Hey yourself. Are you okay?"

"I've been better."

My heart sank. I knew this was all because of me. But before I could start the speech I had rehearsed, she said, "I got a call from the prison this morning."

Whoa. She caught me completely off-guard. "You did?"

She sniffled. "Yeah."

"What did they say?"

"Brian was involved in an altercation last night. They say he started it, but he must have picked on the wrong guy because he was beaten senseless. He's in the medical ward right now with broken ribs and a concussion. I didn't come to school because I felt like I needed to drive up there and see him."

"Of course. I'm so sorry to hear this."

"Would you do me a favor?"

"Whatever you need."

"Would you meet me somewhere tonight so we can talk? I know I'm going to be an emotional wreck after spending time with Brian. I always am. He has a way of draining me of every ounce of self-respect I have."

It was a perfect opportunity for me to address what was building between us and make a major course correction.

I said, "Where did you have in mind?"

"I know we can't meet here in town. How about if I look around up by the prison and find a quiet spot? That is, if you don't mind driving up."

A tiny voice desperately urged me to stick to my guns and tell her we needed to get our relationship back on proper footing. But another, louder voice said, *You can't do that to her now. She's already feeling terrible. Be the friend she needs just for tonight. There'll be plenty of time to talk about those other issues later.*

I said, "Sure, I'd be happy to meet you. Just let me know where when you find a place."

After we hung up, I stared out the window for a full five minutes. The thought of meeting Faith in the shadows of the evening, somewhere away from the area where people knew us, was intoxicating. The idea had a film noir feel to it that set my imagination spinning. And I was able to justify it by telling myself she needed a friend. What kind of person would I be if I denied her request to talk? She just needed to blow off steam about her idiot husband. What could possibly go wrong?

- 36 -

It was after 10:00 the next morning before I finally connected with Mary Beth. I called her every twenty minutes or so because I wanted her to see those missed calls on her phone. I wanted her to know I was trying. Finally, she called. I was talking with Alice and excused myself to step into my office.

I said, "Hey there. Thanks for calling. I was getting a little worried."

"I'm sorry. I saw your calls, but doctors have been in and out all morning. This is the first chance I've had to get back to you." She had definitely softened.

We talked first about her mom. She gave me the rundown on her tests and the doctors' thoughts regarding the likelihood of her pulling through. They thought she had a good chance, but it was going to be a slow process. They predicted several days in the hospital and then a stint in rehab. Mary Beth told me she thought she needed to stay until her mom was back on her feet, which might take weeks.

It's hard to describe how those words hit me. On one hand, I felt a little jolt of excitement. The very idea of having total freedom to do what I wanted with no wife around to answer to, especially in light of my connection with Faith, was heady stuff. But I also knew my relationship with Faith was trending in an unhealthy direction, and more freedom to fuel the trend could be dangerous. Those thoughts and their related concerns were tangled in my gut like a bowl of spaghetti. But at the moment, I needed to give Mary Beth my full attention.

I said, "I agree you should be there with her, but I'll miss you."

"Maybe you could drive up some weekend after she's a little better."

"Or just fly. That would give us more time together."

"That would be good."

Thankfully, Mary Beth and I were back on track, which was a load off my mind. It also gave me confidence that I would be able to do the right thing with Faith. I'm no psychologist, but I don't need to be to understand there's a strong connection between marital tranquility, or the lack thereof, and temptation. When Mary Beth and I were emotionally disconnected, Faith seemed even more attractive. When we healed the rift between us and got back to being our real selves, I suddenly couldn't wait to distance myself from Faith. I hate the thought that I am so incredibly shallow, but denying it is pointless.

After hanging up with Mary Beth, my mood soared. Alice even commented that I seemed more chipper. I simply said Mary Beth's mother was doing better and we were relieved. The rest of the day went well. I had no brush fires to put out and got quite a bit of work done at my desk. Then, at 2:30, I got this text from Faith:

> There's a little place called
> Brady's Pub about two miles
> east of the prison on route 23. I
> hear they have amazing
> burgers.

I thought about telling her something had come up, that I couldn't make it. Maybe she would take the hint and pull back a little. But I figured my not going to meet her would unleash a flood of texts and phone calls that would lead us into turbulent waters, if not about her husband, then about us. And if there's one thing I hate, it's trying to work through a problem over the phone. Texting one or two sentences at a time is maddening, and even a phone conversation deprives you of body language and the look in each other's eyes. I've always said if you have something important to discuss, do it face to face.

And so I responded to her text:

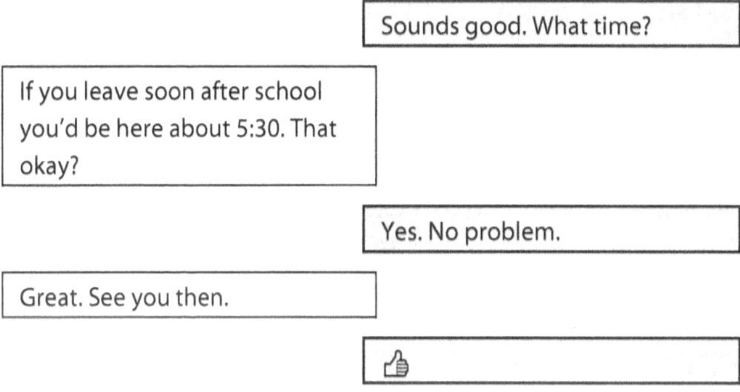

I left at 4:05 to make the seventy-mile trip. Ordinarily, I listen to jazz when I'm driving alone, crooning along with Ella or doing my best Buddy Rich imitation on the steering wheel. This trip, however, was made in complete silence. Or perhaps, I should say it this way: It was silent inside the car. Inside my head the cacophony of colliding thoughts sounded like a hundred people banging on trash can lids.

I'll be honest. I was excited to meet an attractive woman for dinner. The fact that there was almost no risk of anyone we knew seeing us, plus meeting in what sounded like an intimate little dive, raised my blood pressure more than a little. I could picture us in the darkest corner of the pub, leaning forward, speaking in soft tones like a couple of Cold War spies swapping state secrets.

But Mary Beth had a place in my mind too. I was glad to be back on good footing with her. I've never been one who could stand unresolved conflict with someone I care about. I've probably offered a thousand apologies during my lifetime to people who really owed *me* an apology, just so I could hurry up and get the issue resolved.

As I pulled onto route 23, my nerves were stretched tight and my face felt hot. I felt like a sixteen-year-old boy on his first date. I told myself I was being ridiculous. We were just two friends meeting for a burger and some conversation. Get a grip!

As I approached Brady's Pub, I saw Faith's car in the parking lot. Because her windows were tinted, I couldn't tell if she was in the car. I assumed she was; Brady's didn't look like the kind of place a woman would go into alone. Sure enough, when I pulled into the parking space beside hers, she got out of her car. From the serious look on her face, I concluded she'd had a tough day.

"You found it," she said as I exited the car.

"I channeled my inner bloodhound. And followed your directions."

She giggled, and then we hugged in a platonic way and started for the pub. As we were walking, she took my elbow and pressed her cheek against my upper arm. "I'm so glad to see you. I've been looking forward to this all day."

- 37 -

When we walked into Brady's Pub, I felt like I'd been there before. The familiarity came from it looking like the kind of place I'd seen in a hundred movies: A polished oak bar with stairs of liquor bottles surrounded a mirror that allowed the bartender to see every corner of the room with his back turned. And in those corners were the requisite shadowy booths where even more shadowy people, from hard-drinking cowpokes to shifty-eyed Russian spies, whispered their offers to saloon girls and double agents. On this night, a jukebox was playing an Elvis ballad while a rugged-looking waitress dragged herself and about twenty years' worth of ten-hour shifts from table to table trying (but not quite succeeding) to act like she wanted to be there. The place was less than half full, but I assumed that would change as more people got off work. The place had a sign on the front that said the "Brady Burger" had won some kind of award several years in a row. Considering the rural surroundings, I can't imagine it had much competition.

Faith and I took a table in a back corner of the pub. I noticed it was very near a rear exit, which pleased me. This far from home, the chance of someone we knew walking in was remote, but it was good to know we could make a quick getaway if the need arose.

Faith spoke first: "How was your day?"

"I'm sure it wasn't half as interesting as yours. Are you okay?"

She smiled. "I am now. Thanks for coming."

"What happened when you went to see Brian?"

Faith shook her head. "I don't know what's wrong with him. I really don't. He has a wife and daughter. He *had* a decent business doing something he loved. But apparently that wasn't enough to make him happy. He just *had* to try selling drugs even though he knew they'd send him away if he got caught. And of course he did get caught, leaving me to raise Zoey by myself."

She didn't answer my question, but I could tell she needed to vent, so I let her.

"And now even in prison he screws up," she continued. "He can't get with the program and try to get out early on good behavior. Oh, no. He has to be an idiot and get time *added* to his sentence."

"He started a fight?"

"Yeah. He apparently made a racist remark to a black guy who outweighed him by almost a hundred pounds. From the looks of him, the guy almost killed him."

I winced and said, "Ouch. Is he going to be okay?"

"He's *never* going to be okay. It's the one thing I know above everything else. He's a screw-up, plain and simple. His body will heal, but it's only a matter of time before he does something else stupid. One of these times he's going to get himself killed."

I didn't know what to say, so I went with this: "Was he glad to see you?"

She scoffed. "If he was, he didn't act like it. His first words when he saw me were, 'What are *you* doin' here?' Apparently, *Thank you for coming* never occurred to him."

Faith paused when the waitress dragged herself to our table and said, "Whaddaya have?" We both ordered the award-winning burger and soft drinks while she blew a huge bubble with her gum and scribbled on a small pad. I noticed a ring in her left nostril and a tattoo that started below her right ear and disappeared underneath her polo. When she walked away without saying a word, Faith said, "Classy babe."

I turned and looked around the room. "Where?"

Faith giggled. "See, that's why I love it when you're around. You make me smile even when smiling is the last thing I feel like doing."

"And you haven't seen me dance. I'm *really* funny when I dance."

"Aw, I'll bet you're a good dancer. You look very athletic."

"Remember how Elaine danced on Seinfeld?"

"Yeah, that was a hilarious episode."

"Well, they brought me in to serve as a consultant. I taught her my moves."

Another giggle. I loved her giggle. "Mr. Self-Deprecating. I'm going to start calling you that. Mr. S. D. for short."

"Well, that's better than Mr. S. *T.* D."

I have no idea where such a ridiculous comment came from, but Faith belly-laughed. She said, "You're amazing, you know that? I've been moping around all day, on the verge of tears, and ten minutes after you get here you have me laughing."

"Glad to be of service."

Faith leaned toward me and got a mischievous look in her eyes. "But you better watch out."

"Why?"

"Because laughter is a powerful aphrodisiac."

"Oh, get out."

"It is!"

"Is not."

"Yes it is! You can look it up. They've done studies on it. Funny people have more sex than anybody."

"That's ridiculous."

"Is not."

"Is too."

"What have you been reading, *The National Enquirer*?"

"What's wrong with *The National Enquirer*? I'll have you know they were the only paper in the country that uncovered the truth about the two-headed boy that came from outer space."

Then it was my turn to laugh.

We were still chuckling when the waitress showed up with our food and drinks. I wonder what she would have thought if she'd known what was happening right in front of her . . . that the two people she was serving were tumbling over an emotional cliff that would lead them into the darkest period of their lives and result in the tragic murder of the attractive young woman who seemed so ebullient and carefree.

- 38 -

The burgers were amazing. We both agreed they were among the best we'd ever had. And the conversation was equally enjoyable. We talked for over an hour, bouncing from topic to topic yet always managing to avoid the one we should have been addressing. From somewhere far away my conscience called out to me, but I was so captivated by the charming creature in front of me that I couldn't quite discern the message.

As we ate and talked, I noticed things about Faith I found endearing. For example, she was a hearty eater. Some women, Mary Beth included, pick at their food. Faith, on the other hand, took big bites and then, almost as if embarrassed by the amount of food she'd put in her mouth, held her hand in front of her mouth as she chewed. But then she turned around and took another bite just as big or bigger.

She also did this adorable thing where she put her elbows on the table, laced her fingers together palms down, and made a little hammock to sit her chin on. It was the kind of pose you might see in a celebrity headshot, but for Faith it was perfectly natural. And while she sat listening to me talk, her eyes threw off more sparkles than a disco ball under a spotlight.

I also noticed she was an exceptional listener. I told a few stories along the way, and she became engrossed in them, reacting with giggles and gasps and even asking follow-up questions to get more details. Mary Beth has always been what I call a one-eared listener. She listens, but always while she's looking at the TV or shoveling laundry into the dryer or stirring a pot on the stove. She rarely looks at me when I speak. She calls it multitasking and thinks I'm silly for mentioning it. All I know is it felt wonderful to have Faith's undivided attention as I talked.

Eventually, the spell was broken by Faith's cellphone. She took a call from Zoey, who was spending the night at a friend's house. There was no problem, thankfully. Zoey just wanted to tell her they went to the park to feed stale bread to the ducks. Faith sounded duly impressed and winked at me as she listened.

When she ended the call, Faith tucked her phone into her purse and said, "You ready to get out of here?"

"Yup."

I paid the bill in cash, and we walked to our cars. It wasn't yet dark, and neither of us had anyone waiting on us at home, so Faith asked if I'd like to follow her and stop at a state park just off the highway, one we had passed on the way up. "They've got a beautiful little lake with a footpath all the way around it."

"Sounds nice."

Forty minutes later, we parked side by side. She was right; the lake was small but postcard gorgeous. A concrete footpath encircled it with palm trees and park benches every one hundred yards or so. There was also a fishing pier and a small building that doubled as a bait shop and ice cream parlor. About a dozen cars were in the parking lot. A few couples strolled hand in hand, and a man and his son fished off the pier. The sun had become a fireball that was easing its way toward the horizon, giving the entire scene a soft orange glow.

Faith walked around her car, took my hand, and started pulling me toward the footpath. "Come on, big boy, we gotta burn off some of those burger calories."

I didn't resist.

Half an hour later, after we'd been sitting on a bench for at least twenty minutes, I looked at Faith suspiciously and said, "I thought we were supposed to be burning burger calories."

She said, "We are."

"We've been sitting on this bench almost the whole time."

"We're burning them by laughing, silly. Who said anything about walking?"

She was right. We'd been telling stories and laughing almost the whole time. I don't think either of us wanted the evening to end, but it was getting late and almost everyone had left. There were two other cars in the lot, but I think they must have belonged to bait shop and ice cream parlor employees because I didn't see anyone else around.

Faith turned her body so she was facing me and placed her hand on my arm. After so much storytelling and laughter, she suddenly looked very serious.

She said, "I want you to know this was one of the nicest evenings I've had in . . . maybe forever. I can't tell you how much I appreciate you coming up to see me."

"We never did really talk about your meeting with Brian."

"I know. I thought I wanted to. Then when you got here it just felt so good to be with you and laughing again. I decided I didn't want him to take that away from me too. He's already taken so much."

I put my hand on hers and squeezed. "I understand. I'm glad I could help."

The look in her eyes was unspeakably tender. "No, I don't think you do understand. You probably never will."

"I won't?"

"Nope, but that's part of your charm. You're this amazing,

incredible man, and you really have no idea. In just the last few hours you took my breaking heart and turned it into one that's almost bursting with happiness."

"You're exaggerating."

"See? There—you're proving my point. You really have no idea how wonderful you are."

I don't know if it was the chemistry we shared, the kind words we'd spoken to each other, the physical attraction, the privacy, the blanket of stars spread out above us, or all of those things put together, but we stared into each other's eyes without speaking for about fifteen seconds and then slowly leaned in for a kiss. It was soft and tender, tentative I would call it. But good. So very good. And then came another that was more confident, bordering on urgent.

My conscience had given up on me by then. Whatever still small voice I'd heard earlier was now completely drowned out by the roar in my ears and the pounding of my heart.

About a mile before we reached the park, we'd passed a small roadside motel. It featured an office in the middle with two wings of about six rooms stretching to the right and left. The flashing vacancy sign and "free cable" notification made it seem like something from a bygone era. There were three cars in the lot. I paid cash for the room farthest to the right because there was an overhanging oak tree that blocked out the street light and helped make my car harder to see. Faith pulled hers around behind a dumpster so it couldn't be seen from the road.

We were in the room for an hour and a half. That's how long it took us to put out the wildfire our evening together had ignited. I can tell you we came to our senses when it was all over, that we asked for each other's forgiveness and promised never to let such a thing happen again. But I knew it was a promise without a backbone because all the way home my mind wasn't on Mary Beth, and I wasn't begging God for forgiveness. I was thinking about Faith and wondering if the deep dark secret we now shared had tilted the axis of her world as much as it did mine.

I got my answer about twenty minutes before I turned into my driveway. Faith texted me:

Please keep Sunday night open.
PLEASE.

It was yet another opportunity for me to do the right thing. One text was all it would have taken to get things back on track, one text mentioning Mary Beth and my desire to recommit myself to my marriage. I know Faith would have respected my wishes. But of course, I answered like the slave to my flesh I was:

Why wait till Sunday night?

- 39 -

For the duration of Mary Beth's time in Atlanta with her mother, Faith and I continued to see each other and settled into an illicit but no less intoxicating routine. At school, we were super careful not to give off vibes when in each other's presence. We couldn't have been more professional if we'd bowed and curtsied every time we passed in the hallway.

Concerned about phone records, I bought us each a track phone. This enabled us to talk whenever we wanted without anyone knowing. Many nights we lay in bed and talked for an hour or two, never running out of topics to discuss and always finding things to laugh about.

We also found Belle Isle Park and discovered we could just happen to run into each other there at dusk and have the hiking path to ourselves. The advantage of meeting there over simply talking on the phone was that we could touch each other while we talked. Like a couple of high school kids discovering love for the first time, we held hands, snuggled on cool evenings, and kissed.

Believe it or not, sex wasn't a big priority for us. Though neither of us ever said it, I think we mostly avoided it because it was impossible to justify. As long as we were only talking, we could always play up the we're-just-good-friends angle and make ourselves feel better about what we were doing. But on those occasions when things turned sexual, sure, it was fun and exciting, but afterward a fog of guilt enveloped us. Also, having sex is a logistical nightmare for two adulterers who live with other people and do not want to risk being seen (or recorded on a security camera) checking into a hotel.

Looking back, I am amazed at the lengths we went to in an effort to cover our tracks. I've already mentioned the professionalism we maintained at school. I still remember the day Faith came charging into Alice's office demanding to see me. Faith had a temper, and when she got riled up she was a regular bulldozer.

Alice came into my office with eyebrows raised. "Mrs. Connelly is out here and would like to see you." Then she silently mouthed the words, *She's really upset!* I told Alice to send her in.

As soon as Faith got inside my office, I closed the door and asked her to take a seat. She didn't. In a loud voice, she began telling me about how the computer lab in her classroom needed to be updated with new machines. Apparently, the computers kept freezing up, causing no end of frustration for teacher and students alike. But all the time she was saying these things she was pushing me against my desk, loosening my tie, and kissing my neck. I did my best to fend her off while keeping a reasonable-sounding conversation going in case Alice was listening, which she probably was.

Faith thought her little stunt was hilarious. She especially enjoyed how it flustered me. When she left my office, my tie was fixed and any lipstick she may have left behind was wiped off of my neck. She stalked out the door like a social justice warrior who'd just demanded that Congress do a better job of feeding hungry children. The next time we met in private she laughed and laughed about how wide my eyes were when I realized what she was up to.

Faith also made it a point to criticize me occasionally when talking to other teachers. Nothing too bad, mind you. Certainly nothing that would rise to the level of insubordination. Mostly, she accused me of being lax in this area or that, a nice guy who needed to be a little more assertive. I might have been a little hurt by these criticisms, but she assured me she didn't really think these things—she was only covering our tracks.

One day, Jolly Molly Thomas came to see me with a complaint about Faith. "I don't like her attitude. I think she drags down morale around here."

"Oh really? How?"

"She's a nitpicker. She never has anything good to say."

"About who?"

"About *you!*"

"Me?"

"Yes, you."

I acted intrigued and said, "Tell me the worst thing she's said about me."

Jolly Molly thought for a moment and said, "It's not any one thing. It's just that she never has anything good to say. Mr. Vincent, I think you do a wonderful job here, and everyone else does too. But with Faith . . . I don't know, it's like you never do anything right."

That night at Belle Isle Park I told Faith to cool it a little with the criticisms. She scoffed at my concern and called Jolly Molly a childish tattletale, but I said, "You're drawing attention to the very thing you're trying to deflect attention away from. I'm not saying you have to praise me to the heavens to everyone you meet, but a little moderation would be good."

"So, compliment you a little, huh?"

"That would be nice. Within reason, of course."

"Can I tell them what a good kisser you are?"

"That's not even close to being within reason."

Faith did moderate her criticisms, but the incident illustrates what a tightrope we were walking. In trying to cover her tracks, she actually called attention to herself. This, I think, is why so many extremely smart people get caught having affairs. They're basically too smart for their own good. They come up with sneaky little plans that seem ingenious and foolproof, but there's always an X-factor—a Jolly Molly—they don't anticipate.

The bottom line is when you sign up for an affair, you basically agree to spend every day walking through a mine field where one false step could blow your world sky high. It doesn't matter how many landmines you are able to avoid, all it takes is one misstep to render all those thousands of perfect steps pointless.

- 40 -

The closest we came to getting caught was about two weeks after Mary Beth went to Atlanta to be with her mother. We had been talking on our prepaid phones a couple of times a day, and things were going well between us. But on this particular day, Mary Beth was out of sorts. She had turned in her rental car because of the mounting expense and was using her mother's old Toyota Corolla. While in that car she tapped another driver's bumper in a grocery store parking lot.

According to Mary Beth, the other driver was young, foul-smelling, covered in tattoos and piercings, and weighed at least three hundred pounds. She said he was as round as a bowling ball and just as unyielding. He used foul language and tried to intimidate her into giving him cash to get his car fixed. She refused and said she intended to call a cop and fill out an accident report, to which he replied, "Lady, you do not want to do that. If there's a report filed I will know where you live, and trust me, you do not want me to know where you live." As if he might murder her in her sleep or burn our house down or something. She ended up giving him one hundred dollars just to get him out of her life and then hated herself afterward for letting him bully and manipulate her.

When we spoke on the phone a while later, she was still fuming. I understood, of course, and tried my best to be sympathetic, but nothing I said had any cooling effect on her rant. The result? I couldn't wait to get off the phone with her.

Later the same afternoon, I called Faith to set up a Belle Isle Park rendezvous for that evening. We were still pretty new at that point, the excitement was running high, and having Mary Beth chew my ear off on the phone only added to my need for some tenderness. Subconsciously, I think what I really wanted was to get rid of the feeling of being oh-so-very-married.

Consequently, that night more than most others, I was feeling amorous. Faith noticed this right off. I suspected her first clue was that my usual peck-on-the-lips greeting was replaced by a kiss that lacked subtlety in the way Times Square lacks pedestrians on New Year's Eve. And Faith loved it. The kiss was her signal I was willing to take things a little further than usual, which she'd been wanting. In fact, the previous time we met, I'd literally had to push her away and ask her to cool it.

"What's different tonight?" she breathed against my neck when we finally came up for air.

Not wanting to focus on anything else, I said, "Don't question why one wave is bigger than another. Just ride it."

She pulled her head back and gave me a look. "You're Socrates all of a sudden?"

I answered her with another, more passionate, kiss. We were both so into it, I was surprised we heard the voices. Just around the bend, heading for our spot on the bench, a couple was approaching. We had no idea who they were but couldn't take the chance that we might know them. I grabbed Faith's hand, and we stepped off the path into the shadows and stood behind some trees. To our horror, the couple was Carrie Austin, our school librarian, and her boyfriend.

Carrie is thirtyish, very pretty, and well liked. Or maybe it's just that people are drawn to her because her life resembles a soap opera, and they enjoy hearing about her exploits. And hear about them they do. Carrie is an animated talker who has apparently never heard of the concept of discretion. She not only tells you what she does but how she does it and who she does it with. And as for boyfriends, the in-house joke is that she is on schedule to have dated every single male in our county by the end of next year. My favorite thing about Carrie is that she's funny. When she waxes eloquent about her dating horror stories, everyone within earshot doubles over in laughter.

But on that particular evening, no one was laughing. Not Carrie, who was having a fight with her boyfriend, and not Faith and I, who were in the dark shadows less than thirty feet away, standing as still as statues, trying not to make a sound. If Carrie, of all people, found out about us, the whole world would know about our illicit relationship before the top of the hour. I looked around for an avenue of escape, but the ground beneath our feet was littered with sticks and leaves. We couldn't have tiptoed away without being heard.

So we stayed put.

For almost an hour.

Being on your feet for an hour is not so bad if you're walking around and keeping your blood flowing. But standing perfectly still that long starts to mess with your head. I grew dizzy, and pain shot through my ankles and hips.

But at least the show was entertaining.

Carrie was furious with her boyfriend for going to a strip club with his buddies. Apparently, it created a crisis of self-esteem for her. "I'm not good enough for you? What's wrong with me? Go ahead and tell me . . . why am I not good enough for you?" He had no answer—or perhaps he just chose not to share the one he did have—so she changed directions and tore into him for not telling her he went. (Apparently, she found out through the grapevine.) He told her he didn't tell her because he knew she would do exactly what she was doing at that moment: throw a fit. She said, "A fit? That's what you call me telling you how I feel?" At that point she called him "Buster"—never a good sign—and informed him he hadn't seen anything yet. If he wanted to see a fit, she would show him a fit.

I was thinking, *Could you just break up already? Please?* I was willing her to slap his face and march back down the trail. But no, she had plenty of verbal grenades left.

Eventually, Carrie did end the relationship. Her parting shot was that her now-ex-boyfriend was juvenile and needed to grow up. I thought, *Yes, grow up. What a wonderful idea. But please do it somewhere else!*

When they were gone, Faith and I emerged from the shadows and staggered back to the bench, where we collapsed, moaning and rubbing our aching joints. Then we started giggling about what we'd heard and started mocking Carrie and the now thoroughly dumped boyfriend. Faith actually did an excellent Carrie impersonation and threw in a few one-liners of her own creation that were hilarious.

The result of almost getting caught, of hiding in the shadows until our bodies ached, was that all the fiery passion we were feeling earlier completely drained out of us. We decided to quit while we were ahead, gave each other a hug and a peck, and went our separate ways.

Later, as I lay in bed, I shivered when I thought about how close we had come to getting caught. Clearly, we needed to quit what we were doing. But when I thought about how Faith kissed me, how it practically sent smoke rolling out of my ears, I realized I didn't want to.

- 41 -

The Red Chevy Truck Theory.

It's a theory I developed as a result of buying, um, a red Chevy truck. It's the idea that you never notice red Chevy trucks until you buy one, and then you see them everywhere. The same goes for having an affair. You don't think much about affairs until you get embroiled in one, and then, suddenly you run into adultery references everywhere you turn.

Every other song on the radio is about cheating. I'll bet I heard *Me and Mrs. Jones* more times while I was involved with Faith than I have during all the rest of my life put together. Every television or movie plot features an ill-fated affair. Every sermon at church contains some reference to unfaithfulness. And every gossip rag in the supermarket checkout lane features a headline about some celebrity who was caught with the nanny.

We humans have an uncanny ability to fend off these attacks on our conscience. The radio station can be changed, the TV can be switched over to sports, church can be skipped, and the gossip rags can be rendered impotent simply by scrolling through your phone in the checkout line until it's time to pay. I actually found myself doing all of these things in an effort to avoid thinking about what I was doing.

And then one day I couldn't avoid it anymore.

I came home and found Mary Beth in tears.

She'd been home a couple of weeks because her mom had greatly improved, and she was sitting on the sofa with her face in her hands, sobbing. I dropped my briefcase on the kitchen counter, rushed to sit beside her and wrapped my arm around her shoulders. "Baby, what's wrong?" I was looking her over, checking for a bandage or some other indication she might be hurt. I saw nothing unusual, which was good news and bad news. I was glad she wasn't hurt, but I assumed that meant she'd somehow discovered my affair with Faith. I couldn't think of another reason she'd be so upset.

She started to speak but dissolved into tears once again.

I rubbed her back and said, "Take your time," the picture of a patient, loving husband. But my mind was racing full-speed ahead on two tracks: One, I was trying to figure out where Faith and I had slipped up, and two, I was trying to think of what I would say when Mary Beth hurled the inevitable accusation at me. I failed to come to a conclusion on either question.

Faith and I had been so careful. We both knew what was at stake and were determined not to take any foolish chances. I couldn't imagine where we went wrong. Other than the close call we had in the park when Carrie and her boyfriend showed up, I couldn't think of another situation that might have exposed us. Maybe that was the problem. In all likelihood, something had happened that Faith and I were oblivious to, a freakish coincidence that couldn't possibly have been anticipated.

Mary Beth finally dropped her hands and stared straight ahead. Her cheeks were wet and her nose was running. She pressed a balled-up wad of tissues to her face and took a deep breath.

Here it comes, I thought.

"Bill," she said.

"Bill?" I was confused. "Bill who?"

"Bill Hancock."

He was the husband of Anne Hancock, one of Mary Beth's best friends. "What happened? Did he die?"

Mary Beth looked at me and sneered. "No, but he will if I ever lay eyes on him again."

I'd never heard her make such a statement.

"Why? What happened?"

"I just got off the phone with Anne. She found out this afternoon that Bill has a mistress and that his mistress is pregnant with his child!" Mary Beth exploded off the sofa and started pacing and waving her arms. She said, "Can you believe it? Mr. I'm-Such-A-Good-Christian is a liar and a cheat! Anne has supported that man in everything he's ever done. She was at home, changing diapers, while he was out chasing his dream. She's sacrificed her own career so he could have everything he wanted, and now he does this!"

I had a lump in my throat the size of a softball. I opened my mouth, but nothing came out, which was okay because Mary Beth wasn't finished. Not by a long shot.

"Can you believe the girl is seventeen years younger than him? For crying out loud, she's not even twenty-five! She's a kid! He's almost old enough to be her father! He's like some dirty old man you read about in the news. And he got her pregnant! Can you believe it? He's not only a snake in the grass, he's too stupid to use protection!"

As rants go, it was epic. Mary Beth was as furious as I've ever seen her. I decided to say nothing until she ran out of steam.

She continued: "I was over at their house two days ago and he was doting on Anne like she was some kind of princess. I remember thinking how lucky she was to have someone who loved her so much. Ha! All of it—every bit of it—was a sham!"

She flopped onto the sofa and lay back against the cushions, staring up at the ceiling. I said, "How did Anne find out?"

"She found his second cellphone, the one he bought on the sly so he could talk to his girlfriend without her knowing."

My track phone was five feet away from us, in my briefcase.

"So when she found it he admitted it?"

Mary Beth looked at me like I was stupid. "How could he do anything else? The only reason a man buys a second cellphone is because he's a liar and a creep."

The comment felt like a kick in the ribs. I hoped what I was feeling wasn't written all over my face. I said, "What's Anne going to do?"

The question sent Mary Beth off on another rant. "Oh, if I know her, she'll take him back. She's been taken care of for so long she doesn't have any confidence in herself to make it on her own. They'll probably go to counseling, and he'll act all sorry, and the first thing you know he'll be back home, and it'll be right back to what it was before, which means him doing whatever he wants. I tell you, if I was her, I'd kick him out in the street. He could go live with his little bimbo and just write me a nice fat check every month. No way I'd even want him near me."

For a fleeting instant I had the feeling Mary Beth was sending me a message, that perhaps she'd concocted the situation with the Hancocks just so she could do this rant for my benefit as a way of warning me that she knew what I'd been up to. Then I thought, *No, Mary Beth wouldn't do it that way. She would just tear my head off.* Still, it seemed so strange that every word she spoke about Bill Hancock was also applicable to me. All except the part about his mistress being pregnant. Suddenly, I was very glad Faith and I had downplayed the sexual aspect of our affair.

Suddenly, Mary Beth snuggled up to me, pulled my arm around her, and laid her head against my shoulder. "Hold me," she said, so I did.

We sat there for a long while, saying nothing. She sniffled and wiped her nose a couple of times. Otherwise, I might have thought she had fallen asleep. Apparently, she'd run out of steam and was experiencing the physical lull that comes after a huge adrenaline rush. Part of me wanted to say something, but I decided just to hold her, again playing the concerned husband.

After about ten minutes, Mary Beth sat up and gave a deep sigh. Then she turned and looked me in the eye. My heart thumped a little harder as I thought, *This is it. She's now going to tell me she knows everything.* Instead, she took my face in her hands and gave me much more than a run-of-the-mill kiss. Then she said, "Thank you for not being like Bill Hancock" and got up and walked out of the room.

- 42 -

She walked into our bedroom and closed the door, which was her way of saying she wanted to be alone. It's a good thing, because I don't think I could have spoken a word without breaking down in tears. My hands were shaking, and I wasn't sure my legs would hold me up if I tried to stand. But I knew I couldn't just sit there on the sofa, looking like a wanted felon who just realized he walked into a police station by mistake. I had to move.

Thankfully, my legs did hold me up. I picked up my briefcase and walked into my office, shutting the door behind me. It was all I could do to keep from screaming and pulling my hair out. In my entire life, I don't think I ever hated myself as much as I did right then. It was as if a blindfold had been removed and I suddenly saw the person I had become. Yes, I'd had guilt pangs and moments of regret along the way, but the excitement and pleasure I was experiencing motivated me to find a way to suppress them.

Oh, the memories—the *painful* memories—that came flooding back. My mind was suddenly a movie screen where I saw a replay of the flirtations Faith and I had shared, the kisses, the phone calls, the rendezvous, the sex acts, and worst of all, the lies I had told Mary Beth. Every excuse I'd ever made to get out of the house and go meet Faith rolled through my brain like credits at the end of a movie. I also saw Mary Beth's trusting expressions, the smiles and winks of a woman who thinks she has a devoted husband.

One memory in particular was especially painful. I'd concocted a reason to get out of the house and go meet Faith. Based on the phone conversations Faith and I had had that day, it seemed likely to be one of the rare occasions something sexual would happen. We both seemed to be in the mood, which, I won't lie, was thrilling, except that Mary Beth, in complete innocence, called to me from the bathroom before I could get out the door. I'd heard the water running in the shower and knew she hadn't had time to dress. I pushed the door open and stuck my head into a cloud of steam. "You need something?"

She was wrapped in a towel, and her hair was wet. She smiled in a way that told me exactly what she wanted. She said, "How long will you be gone?"

"Um, I don't know. Hopefully not more than an hour."

She walked up to me and grabbed the front of my shirt with both hands, pulling me in for a kiss. It was the kind of sexy moment every husband dreams of, the kind of moment half the married men in America would kill for, and all I could think about was extricating myself and heading off to see Faith.

Mary Beth ended the kiss with a loud smack and looked into my eyes. "Your wife wants you to hurry home."

"She does, huh?"

"Yes, she does. Do you need to write it down, or do you think you can remember?"

"My memory's not the greatest, as you well know, but I think this is something I'm likely to remember."

"See that you do."

And with that, I was gone. The crazy thing is, I was glad to be out of there. And all the way to my rendezvous with Faith, I was frustrated—you could even call me angry—that what I'd been sure was going to happen with Faith would now have to be put on hold because the last thing I could do was come home sexually spent with Faith's scent all over me. I'd become pretty good at lies and excuses, but there was no way I would ever be able to explain that.

Faith noticed how sullen I was when I finally arrived and asked what was wrong. I told her what had transpired, which sent her into the same kind of funk I was in. We spent about fifteen minutes brooding about our circumstances and then went home.

Sitting there in my office, reliving that evening in my mind, I felt sick enough to vomit. How in the name of all that is holy had I become such a horrible, lost person? Mary Beth had been enraged by Bill Hancock's philandering; she'd be even more enraged by mine. The thought of her anger exploding in my face was truly terrifying, and yet I knew it would be justified.

Should I march into our bedroom and confess everything to Mary Beth? A part of me said yes, it would be the honorable thing, and I would get what I deserved. The only thing that stopped me was thinking about the pain I would subject Mary Beth to. Her life would be wrecked, at least for the foreseeable future. She might forgive me someday, but I had no doubt she would spiral into a period of darkness.

I got down on my knees and prayed. I've said a lot of prayers in my life, but none with that kind of fervor. Over and over again I begged God to forgive me. I thanked him for Mary Beth, for giving me such a good wife, and I apologized for not appreciating her the way I should've. I asked him to show me the way forward, to reveal to me the best way to get out of the monumental mess I had created for myself. I've been mostly a guy who prays two- or three-minute prayers, but that night I went on and on.

Eventually, I got to my feet and sat at my desk. I wiped my eyes and blew my nose. If Mary Beth had walked in, I would have had no answer for why I was so emotional. But she didn't. I sat there for several minutes, barely conscious of my surroundings.

Then my emotions shifted.

My self-loathing subsided enough for me to think clearly about a plan. Without question, I was going to end it with Faith and try, somehow, some way, to get some self-respect back. The only thing I had to decide was how. I could call her, but breaking up by phone seemed cowardly. I felt she deserved the opportunity to say whatever she would want to say to my face. That left one other option.

I would ask her to meet me at Belle Isle Park.

PART 3

"No adultery is bloodless."

—Natalia Ginzburg

- 43 -

I have a black suit. It's my best suit, fairly expensive with fine tailoring. Mary Beth says it looks good on me and I should wear it more often. I jokingly tell her it makes me feel like a funeral director. About an hour before Faith's funeral, I pulled it out of my closet and put it on, hoping it really would make me feel like a funeral director. Feeling like a funeral director would be better than feeling like a killer.

I do understand I didn't kill Faith. I didn't encourage her to take off running, and I didn't swing the crowbar that crushed her skull.

Tell it to my heart.

The day she died, my heart started accusing me of killing her with all the fervor of a high-powered prosecuting attorney. The worst times were at night when I tried to go to sleep. I even started listening to music or watching television to keep the voice at bay, but Mary Beth started to wonder what had gotten into me because I have always preferred quiet at bedtime. To tamp down her suspicions, I went back to the quiet and suffered. Many nights, it was one or after before fatigue managed to silence that belligerent inner voice.

Standing before the mirror, I thought I looked pretty good. I'd gotten a haircut the day before, and my face was shaved smooth with a new blade. My shirt was a crisp white, the knot in my tie was centered nicely, and the creases in my suit were as sharp as the drycleaner's press could make them. By all appearances, I had everything under control. In truth, I felt like I was on the verge of a breakdown. My head hurt, my hands were shaking, and my stomach felt queasy. And I was scared. I had no idea what would happen when I tried to deliver Faith's eulogy. Would I be able to muddle through? Would my emotions get the best of me? Would I break down and confess everything? I was in such a fragile state I honestly couldn't predict what would happen. The only thing I knew was I had to give it a go. For me to refuse to pay tribute to one of my teachers would create all kinds of questions I didn't want to answer.

The car was quiet as Mary Beth and I drove to the church. She had noted my nervousness and tried to encourage me before we left the house by talking about how comfortable I always seem in front of people. I told her this was not a school assembly or a PTA meeting. She agreed and fell silent, most likely figuring she'd done all she could to help me.

We were about halfway to the church when I had an overwhelming desire to pull into a Target parking lot, turn to Mary Beth, and confess everything. Even if she'd hate me and file for divorce, I felt it would be better than listening all day every day to the accusations of my heart. I'd simply call ahead to Pastor Dwayne and tell him I was sick and couldn't make it. It wouldn't have been a lie. I was the sickest man I knew.

But somehow, I kept driving. There's no telling what my blood pressure was right then. I'm surprised the steering wheel didn't snap in two I was squeezing it so hard. I don't know if Mary Beth saw my white-knuckle grip. I wanted to steal a peek at her but was afraid I'd see her giving me a suspicious look.

Woodcrest Community Church—or WCC, as the members often called it—owned one of those church buildings that tries to look modern (lots of severe angles and mirrored glass) while still retaining some sense of tradition (a steeple with a cross). When we stepped into the lobby, Pastor Dwayne happened to be walking by. He looked to be in his thirties and was bald and pudgy. He was also in need of a new suit, as the one he was wearing appeared to have stopped fitting him about twenty pounds ago. I wondered how long it had been since he'd been able to button the jacket. I also noticed his shoes needed a good polishing. Anything to keep my mind occupied.

I'm not sure how he knew who we were, but he did and greeted us warmly though with an overtone of reverence befitting the occasion. He shook my hand firmly and told me how glad he was I agreed to help out.

Mary Beth and I followed him to his office, where he invited us to sit. He opened a desk drawer and pulled out a half-sheet of paper that had the order of service typed on it. I saw my name listed fourth on the agenda, just after a vocal solo by someone named Becca Talbot.

Pastor Dwayne said, "I'll need you to sit on the front row so you can have quick and easy access to the platform. As soon as Becca finishes her song, just get up and go. Our sound guys will adjust your volume on the fly. When you're finished, just go back to your seat. Or you could go sit with Mary Beth if you prefer."

For all his weight and wardrobe issues, Pastor Dwayne seemed to have his act together. I wondered what he'd think if he knew he was looking at the man who had contributed to the delinquency of one of his church members and then led her to her death. Would he have forgiven me or thrown me out? I suspect my secrets would have tested the charitable nature of even the most dedicated pastor.

Before the service started, I met Joe and Doris Jackson, Faith's parents. Doris was the image of Faith, only twenty years older. Which means she was beautiful. Or perhaps I should say she *would* have been beautiful if her countenance hadn't been so tightened by grief. Joe seemed quite a bit older than his wife and almost in a stupor. His mouth was open slightly, and his eyes were a little glazed. Doris hugged me and thanked me for everything I had done for their daughter. She said, "Faith always talked about you and what a nice man you are."

My eyes watered, and I was barely able to croak out the words, "Thank you."

When we left them, Mary Beth took my arm and led me toward the auditorium. I pulled a handkerchief out of my pocket and dabbed at my eyes. When no one was within earshot, she whispered, "You're going to be fine."

She spoke those words just as my eyes fell on the stage area at the front of the auditorium, where I saw a casket surrounded by a brilliant array of fresh flowers. The lid was open, and in the muted light I saw the profile of an attractive face that might have looked peaceful were it not for the blunt force trauma I knew was hidden by her hair and the satiny pillow on which her head rested. It was the first time I'd seen Faith since I left her lying on the trail in Belle Isle Park. I had assumed the casket would be closed. What is it about people that makes them want to look at dead bodies? Isn't it better to remember people as they were when they were alive?

Mary Beth sensed my uneasiness and squeezed my arm. "You okay?"

I knew I had to be. I couldn't let myself fall apart. "Not really. I've never been good at this kind of thing."

"Think of her parents and how much they need to hear the kind words you have to say."

I took a deep breath and said, "You're right."

The auditorium was about half full when I settled into my front-row seat just before the top of the hour.

$$- 44 -$$

Pastor Dwayne opened the service. He had a kind and gentle way about him. I thought he might be someone I would like if we found ourselves living next door to each other. As for what, specifically, he said, I have no idea. I was in a fog. I didn't come back to reality until Becca Talbot, who was younger than I expected—perhaps only in high school—made her way to the podium and sang a song about meeting God face to face. How she managed to be so young and show such poise, I don't know.

About halfway through the song, I glanced to my right and saw Jack and Doris, Faith's parents, fighting back tears. I wondered why they were sitting in the second row until I looked at the first row and saw the man who had to be Faith's husband, Brian. He'd obviously been granted a leave from the prison to attend his wife's funeral. Somewhere close by there would have to be deputies monitoring his movements. I would have expected him to look sad, but he looked angry. He wore an ill-fitting suit with no tie and sat with his shoulders hunched, staring at the floor like a teenager who'd just been told he'd been grounded for a month. There were two empty seats on either side of him, a clear indication of how Faith's family felt about being near him.

I looked away and tried to focus on the job at hand. My remarks were typed out, double-spaced, on two sheets of paper. I planned to simply read them and sit down. I would not be throwing in anything off the cuff. My only goal was to get up and down without telegraphing to the audience that I was involved in Faith's death.

And then Becca was finished.

On wobbly legs, I stood and climbed the three small steps onto the stage. When I reached the pulpit I was careful not to look at the audience. Instead, I concentrated on opening my folder and laying my notes out flat. I took a deep breath and then looked up.

There were perhaps sixty people in the room, most of them teachers and employees of our school. I saw serious expressions on the faces of Adam Brooks, Jolly Molly, Alice, and all the way in the back row, Mia Li, the investigator I'd hired to check out Angela Wells. I was so shocked to see her my jaw almost dropped.

Almost being the operative word.

As surprised and confused as I was by her presence, I knew I couldn't allow anyone to see through my façade. I figured I would find out soon enough what Mia was doing there. So I glanced down at my notes and began:

"Good afternoon. I'm Jason Vincent, the principal at Lake Arbor Elementary, where Faith was a second-grade teacher."

I spoke about how she'd been out of teaching for a while but jumped right back into it without missing a beat. I talked about how well liked she was and how her students especially loved her.

"Maybe it was because she had a child of her own about that age, but she developed an amazing rapport with her students. The kids in her class looked up to her with something bordering on hero worship. Even students that weren't in her class sensed she was someone they could trust.

"I'll never forget the time one of our more challenging students climbed over the chain-link fence that surrounds a retention pond on our school property. He was angry about something and was threatening to drown himself. We didn't think he actually would, but we had to get him out of there and I was ready to pick up the phone and call the police. That's when Faith asked me to let her talk to him.

"She walked down to the fence and sat down cross-legged. She pulled a weed out of the ground, stuck it in her mouth, chewed on it like she was just there to catch a few rays on a lazy afternoon. None of us could hear what she was saying, but we could tell by the boy's body language that he was responding.

"Soon, he was sitting down cross-legged too, right in front of her with only the chain-link fence separating them. They were talking back and forth, and then, suddenly, the boy laughed. I still remember my secretary, Alice, saying, 'She's like the horse whisperer, only with kids.' And she was. Faith had an uncanny ability to connect with children."

I continued on with another anecdote about the time Faith dressed up like a man for a school assembly skit and had the kids roaring with laughter. I snuck a peek and was thrilled to see Faith's mother smiling, though her father still looked as if his mind was somewhere else. Brian was still staring a hole in the floor. The one thing I had wanted to do was bring some life and a sense of celebration to the proceedings. At least I was partially successful.

When I finished and sat down, I almost fainted with relief that I hadn't lost my composure or in some other way betrayed my terrible secret.

After the service, numerous people approached me and talked about what a good job I did eulogizing Faith. I was gracious but kept working my way toward the door. There was to be a funeral procession to the cemetery, and I used that as an excuse not to linger and visit. I couldn't, however, escape quite fast enough. Joe and Doris cornered Mary Beth and me in the lobby.

Doris gave me an awkward hug and blinked back tears as she told me how much my words meant to them. "Faith used to talk about you all the time," she said as I cringed inwardly. I didn't dare look at Mary Beth.

"Your daughter was a blessing to our school," I said, trying to keep things more professional than personal.

"And *you* were a blessing to *her*. She always said you were the best principal she ever worked for."

I smiled and said, "Well, she didn't work for that many."

I really wanted to get away from them.

Thankfully, the funeral director came by and gently encouraged us to make our way to our cars so we could begin the procession to the cemetery. I wanted to hug him.

As Mary Beth and I were climbing into our car, I looked up and saw Mia Li leaning against a large oak tree. Her legs were crossed, and her arms were folded. And she was staring right at me.

- 45 -

When I was a teenager, some buddies and I spent part of one Halloween night in a cemetery. We'd heard some girls were going there after dark to read the grave markers and make up scary stories about the dead. We decided to get there ahead of them and add an extra dash of fright to their recipe for a scary evening. It turned out just like we'd hoped. We came flying out from behind the headstones, screaming like banshees, and scared them half to death. We ended up joining them for the rest of the evening. We all had a blast.

That trip to the cemetery was as fun as this one was going to be miserable.

The procession crawled along at thirty miles an hour, which prompted impatient drivers to speed around us to get to the next intersection before we jammed everything up. If that's not bad enough, some of them even gave us dirty looks as they passed, as if we were enjoying hauling a dead friend to her final resting place and clogging up the traffic was just icing on our cake. I remember a time when drivers showed respect for a funeral procession, even pulling to the side of the road until it passed. Those days are gone.

What, under normal circumstances, would have been a fifteen-minute trip, stretched into thirty because of our reduced speed. My nerves were on edge, not only because we were slogging through a sea of obnoxious drivers, but also because the day's activities and what they represented for me had ratcheted up my stress level to unprecedented heights. I guess I didn't realize how much it was showing because, about halfway to the cemetery, Mary Beth caught me off guard when she said, "Jason, can I ask you something?"

I looked at her and said, "Sure."

I could tell from the measured way she spoke that she was choosing her words carefully. She said, "Is there something wrong? I mean beyond the obvious."

Oh boy. Here we go.

"I don't know what you mean."

"What I mean is . . . I get it about Faith's death hitting you hard. She's someone you saw every day, someone you were friends with, someone whose death leaves a void in your school and in a lot of people's lives. But I've been watching you today and you seem . . . I don't know . . . more jumpy than I would expect."

"Jumpy?"

"Maybe that's not a good word. I mean, I get the sadness, but you seem more than just sad. You seem fidgety. Nervous. Like you're teetering on the edge, which is not like you. You've always been a rock at times like this. Like when your uncle Ted died. You weren't this upset, and you grew up around him. You'd only known Faith for less than a year."

I realized I had to pull it together and do a better job of hiding my anxiety. But I could think about that later. For the moment, I needed to bluster my way through this conversation. We were maybe ten minutes from the cemetery. I shifted my brain into that often-used gear most men possess, the one that enables us to conjure up a line of bull when we get into a tight spot.

I reached over and took Mary Beth's hand. "You know what's

weird? I *feel* what you're seeing. I sense I'm too worked up over this, too. I was embarrassed back at the church when my tears welled up. Ever since Pastor Dwayne asked me to speak, I've had a knot in my stomach. I've had to sit around and think about what to say about Faith, which makes everything feel even sadder, if you know what I mean." I paused, as if reflecting on the meaning of life. "I mean, I think about how she was working so hard to keep things together while her husband was in prison, and then about Zoey, who's only six and will never see her mother again . . . and how they don't even know who killed her. I don't know. It just stinks. The whole thing. Maybe if I can just get through this next hour I can start to unwind a little bit."

It was a pretty good speech. Some of it was even true. But I still half-expected Mary Beth to say, "Oh, cut the crap and tell me what's going on." But she didn't. She squeezed my hand, then lifted it to her lips and kissed it.

Crisis averted.

For the moment.

I knew I had to calm down, quit moping, dry up the tears, and start acting like myself again.

At the cemetery, about thirty people gathered around a hole in the ground that was covered by a green canvas tent and surrounded by a thin carpet of synthetic turf. Underneath the tent, there were two rows of flimsy chairs for the family. Brian Connelly, Faith's husband, sat in the middle of the front row, and again, no one sat next to him. I noticed a plain white panel van was sitting at the end of the line of vehicles that made up the procession. There was grillwork between the front two seats and the back of the van, indicating it was a prison van used for transporting prisoners. Two young men I pegged as prison guards stood at the back of the tent, keeping an eye on Faith's husband. If he even looked like he might try to run off, I figured they'd pounce on him.

Sitting on the end of the front row were Joe and Doris Jackson. They wept yet again for their daughter, or at least *she* did. Poor Mr. Jackson still looked dazed. I wondered if he would snap out of his trance someday and have to be told his daughter was dead. He looked for all the world like a man who had blocked out reality.

Pastor Dwayne did another good job reading Scripture and making some heartwarming comments about how our dear beloved Faith was now in the arms of Jesus. And to think, just a few days earlier she'd been in *my* arms. She'd definitely taken a big step up.

- 46 -

Mia Li's presence at the funeral surprised me until I remembered something I'd picked up in the hundreds of crime novels and movies I'd digested over the years: Killers often show up at the funerals of their victims. Or maybe that's just a plot device that works well in books and movies but has no basis in real life. I wasn't sure, but I convinced myself it was the reason she was there.

But there hadn't been anyone there who seemed suspicious. There were a few of Faith's relatives I didn't know and a small handful of people I assumed were church members, judging from the way Pastor Dwayne interacted with them. But everyone else was from the school. Angela Wells wasn't there, nor was anyone fitting Machete or Crowbar's description. I kept my eyes open, even scanning the distance, in case one of them might be watching.

On the way home from the cemetery, I asked Mary Beth if she wanted to stop by Culver's for ice cream. Or was it frozen yogurt? Or custard? I couldn't remember. I only knew she loved their turtle sundaes. Our tradition was to get one and share it. She always said when we stop eating one ice cream with two spoons it will be time to go to marriage counseling, whatever that means.

As we plowed through the sundae, our mood lightened. Actually, my mood didn't, but I put every ounce of energy I had into pretending it did so Mary Beth could feel better about me. It pains me to admit I was so disingenuous, but I knew of no other way to put her at ease. By the time we finished the sundae, I had a drip of it on my crisp white shirt, and Mary Beth joked about how, the next time I managed to eat ice cream without getting any on me, it would be the first time and we would plan a celebration. In other words, things felt back to normal.

That night, I waited until Mary Beth had been in bed for a while and then stepped into my office and closed the door. It was after ten, but I pegged Mia as a night owl because of her age. When I was in my twenties I rarely went to bed before midnight, and I didn't think most young people today were much different. So I texted her:

She must have had her phone in her hands because she texted back immediately:

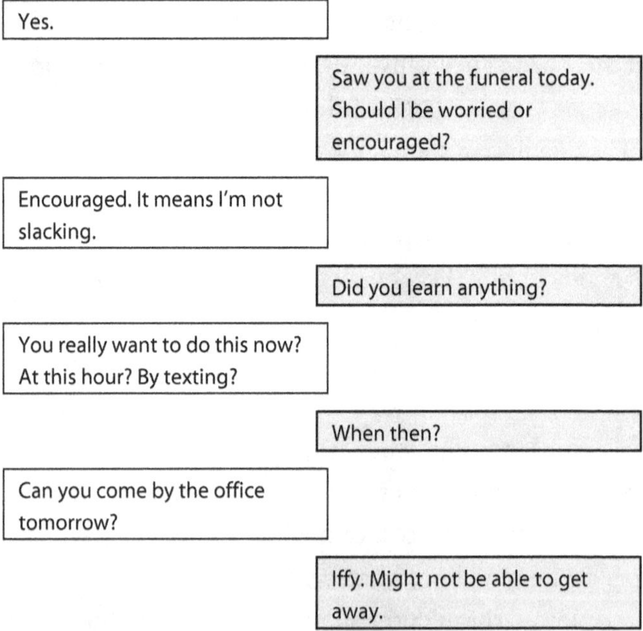

Can you call?

What time?

Anytime as long as it's DURING BUSINESS HOURS.

Understood. Sorry.

It's okay.

Just tell me this. Have you made any progress?

Yes and no.

Seriously? That's the answer you're going to leave me with to sleep on?

LOL Just teasing. Yes. I've made some. But still lots of unanswered questions.

Some is better than none.

True. Get some sleep and call me tomorrow.

Will do. Thanks.

No, thank you. I just billed you 20 bucks for this.

What?!

Relax! I'm kidding!

Really?

Go to bed, Jason. Call me tomorrow. Or I WILL start billing you.

Okay. Sorry. Goodnight.

The more interaction I had with Mia Li, the better I liked her. She seemed more than competent and had a great sense of humor. Working with her had to be better than working with some crusty old burned-out ex-cop who's just trying to make a little money to keep his fridge filled with beer.

She said she had made "some" progress. I couldn't wait to find out what it was. Somewhere out there a murderer was walking around free . . . as was a beautiful imposter who apparently knows about my affair with Faith. The murderer and the imposter had to be connected somehow, didn't they?

My ultimate fear was I might never get to the bottom of this mystery and that my need for secrecy might prevent me from going to the police, who, with all due respect to Mia, were much more equipped to deal with this situation than a PI. What if it came down to either me coming clean about my sins and flushing my life down the toilet or the murderer going free? How would I choose?

Thinking about it gave me a headache, and I knew I wasn't going to answer the question right then, so I got up and trudged toward our bedroom.

When I crawled into bed, Mary Beth wanted to snuggle, whispering something as she turned to face me. She spoke so low the rustling sheets kept me from hearing her clearly, but I think she said, "I'm glad this day is over. Now we can get back to normal."

- 47 -

After telling Mia I would call her the next day, I decided I didn't feel comfortable contacting her by phone if I didn't have to. I didn't want the call to be logged on either of our phone records. When things go sideways, phone records always end up front and center. If I was going to fly under the radar and keep my shameful behavior a secret, I had to leave as few traces of myself as possible, which meant I needed to see Mia in person.

It wasn't hard to get away from school, though it did require another lie. I told Alice I had developed a sore throat over the weekend and had a doctor's appointment. She practically shooed me out the door and grabbed a bottle of Lysol disinfectant to ward off my germs. I told her that, if anyone called for me, she should not tell them I had gone to the doctor, only that I had stepped out for a while and would return the call when I returned. I knew Mary Beth, if she called, would dial my cell.

Luckily, Mia was in her office and buzzed me in.

"Where'd you park?" she asked as I came through the door.

"Down the street, in front of the record store."

She beamed. "You're learning."

"Sadly, yes."

"Why *sadly*?"

I shook my head. "I have become all too good at lying and deceiving. I wish I could turn back the clock to when I was just a clueless, bumbling, *faithful* husband."

Mia nodded as if she understood. "We're going to try to get you back there. Come on back."

We walked into her back room where the computers were humming and Dr. Watson was stretched out on the floor. He didn't even bother to raise his head. Mia motioned me to a chair as she plopped down in her own, leaned way back, and put her feet up on the desk, ankles crossed. She was the picture of relaxation, which made me wonder if she was taking my problems seriously enough. I didn't have to wonder long.

"I suppose you'd like to know what I've learned," she said.

"I would indeed."

"First of all, your mystery lady, Angela Wells, has a checkered past."

Ed Dickerson had told me about the criminal solicitation and misdemeanor assault. I was happy to hear Mia had come up with the same information. Only, she didn't come up with the same information. She came up with more.

"What has she done?" I asked, feigning ignorance.

"Criminal solicitation and misdemeanor assault are on her record, though she never did any time, which is not unusual. To me, the more interesting bit of information is that, two years ago, she was questioned as a person of interest in a homicide investigation."

The metronome in my chest increased its tempo. "A homicide investigation? Who was killed?"

"A man named Jasper Royal."

I ran a quick scan of my mental database. "The name doesn't ring a bell."

"Good. If it did, I would have a very bad feeling about you."

"Why?"

"Because he is—or rather, *was*—a pornographer. One of the biggest in the country."

"He lived here?"

"Over on the coast. Big mansion on the beach, currently valued at 3.5 million dollars. Business was apparently very good."

"And he was murdered?"

"Thoroughly and completely."

"How?"

"Beaten to death."

I swallowed. "With a crowbar?"

"Maybe. The murder weapon was never found. But it was a severe beating, definitely the kind a crowbar could deliver. His skull was crushed from multiple blows."

"And Angela Wells was a suspect?"

"I didn't say that. I said she was a person of interest."

"Which means . . . "

"Which means she was his girlfriend at the time and might've had some information the police would be interested in."

"His girlfriend? Was she also one of his . . . models?" I couldn't help thinking about how attractive Angela Wells was.

"Yes, she was, but it was some time ago. Apparently, after she graduated from model to girlfriend, he kept her away from the cameras."

"And did she have any information that was helpful to the police?"

"Apparently not. The murder was never solved."

Mia paused and gave me a moment to fit a few pieces together. Angela Wells, the mystery woman from my media interview and whom I caught driving by my house, was a criminal and the former girlfriend of a big-time pornographer who was beaten to death, possibly with the same weapon, or at least the same *kind* of weapon that killed Faith. Fascinating, but I saw no connection to me . . . no reason she would be stalking me. And then I had a thought.

"Was there a connection between her and Faith? Were they maybe . . . friends or something? Might Faith have said something to her about our affair? Something that set her off when Faith was killed and made her want to target me like I was responsible?"

"I checked. I looked at their employment records to see if they ever worked for the same company. I even went back to their childhoods to see if they ever attended the same schools or played on the same soccer team. The same with their college histories. But nothing overlaps, at least not I've been able to find."

"Do you have any theories?"

"Nope, but it's early in the game. There's still a lot of snooping I can do."

And then I had another thought.

"There's a teacher at our school. His name is Adam Brooks. He's the head of our PE department. One of my teachers thinks he was having an affair with Faith at the same time I was."

Mia's eyes popped open. "Wait, what?"

I sighed. "I know."

Mia's feet hit the floor, and she leaned forward. "Do you mean she was cheating on her husband with you, cheating on you with this Adam Brooks guy, and cheating on Adam Brooks with you?"

"You put it so eloquently. But yes, something like that. At least that's what one of my kindergarten teachers says."

"How does she know?"

"She says she saw them kiss in a mall parking lot a few days before Faith was killed."

"Holy Moly. You believe her?"

"I have no idea what to think. She seemed 100 percent sure about what she saw until I encouraged her to talk to the police. Then she started backpedaling."

We batted that whole scenario around for a few of minutes. Then, Mia said, "I'll definitely look into Mr. Brooks. He's a person of interest if there ever was one."

Two minutes later I was standing at the front door, shaking Mia's hand, and thanking her for the work she'd done. Though none of it explained anything, I felt there were some threads that, if pulled, might lead to something. Just as I turned to go, I remembered to ask Mia why she had come to Faith's funeral. She said, "Don't you ever watch cop shows? The murderer often attends the funeral of his victim. I just wanted to see if anyone interesting showed up."

"But how would you know?"

Mia smiled. "I wouldn't by sight, but I did get the tag number of every car within a hundred yards of the church building."

I was impressed. "Wow. And did you learn anything from those tag numbers?"

"Not yet. My guy should have a list of vehicle owners to me in a day or two. I'll email it to you, and you can look it over. See if any of the names jump out at you."

"Your *guy*?" I was afraid she might be working with a cop, which could spell trouble for me. Big trouble.

"My go-to tech guy. Weirdest little man you've ever met. Dresses like a 1960s nerd and blinks his eyes hard like this every few seconds. Probably hasn't had a date in . . . to be honest, he's probably never had a date. But he's the most tech-savvy guy I've ever met. I don't think there's a database he can't get into. He's an absolute genius."

"And he's not a cop?"

"Nope."

"Am I paying him?"

"You are."

"Is he expensive?"

"He gives me a discount because he's in love with me."

"But you're not in love with him?"

"I'd fall for an orangutan first."

"And he's okay with that? And still working with you, I mean?"

"As long as the checks don't bounce."

I shook my head. "You are really something."

She grinned. "Which is why he's giving you a 20 percent discount."

- 48 -

The problem with telling people you're going to the doctor is that when you return, they want to quiz you. *What did you find out? Did you get a prescription? Are you contagious?*

Alice, who had a tendency to mother me at times anyway, delivered all the requisite questions right on schedule and then started doting on me. She offered to make me some hot tea and to clear my schedule for the rest of the day. I told her I was actually feeling much better and would be fine. My only concern was she might have an occasion to speak with Mary Beth and mention my midday trip to the doctor's office. I decided the chances were slim, however, and I could afford to put it out of my mind for the time being. I had much bigger concerns.

Inside my office with the door closed, I leaned back in my chair and closed my eyes. I must have been exhausted from the stress and lack of sleep because the next thing I knew, it was twenty minutes later, and my desk phone was chirping. I jumped at the sound and rubbed my eyes as I reached for the phone. Alice said, "Do you feel up to seeing Ms. Thomas?"

Jolly Molly was back. I wondered what she wanted this time.

"Sure, send her in."

When she stepped into my office I noticed she didn't look well.

Usually, she was the picture of vitality. Her hair was always perfect, and her makeup left no detail of her face unimproved. And her clothes, which were always stylish and attractive, normally bore nary a wrinkle, even at the end of a long, hard day of chasing kindergarteners. It was enough to think she had an iron stashed in her classroom. But on this morning she actually looked disheveled, like she'd slept in her clothes and gotten up too late to do her hair.

I said, "Molly, are you okay?" I thought she was going to tell me she was sick and needed to go home.

Her response was subdued: "Yes, I just need to talk to you for a moment."

"Sure. Have a seat."

She sat down in front of my desk and stared at her hands, which were folded in her lap. I watched her take a deep breath, as if to steady herself. For the life of me, I couldn't imagine what she might say, but I could tell it was weighing heavily on her.

When she continued staring at the floor, I tried prompting her. "So what's up, Molly? I can tell you're upset about something."

She took a deep breath, looked straight at me, and said, "I have a confession to make."

"And what would that be?"

"I lied about Adam."

"Are you referring to what you said about him and Faith, about seeing them at the mall?"

She nodded and looked down in shame. "Yes."

"I see." I really didn't. Not at all. But it seemed like the thing to say. "What part of what you told me was a lie?"

"I did see them at the mall, in the parking lot, by her car. But they weren't together. She was walking from the mall, and he was walking toward it. They crossed paths and stopped to talk for a moment and then went their separate ways."

Molly had no way of knowing the impact of her words. I'd been deeply wounded by the thought that Faith had been cheating both *with* me and *on* me. I'd also been racking my brain, trying to make sense of Molly's claim in light of the fact that Faith never had a good word to say about Adam. In short, her little fabrication had added more than a few stories to the skyscraper of stress my life had become.

I was tempted to yell at Molly and demand an explanation. Instead, I spoke softly, like a lenient father speaks to his adolescent daughter after a first offense: "Can you explain to me why you lied?"

Molly teared up. She pulled a tissue out of her sleeve—something my grandmother used to do—and dabbed at her eyes. She said, "I was hurt and wanted to get back at him."

"Did he do something to you?"

It took her a moment, but she sniffled and wiped and finally said, "No. Not really."

Talking to Molly was never easy because she gave out information in tiny bits and pieces and seemed intent on being as vague as possible. Most of the time I didn't mind, but lately, with her being a player in the greatest drama of my life, her communication style was really getting on my nerves. Trying to remain patient, I said, "Molly, you've got to explain this. You can't come in here with vague answers to important questions and think I'm going to let this go. Did Adam do anything to you or not?"

Molly blew her nose, which turned out to be a very unladylike endeavor. With a mighty expelling of air through her nose, she produced a honking sound that would have been hilarious had we been characters in a sitcom.

Finally, she got to it. "A few weeks ago, Adam and I had a moment in his office after school. I mean, nothing happened, like sex or anything . . . we were just talking. Well, mostly talking. It was pretty personal and kind of intense, if you know what I mean. We both said some things that made it seem like we might, you know . . . have a thing for each other or something."

She stopped as if what she'd said explained everything.

Prompting her yet again, I said, "So?"

"So I went home, thinking it was something it wasn't. I spent an entire weekend fantasizing about us being together and . . ."

"Molly, he's married. He has a child." I said it the way I would have told her water was wet or the earth was round.

She seemed to shrink at the reminder of Adam's marital status, and even more tears spilled onto her cheeks. "I know, but for someone like me who wants to be in a relationship so bad, I didn't care. I wanted to believe, you know?"

"And so your heart got broken, and you were angry and wanted to get back at him."

She nodded without raising her eyes to look at me. "Pretty much."

I sighed and shook my head. "Molly, Faith was murdered, and you were ready to throw Adam into the police-investigation grinder just because . . ."

"I was never going to tell the cops. I just wanted to cause a little trouble for him around here. I knew Faith wouldn't be around to deny the affair, so it would all be on him. I wanted to see him squirm."

I sighed and rubbed my forehead. This was unbelievable. "So you wanted him to lose his job and maybe his marriage all because he hurt your feelings?"

"No, I just thought . . ." She closed her eyes tight and shook her head. "Honestly, I don't know what I was thinking. I *wasn't* thinking. I was just acting on the anger I felt. I couldn't think of any other way to make him hurt the way I was hurting."

Then Molly's eyes popped open, and she gasped. "You didn't tell the cops what I told you about him, did you?"

"No, I didn't. Because it all seemed implausible to me. I couldn't picture them being dumb enough to kiss openly in a mall parking lot. But what if I *had* told the police? Can you imagine what it could have done to his marriage and reputation, not to mention Faith's memory? The police would've had to interview people in Faith's family to see what they knew, which means Zoey would've probably heard things about her mom that would've been extremely hard for her to process. As if she doesn't have enough to process already."

"I know. That's why I'm here. I want to set the record straight and get this off my chest. It's really been bothering me."

I sat there a moment, not wanting to let her off too easy. "This absolutely cannot happen again. Ever."

"Oh, it won't. I've learned my lesson."

"And what lesson is that?"

"Don't flirt with married men."

"How about this one too: Don't seek revenge by telling lies about people."

Sheepishly, Molly said, "Yeah, that too."

I sat there for a moment, then said, "I'm glad you told me . . . glad you came clean. The story never really sounded quite right to me, but I didn't want to not believe you. I've known you a long time and always considered you an honest person."

"Can you forgive me?"

"I can forgive you, yes. But you deserve to go on suspension. I can't have people on our staff trying to hurt and undermine each other. We have to be a team around here. We cannot let our private lives and personal animosities get in the way of what we're doing for the kids. This little plan of yours could have gone wrong about six different ways, and innocent people could have gotten hurt. I mean *really* hurt. In life-changing ways."

"I understand."

Molly seemed willing to take the suspension without trying to talk me out of it. I expected her to beg me not to suspend her because it would have been so difficult for her to explain to her friends and coworkers why she wasn't going to work. Perhaps because of her humility, and partly because I had committed far greater sins than she had, I said, "But I'm going to let it go this time because you've never done anything like this before and because you fessed up and nobody got hurt. But I am going to write a report and file it, and if you ever do anything like this again, you won't be suspended, you'll be fired."

"Thank you, Mr. Vincent. I promise it won't happen again."

Molly went out the door, sniffling, and I sat at my desk trying to sort through the implications of what I'd just learned. I was glad Faith had only been cheating with me and not on me. And maybe it simplified things a little by eliminating the Coach Brooks angle altogether. But I was still no closer to figuring out how Angela Wells fit into things and how on earth she knew Faith and I were having an affair.

- 49 -

On my way to school the next morning, I stopped at a 24-hour Wal-Mart and bought another prepaid phone. I'd gotten rid of mine after Faith was killed, but now that I was communicating with Mia, it seemed wise to pick up another one. I couldn't be running to her office every time I wanted to talk to her, and I still wanted to keep our calls from being logged in our phone records. The trick was to not slip up and allow Mary Beth to find the thing. If there is a room somewhere in heaven (or hell) that logs the stories of philandering husbands, surely there must be a section dedicated to all the affairs that were blown up by the wife's discovery of incriminating evidence. Keeping the phone well-hidden would give me yet another thing to worry about, but I didn't see any way around it.

I walked out of Wal-Mart at 6:20 a.m., and when I got to my car, I found an envelope stuck under the driver's side wiper. There weren't many other cars on the lot at that hour, but I noticed none of them had an envelope stuck under a wiper. It didn't appear the envelope was part of some poor businessman's shoe leather advertising campaign. I whipped my head around but saw nothing suspicious. There were no cars driving away, no hooded figures peeking out from around the corner of the building, only an older gentleman and his wife toddling out of the store with their Velcro sneakers and canes.

I picked up the envelope, got into the car, and drove away. Yes, I was dying to open it, but I was sure I was being watched, even if I failed to spot anyone. Whoever left the envelope had obviously followed me and was almost certainly sitting somewhere in a car with tinted windows, watching for my reaction. I was happy to disappoint him. Or her.

I took a circuitous route to the school, constantly glancing at the rearview mirror. I expected to see Angela Wells' black BMW tailing me. Once I even pulled into a gas station and watched the next fifty cars go by to make sure a BMW wasn't following me from some distance back.

The thought occurred to me I was becoming paranoid, that I would probably open the envelope and find a flyer advertising bounce houses and clown services for children's backyard birthday parties. I did buy some gas while I was sitting at the pump because I needed it anyway, and then I pulled to the side of the convenience store where there was very little foot traffic.

After looking around and seeing nothing suspicious, I stared at the envelope. It was plain white, letter-size, and there were no markings on it of any kind. I also noted the flap was tucked in instead of sealed. I sniffed the envelope but detected no unusual scent. Finally, I opened it.

Inside was a single sheet of white copy paper, folded in thirds. I can't say I was surprised by the message because an oppressive weight of dread settled on me the moment I saw the envelope. I knew it would be nothing good, and I was right. Written on the paper were five words, all lowercase, typed, italicized, with no period at the end:

i know what you did

- 50 -

I can't exaggerate how terrified I felt. Someone seemed to have me in their crosshairs. I was being watched and followed. Someone knew when I left my house and when I was inside Wal-Mart. I wondered if my surveillance was part of some kind of team effort. Were there people keeping tabs on me and reporting to others who were doing the hands-on work? I tried to remember if I saw any suspicious-looking people inside Wal-Mart who could have been keeping an eye on me, making sure I was where I wouldn't see someone approaching my car with an envelope.

Or perhaps there was some kind of tracker on my car. I'd read about tiny magnetic trackers that were virtually invisible when attached to the bottom of a vehicle. Such a gizmo would allow someone to know where I was at all times and to follow me from a distance so I would never know. That possibility was even more frightening.

And then there was the message itself: *I know what you did.* Was it a reference to my affair with Faith? If so, the author of the message was correct: I *did* do something. But what if it was a reference to Faith's murder? What if the person somehow knew I was involved with Faith and assumed I killed her to keep her from ruining my life and reputation? In that case, the author was mistaken.

And then another thought struck me: What if the note was from someone who knew I fled the scene of the crime? Perhaps someone had been in the park that night but had stayed hidden throughout the encounter, much the same way Faith and I did when we were surprised by Carrie Austin and her boyfriend. This was a possibility that had nagged me from the beginning. Mia and I were focused on the people we identified as possible players in this mystery. But what if there was a player in the game we knew nothing about? This was perhaps the most terrifying thought of all . . . one that could easily produce the note I held in my hand.

Sitting in the car beside the convenience store, I was tempted to drive straight to the police station and tell them what I knew. Would they keep me in custody until they could investigate my claims? Would they arrest me for obstruction of justice since I had told one lie after another from the get-go? If the TV shows were accurate, I would get one phone call. That, of course, would go to Mary Beth to tell her I was, at the very least, being held for questioning. It hurt me to think about what such news would do to her.

Still, the temptation to give myself up was strong. I'd been embroiled in this nightmare for almost a week, and it was almost more than I could take. Before Faith's murder, I saw myself as a nervous, stressed out guy because of the affair. But this was a thousand times worse. My marriage, career, and reputation were still on the line, but now someone was dead and I was an eyewitness. And someone was messing with my head, and there was no telling what lay in store for me down the road. If I went to the police, would it have the same effect turning on a light has on cockroaches? Would my enemies suddenly scurry away to hide in the darkness and leave me alone? Would I ever find out who they were?

With these thoughts swirling in my mind, I turned out of the gas station parking lot and headed to the school. It's not because I was determined to fight on. I genuinely thought I might choose at some point to chuck everything and turn myself in. But the one thing I wanted to do first was talk to Mia. I wanted to get her take on the envelope.

I arrived at the school just as Alice did. I greeted her in the parking lot and walked with her toward the building. Normally, she was fresh and ready for action in the mornings. She's had her coffee and comes in singing or telling some funny story about something her husband said the night before. This time she seemed a bit standoffish. She said hi, but didn't engage me in the kind of banter we were accustomed to.

"You feeling okay?" I said.

"I'm all right."

We'd worked together long enough to have taken on some of the characteristics of a married couple, such as an ability to read between the lines of each other's comments and to hear nuances in the other person's tone of voice. I knew from Alice's clipped answer that something was wrong. And since it had never been our style to beat around the bush with each other, I said, "What's wrong?"

She looked at me, then looked away.

Every husband in the world who's been married more than a week has been on the receiving end of one of those looks. And none of us has ever construed it as a precursor of good things to come. Naturally, my mind raced forward, leaping frantically toward the worst possible conclusions. It even flashed through my mind that she, too, had gotten an envelope, one that spelled out my sins in the goriest of details.

I stopped walking and said, "What was that look?"

Alice stopped too and turned to face me. "I'm sorry. I'm having a bad morning."

"Why? What's wrong?"

She glared at me. "Did you go to the doctor yesterday?"

Uh-oh.

It was clear she already knew I didn't, so there was no point in denying it. "No."

She turned on her heel and marched toward the building. I didn't try to keep up. People were around, and I didn't want to have the conversation we needed to have with anyone else in earshot. I knew that, once the bell rang for first period, things would quiet down and we'd be able to talk. In the meantime, I had to figure out what I was going to say.

- 51 -

I stood in my doorway and asked Alice to come into my office. She marched past me without looking me in the eye and plopped down in the chair in front of my desk. I closed the door and walked to the window behind my desk and looked out at the parking lot. With my back to her, I said, "How did you know I didn't go to the doctor?"

Alice said, "If you hadn't been in such a hurry to get out of here yesterday, you would know."

I turned and looked at her. "What does that mean?"

"Yesterday, when you left, I called after you to tell you my daughter-in-law just got a job at Dr. Carlson's office. He *is* your doctor, isn't he?"

"Yes."

"Well, guess what ... she's the new receptionist. She sees everybody who comes through the door. I was going to tell you to say hi to her, but you were in such a hurry, you got out the door before I could catch you."

I nodded, accepting that I'd been busted, but Alice wasn't finished. "So Jenny and David and the kids came over for dinner last night, and I asked her if she saw you. She said no and assured me you did not have an appointment and were not in the office."

"Alice, I'm sorry."

"So am I. You've never lied to me before. At least not that I know of."

All I had wanted was to end my affair with Faith and get back to being a good person. I wanted to protect the people closest to me and spare them the pain of disappointment. And yes, I wanted to spare myself, as cowardly as it might sound. And in sparing myself, I would have been sparing others. I truly felt it was a noble goal, especially if I spent the rest of my life being a good an honest man. But now things seemed so hopelessly tangled that a complete implosion could happen at any moment. I felt so sick about all of it. And even though it was unintentional, I was starting to hurt people I cared about. People I loved. Like Alice.

I pulled out my chair and sat down. I spoke in a humble, measured tone.

"Alice, I truly am sorry I lied to you yesterday. Obviously, I didn't want you to know where I was going. Part of me wants to open up and tell you everything right now so you can maybe understand my thought process. But I can't do it. Not yet, anyway."

Alice's expression showed not the slightest bit of sympathy. "Are you cheating on Mary Beth? Because if you are, so help me . . . "

"What? No, I'm not. Is that what you think?" It wasn't a lie, but if I'd said it a week earlier, it would have been. "Alice, no. Get that thought out of your head."

She softened a little. "Are you sure?"

"Yes, I promise."

"Well, what was I supposed to think? When a man leaves his workplace in the middle of the day and lies about where he's going . . . anybody would think some hanky-panky was going on."

I nodded heartily, agreeing. "I understand. It was a logical conclusion to jump to. But I am looking you in the eye right now and telling you that I am not cheating on Mary Beth."

Alice looked at me decidedly more sympathetically than she had a moment before. Then she said, "And you can't talk about it?"

I hung my head and shook it. "No, I can't."

"Does it have to do with that imposter reporter who showed up at your media interview?"

Alice was sharp. I held her gaze for a moment and said, "I can't say."

"Which is the same as saying it does because if it didn't you would say so."

"I wish I could say, Alice, but I can't."

Her eyes brightened, and she said, "Ooooh, I get it."

"What?"

"Something's up with that woman, and you're working with the police."

"Alice . . ."

"That's it, isn't it?"

"Alice, please. I cannot talk about it. I know we've told each other a lot of personal things over the years, and I cherish that kind of trusting relationship, but on this one I need to ask you to respect my situation. I can't talk about what I was doing yesterday. And if there comes a time when I have to leave again, I need you to understand and not give me a hard time about it."

"Just answer me this."

"Alice . . ."

"Please."

I stared at her for a moment and then said, "Okay, what?"

"Are you doing anything illegal? Because I can't cover for you if you're breaking the law. That would make me an accessory."

"Unequivocally, no. I am not breaking the law in any way, shape, or form."

She sighed, then thought for a moment and said, "Okay, then here's the deal: I believe you and I'm choosing to trust you on the basis of our years together and the man I believe you to be. As of this moment, I am on your side. I won't ask you anything more about this, but if you need anything from me . . . if you need me to run interference for you or help you in any way, all you have to do is ask."

Tears came into my eyes. I wanted to say how much I appreciated what she said, but I was afraid if I spoke I would break down. Finally, I nodded and croaked out a weak "Thank you."

Alice stood up and started for the door, then hesitated. "One more question. Does Mary Beth know about any of this?"

"No. I'd like to keep her out of it if I can. It would worry her to death."

"At the risk of sounding like your mother, it's not good to keep secrets from your wife."

"Trust me, I know."

"It's also not good to leave your prepaid phone sitting on your desk where your secretary can see it."

I looked down and there it was. I had unpacked it and left it sitting right there in plain sight. When I looked up, Alice was on her way out the door. She looked at me and winked as she disappeared.

- 52 -

I muddled through some work and made it a point to be seen around the campus. I tried to be the picture of cheerfulness, chit-chatting with some of the staff and throwing out a few witty one-liners. It was all PR. Alice already knew there was something up with me; I didn't need other people thinking I seemed off. Just before ten, I was able to retreat to my office and call Mia. I knew she wouldn't recognize my new number and no name would come up on her Caller ID. When she answered, I said, "Hi, Mia. It's me."

"Jason?"

"Yeah."

"Are you at work?"

"Yes. In my office."

"Can you come by later?"

"Why, do you have something for me?"

"Maybe. I've learned some things, but I have no idea how important they are."

"I've learned some things too, but it's going to be hard for me to get away from the office."

"Can you talk privately right now?"

I glanced at the door. It was quiet in the outer office, which meant

217

people were busy, but it also meant I would have to keep my voice down. I said, "Yes, but I'll need to talk softly."

"That's fine. Why don't you go first."

"Okay. First of all, I learned that Adam Brooks is not a suspect."

"How do you know?"

"Because the woman who told me he was having an affair with Faith, who said she saw them kissing at the mall, came in and recanted her story."

"You've got to be kidding me. Why would she make up a lie that could get someone caught up in a murder investigation?"

"Let's just say she felt jilted even though I don't think she really was. Apparently, they flirted, and she read more into it than he intended, and when it became apparent to her, she became angry."

"Oh, for crying out loud. What is she, in the fifth grade?"

"She's actually a nice person, but her weakness is she's desperate. If you knew her, you'd understand."

I couldn't see her, but I pictured Mia, who seemed about as far from desperate as a polar bear's genetic code is from a caterpillar's, rolling her eyes and shaking her head. "I guess it's just as well because I didn't find out anything interesting about Adam Brooks. So what else do you have?"

"This is the big one. Someone left a note on my car."

"What kind of note?"

I told her the whole story of the trip to Wal-Mart, the envelope, and the brief, type-written message. When I finished, I said, "Somebody's obviously following me."

"Looks that way."

"How do you think they're doing it? Visually? Or with some kind of tracking device?"

"Could be either one. It would be easy to park somewhere near the entrance to your subdivision and just watch for your car to come out. But a tracker would be much easier and less risky. They could follow you from a distance, and you'd never see them."

"How do I find out if my car has a tracker?"

"You could crawl under it and look around, but those things can be hard to spot. With the new technology, they're amazingly small."

"Is there some kind of scanner or something that would detect it?" I'd read of such things in novels and assumed they were real.

"Of course. When it comes to electronic surveillance, there's a gizmo for almost anything you want to do."

"Do you have one?"

"No, but my friend I was telling you about—the weird one who blinks—would have something like that. His house looks like every Radio Shack in the country gave him their inventory when they went out of business."

"Can we have him check it out?"

"I'll ask him and get back to you. I'm sure he'll do it."

Encouraged, I took a breath and said, "Okay, what do you have for me?"

"Well, I've been looking into the mysterious Ms. Wells, and I made an interesting discovery. She has a brother who was in the same prison as Faith's husband. His name is Oscar Wells. He did four years for aggravated assault and just got out last year."

Instantly, I sensed this was vital information, but it took a moment for my mind to process it and start connecting dots. Mia kept quiet, allowing me to do just that. Finally, I said, "Are you thinking what I'm thinking?"

"Probably. What are you thinking?"

"I'm thinking you found the missing link, the thing that brings this whole mystery together. Faith's husband, Brian, must be orchestrating everything from prison with Oscar Wells, his old prison buddy, serving as his hands and feet. He probably wondered if Faith was cheating on him while he was doing his time and asked Oscar to find out. Oscar then followed Faith, who would have had no idea she was being followed. She led him right to our regular meeting spot in the park. Oscar then reported back to Brian, who became furious. He then asked Oscar to confront us in the park the night Faith was killed."

"But just to scare you, because you said you felt like Faith's death was an accident."

"Exactly. Oscar and his buddy were just supposed to put a scare into her and make her want to end the relationship. Then, when it went sideways, Faith was killed. When Brian heard about it, he decided I needed to pay. He obviously blames me for her death."

"Um, what about the guy who killed her? The guy you call Crowbar. Don't you think he had a little something to do with it?"

"I'll bet you anything Oscar, who has to be Machete, killed Crowbar because he knew he couldn't go back to Brian and say, 'Oh, by the way, the dude I got to help me scare your wife ended up killing her.' Machete killing Crowbar actually served two purposes. It eliminated one of the two people who knew Oscar was in the park that night, and it gave Oscar something at least somewhat positive to report to Brian. 'Your wife was killed, but I got the guy who did it.'"

"Which leaves only you to deal with."

"Right. Brian sees me as the ultimate reason his wife was killed, so he's got Oscar and his sexy sister working to set me up for something. Mia, it makes perfect sense."

Mia was less enthusiastic than I was but couldn't deny the almost scary way the pieces fit together. "I'll admit, it sounds logical, but I'd like to do a little more digging," she said. "I'd like to see if I can connect Oscar Wells and Damien Robillard, the guy who was found hacked up in the park the night Faith was killed. And I'd like to see if I can find Oscar. Where does he live? Does he have a job? Maybe if I can find him, we can positively ID him as Machete. You said he had a distinctive voice and manner of speaking."

"That's a great idea. Yes, he has a rich baritone voice, almost like a late-night radio announcer. And he spoke like a corporate CEO instead of a thug. No street lingo at all."

Mia was silent for a moment.

I said, "What are you thinking?"

She said, "Let's say we're onto something. Let's say it all went down the way you're saying and we're able to gather enough evidence to, if not prove it, at least plug all the obvious holes. Then what? I mean, if we go to the police with our theory, everything you've been trying to avoid—specifically, your involvement with Faith and the consequences thereof—becomes a reality."

The exhilaration I'd been feeling only seconds earlier drained out of me. Mia was right. If we really had just solved Faith's murder, we had all kinds of information the police didn't have and would never get because they didn't know about my affair with Faith. They didn't know Oscar and Angela Wells even existed. They didn't know Oscar was connected to Faith's husband. They didn't know to look for a connection between Oscar and Damien Robillard, the other murder victim. And they would never know these things unless we told them.

And if we told them, I was toast.

But if we didn't, the story of Faith's murder, not to mention Damien Robillard's, would never be known, and Brian Connelly and Oscar Wells would walk away without paying for their crimes.

Mia sensed what this realization was doing to me emotionally. I could hear the sympathy in her voice when she said, "Jason, let's not worry about the endgame right now. Let's make sure we've got what we think we've got. We might find out there's a piece that doesn't fit. Then, when we're sure, we'll figure out what to do. Maybe there's a way to accomplish all of your goals."

"Maybe," I said, but I didn't really believe it.

"In the meantime, you've got to be careful. You don't know what they might be planning for you. Do you have a gun?"

"No. I've thought about getting one several times, but Mary Beth is no fan of firearms."

"I wish you did, but by the time you could get a concealed carry permit, this situation might be resolved."

"That's comforting."

"I mean resolved in a good way."

"Yeah, right. Look, I need to get off of here. I hear voices outside my office door. I think Alice's is going to buzz me any second."

"Okay, I'll check on Mr. Robillard and see if I can find Oscar Wells. He might be right under our noses. You let me know if you get any more messages on your windshield."

"Sounds good."

"And Jason . . . be careful."

"Will do."

Not more than a minute after I hung up, Alice did indeed call me. During those few seconds it hit me that I was in serious danger. If we did indeed have this situation figured out, and Brian Connelly knew I was cheating with his wife, I could see why he would want me dead.

- 53 -

The next day at school was routine. It was what happened after school that was significant. Early in the afternoon, Mary Beth texted and asked if I would stop on my way home and pick up a couple of steaks. She hated pork and was lukewarm about chicken and turkey but loved steak. Not ground beef or pot roast or brisket, just steak. I told her once that it didn't make any sense; that it was like disliking football and basketball and hockey but loving baseball. She made it clear my life would go much better if, rather than questioning her meat preferences, I would just feed her steak on a regular basis and keep quiet. That's what I've done ever since.

I pulled into a Publix supermarket on my way home and went inside. I found the two thickest ribeyes in the meat case and headed for the frozen food section. When I got to the checkout lane, I laid the steaks and a half-gallon of cookie dough ice cream on the conveyer. I felt about ice cream the way she felt about steak. I figured there was no reason we couldn't both indulge our taste buds. A friendly white-haired woman about my mother's age was ringing up the couple in front of me.

I sensed someone step into line behind me, but I didn't turn to look until the person said, "Hello, Mr. Vincent."

I turned and found myself looking at one of the strangest little men I've ever seen. His cheeks were scarred by childhood acne, his ears were so large they seemed to have been made for someone twice his size and given to him by mistake, and his eyes were different colors. Drastically different. I noticed also that he blinked hard every few seconds and that his smile twitched. He was wearing cargo shorts, white socks, and black wingtip dress shoes.

People in professions like mine meet hundreds, even thousands of people over the course of time. It's not unusual for someone to walk up to me in a supermarket or mall or restaurant and say hi, calling me by name, without me having the first clue who they are. I assumed the strange little man who spoke to me was someone I had encountered at school, so I said, "Hi, how have you been?" as if I'd known instantly who he was. Why I felt the need to try to bluff my way through the moment I don't know.

He said, "Keepin' busy."

"That's great."

When it was my turn to check out, I exchanged pleasantries with the cashier, swiped my card, dropped my purchases into a plastic bag, and turned to bid a good day to the little man. It was then I realized he wasn't holding any groceries. Or gum. Or even a gossip rag from the checkout lane magazine display. He simply smiled and blinked and followed me out of the store. I'm sure the checkout lady thought we were together.

I kept glancing over my shoulder, and sure enough, the little man kept following three or four steps behind me. When we were almost to my car, I stopped, turned to face him, and said, "Can I help you?"

He blinked and grinned. "No, but I can help you."

That's the moment I realized the man was not someone from my school life. I had no clue who he was, but with everything going on in my life, a feeling of apprehension swelled in my chest. Mia's last words to me had been a warning to be careful. I was glad there were lots of people around. I said, "Who are you?"

The man blinked hard a couple of times, stuck out his hand, and said, "Mayford Wing, at your service."

I'd never heard such a name. "Do we know each other?"

"No, but we have a mutual friend."

"And who would that be?"

"Mia Li."

It all came together in my mind. Mia had told me about a weird little blinking friend of hers who was some kind of electronics genius. She said he could tell me if my car had a tracker on it. I said, "Oh, yeah. Mia did mention you, but she didn't tell me your name, and she certainly didn't tell me you would be approaching me at the market."

Mayford smiled and blinked. "Sorry, but it served my purpose perfectly."

"And what would your purpose be?"

"To determine if your car has an electronic device planted on it. I assumed you wouldn't want me to do the check in the school parking lot or in your driveway at home."

"Uh, yeah, that's true."

"So I did it here."

"You've already done it?"

"Yes, sir."

"But . . . did anyone see you?" I pictured him crawling around looking underneath the car.

"No, sir. I just needed to get within a couple of feet of the car with this." He held up a little round disc about the size of the lid on a small jar of pickles.

"It's some kind of scanner thing?"

"Yes, sir. Would you like to see it work?"

"Um, sure. Why not?"

Mayford grinned and headed for my car. I could tell he was pleased to have the opportunity to show off his toy.

When we reached the car, a little green light on the disc he was carrying lit up. He showed it to me and said, "There you go."

In traffic, green is the color you want. I assumed it would be the same in the tracker scanning business so I said, "That means my car is clean?"

"No, sir. Green means yes, there's an electronic device within ten feet of us. I walked around the other cars to make sure it wasn't one of them. Yours is definitely the one with the tracker. By the way, the red Ford Edge over there has one too. I noticed it when I walked into the store."

"It does?"

"Yes, but it doesn't have anything to do with you. It's probably just a suspicious wife trying to find out if hubby is really working late at the office all those evenings. Or maybe a husband who wonders if his wife really goes to the yoga class she talks about. Suspicious spouses are some of my best clients."

I was speechless. And I was afraid. It is a truly frightening thing to know someone is tracking your movements, especially when you're pretty sure the man tracking you believes you are responsible for his wife's death.

I looked at Mayford, who was blinking to beat the band. "What should I do?"

"Two things. One, talk to Mia. She's amazing. She'll know just what you should do. And two, keep this." He handed me the scanner. "I'll want it back when your problem is cleared up. Or if you want to keep it I'll sell it to you for a couple of hundred dollars. I built it myself."

"Why would I need to keep it if you've already told me my car has a tracker?"

Mayford shrugged. "Maybe you have a second car."

"I do. My wife drives it."

The little man blinked again and smiled at me, as if to say, "There you go."

I slipped the device into my pocket and looked around. No one was within earshot, but I still felt odd talking about my situation in a wide open public place. In fact, I felt like someone was probably watching us right then. Mayford must have read my mind because he said, "I doubt they're watching us right now."

"How can you be so sure?"

"I can't. But there would be no point since your car has a tracker. Instead of following you around, all they have to do is monitor your meanderings on a laptop. They might know your car is here but have no way of knowing what you're doing or who you're talking to. It's another reason I thought a place like this would be perfect for our meeting."

I felt hopelessly in over my head. "Thank you for doing this," I said.

"I'd do anything for Mia. She's the best."

And with that, he turned and walked away, leaving me to drive off in my car that was equipped with a tracker that would report my location to whoever was working for the man holding me responsible for his wife's death. It was the most terrified I'd ever been, and I couldn't talk to Mary Beth about it without imploding our marriage.

- 54 -

That evening, Mary Beth was in a great mood. When I walked in from work she was humming a sprightly tune and practically dancing around the kitchen. She dropped a sprig of something green into a pot—it looked like something a conscientious gardener might spray with Roundup—and waltzed over to give me a welcome home kiss and relieve me of the steaks and ice cream. I, of course, acted pleased and eager to reciprocate but in fact felt even more shame and guilt because of her outpouring of affection and good humor. I simply did not deserve this woman.

"How was your day?" she cooed.

I could have told her the exciting news that someone who wanted to do me harm had placed a tracker on my car, but I opted for a more ambiguous response: "It was okay. How was yours?"

She started loosening my tie and said, "I, dear sir, am glad you asked."

I gave her a playful look of suspicion. "You haven't been nipping the cooking sherry have you? You seem awfully happy."

She showed me her pouty face and said, "Isn't a wife allowed to be glad her husband is home from work?"

"Yes, a wife is, most definitely. But when she treats him like he's returning from a foreign war instead of from his office a few miles away, he's bound to wonder what she's up to."

"I'm just happy, that's all."

I was sure I knew why. She'd recently talked to one of her old coworkers, who was now director, at the homeless outreach. She'd made some sweeping changes that addressed some of the complaints Mary Beth used to harp on and was now begging Mary Beth to come back and be her lead assistant. More than once, Mary Beth had talked about how, if some of the administrative frustrations of her old job could get worked out, she wouldn't mind going back. But I didn't mention any of this.

Instead, I played along in the spirit of the moment: "Well, I know you didn't win the lottery because you always say only idiots and people who are bad at math buy lottery tickets, and you're neither. So it must be the Publisher's Clearing House Sweepstakes. Let me guess . . . they came with their camera crew and a bouquet of flowers and a big cardboard check and knocked on the door."

"Now you're making fun of me."

I contemplated briefly and then nodded. "Correct. I *am* making fun of you."

Mary Beth slapped me on the behind and told me to go wash up before she decided to let me wear dinner instead of eat it. We've had a thousand—maybe a million—playful moments like that over the years and they almost all end with my rear end getting slapped or pinched or playfully kicked. On this occasion, I did what I usually do: I exited the room, screaming, "Abuse! Officer, this woman hit me!" Mary Beth giggled as I made my way to the bathroom.

The sound of her joy, of her giggling, triggered a surge of emotion so strong it caused my breath to catch and my eyes to sting. I had always loved her giggle. The very first night we met it struck me as one of the things I liked best about her. Every time I heard it, it made me smile. I told her this once and she seemed hurt. Clueless, I begged her to tell me what was wrong. She said, "No woman wants to be told by the man she loves that she has a great giggle. Tell her she has beautiful eyes or hair or skin or even a beautiful body, but don't tell her she has a great giggle. Scooby-Doo has a great giggle. Do not compare the woman you love to a dog. Ever." The logic of the speech escaped me and still does, but I did learn to love her giggle silently.

That evening, as I headed for the bathroom to wash my hands, I was almost paralyzed by the notion that I could be on the verge of never hearing her giggle again, either because something could happen to me or because Mary Beth might discover my unfaithfulness and want nothing more to do with me. I looked at myself in the mirror and thought I looked old and tired. I marveled that no one had asked me what was wrong with me—if I had a disease or something—because, to my eyes, I looked sick.

Finally, with clean hands and a pasted smile on my face, I ventured back into the kitchen, where the steaks I'd brought home were sizzling on the stovetop grill. She smiled and said, "So . . . you want to hear my news or not?"

Just then, my prepaid phone vibrated in my pants pocket. I had forgotten to put it in my briefcase. Mary Beth didn't seem to have heard it, but that might have been because of the sizzling of the steaks or because she was a few feet away and arranging some pots on the stove. I couldn't take the chance she'd hear it the next time. I had to get that phone out of the room.

In response to Mary Beth's question about hearing her news, I held up my index finger as if checking the direction of the wind, and said, "Hold that thought. I'll be right back." Then I dashed out of the room.

In my office, I pulled out the phone and looked at the screen. I had a message from Mia that said,

Call me. Urgent.

I thought about doing it right then. She'd obviously learned something important. But I knew if I did I would arouse Mary Beth's curiosity, which I simply could not do. She would ask questions, and I would stammer like—I was going to say like a man caught kissing his neighbor's wife, but the metaphor hits a little too close to home. I dropped the phone into my briefcase and took care of one little task so I would have something to say to Mary Beth upon my return to the kitchen.

When I walked in, she said, "Where'd you go?"

"My phone was almost dead. I wanted to plug it in and let it charge while we're eating." It was actually true. My phone—my real one—was down to 30 percent, an unusually low number for me. Mary Beth showed no suspicion whatsoever.

"So . . . what's your news?" I said as I wandered over to admire the steaks.

She took my hand and said, "I'm pregnant."

- 55 -

Women always have the advantage at moments like this. They've had the news, processed it, and started to envision a new reality, while we guys, bless our hearts, are blindsided. In my case, I was expecting to hear she was going back to work. She'd been making noises about it but had not said one word about wanting to have a baby. What man wouldn't be knocked for a loop?

It was this loop, my sudden, head-over-heels tumbling into a strange new reality, that caused Mary Beth's countenance to darken. She instantly assumed I wasn't happy about adding a little person to our family. And if I wasn't happy about it, that raised issues regarding my selfishness, and perhaps even more important, my truthfulness, because I had said on many occasions that I would love for us to have a baby. In her mind, I should have been waltzing her around the dining room like we were recreating a scene from *The King and I*.

I couldn't tell her how terrified I was that by the time our baby arrived our family might not exist.

Mary Beth, with hurt in her voice, said, "You're not happy? I thought you would be ecstatic."

I snapped to my senses and vanquished every negative thought, at least for the moment. I grabbed her hands and said, "What? Yes, of course I'm happy! Are you kidding? This is what I've wanted for years! You know that."

"But you looked like I just told you I had cancer."

I chuckled. "You know why?"

"Why?"

"Because I was sure you were going to tell me something else. I would have bet everything we own you were going to tell me you were going back to work as Lisa's assistant. When you said something entirely different, it just took me a second to adjust. And besides, why would I expect to hear you say you're pregnant? We use birth control. Don't we?"

"We? Who is this 'we' you speak of?"

"Okay, you. *You* use birth control, don't you?"

Mary Beth looked at the floor and said nothing.

"I'll take that as a no."

She said, "Remember the night a while back when we were at Disney Springs and we sat down to eat ice cream beside the young couple that had the twins?"

"Yeah."

"Do you remember what you said?"

"No."

"You said, and I quote, 'Babies represent everything I hate: slobber, vomit, screaming, and poop. So why do I want one?' Do you remember that?"

"Sort of."

"Well, that was the night I quit using birth control. To me, you were saying you still wanted a baby, and right then and there I decided I was ready too. I'd been thinking about it for a while, and right then and there, all of my thoughts and feelings started to flow in the same direction."

"Why didn't you tell me?"

"I knew you wanted a baby, so it wasn't like we needed to discuss it. I thought a surprise would be fun. Was I wrong?"

I got out of my chair and knelt before her, taking her hands in mine. "No, honey, you weren't wrong. You were very, very right. I just . . . I had no idea."

Mary Beth said, "Well, sir, husbands and wives are allowed to keep secrets from each other as long as they're good secrets."

Unbeknownst to Mary Beth, her comment was a kidney punch delivered with the power of a heavyweight champ. There was probably no husband or wife either of us knew who was keeping more secrets than I was. And not good secrets. I hid what I knew had to be a sick expression on my face by lowering my head, and kissing her hands. She withdrew one of her hands and ran her fingers through my hair. It was a tender moment for her, a shameful one for me.

As we made our way to the bedroom, Mary Beth said what I'm sure many women who are pregnant for the first time think, that she would soon be physically unattractive to me. "I know you're not attracted to fat women, and that's what I am going to be real soon." I am not the smartest guy in the world, but at least I knew better than to enter into that discussion.

Later, in bed, with Mary Beth in a cuddling mood, I wondered how long it would take her to get tired of lying with her head on my bony shoulder and retreat to her pillow and her usual spot on her side of the mattress. When she did, and when I was sure she was asleep, I intended to slip out of bed and go call Mia.

Call me. Urgent.

Whatever Mia had to tell me would be even more significant now because the stakes had been raised. It wasn't just our marriage that stood to suffer if the situation I was in unraveled . . . our baby would suffer too.

Our baby.

I could barely wrap my head around the idea.

Lying in the darkness, I wondered if someday he or she would love me or despise me. It was exactly what I'd been wondering about the child's mother.

- 56 -

Mary Beth wasn't just in a cuddling mood, but also a talking mood. A reminiscing mood. A dreaming-about-the-future mood. The pregnancy had set her mind spinning, and there was no way I was going to mess up the moment by trying to finagle my way out of bed to go to my office. I hadn't given her much lately; I was certainly going to give her this. And besides, I was enjoying the moment too. I wondered how many more like it there would be in my future.

We both ended up talking ourselves to sleep sometime after midnight. I woke up at 1:30, and sure enough, she had retreated to her side of the bed. Mary Beth is one of the great cuddlers of all time, but when it's time to sleep she doesn't want to be entangled. I slipped out of bed as quietly as I could and padded to my office.

There was a voice in my head chastising me for thinking about calling Mia at such an hour. Whatever she'd learned would keep for a few more hours. Naturally, I dialed her number. It was the word "urgent" that overrode all other considerations.

She didn't answer.

Her phone must have rung six or seven times before her voicemail recording came on. At the sound of the beep, I stammered out a message that was part apology for bothering her at such an ungodly hour and part plea for her not to keep me in suspense. When I ended the call, I stood there staring at my phone, willing it to ring. I told myself she was groggy from sleep and couldn't get to it before it kicked over to voicemail and that she'd return my call in a minute or two. When it didn't happen, I sat down behind my desk, not knowing what to do with myself. Any other fool would have gone back to bed. I chose to sit there and conjure up disaster scenarios.

From prison, Brian Connelly had somehow learned his wife was cheating on him. No doubt he had asked his old inmate buddy, Oscar Wells, to follow her and report back. Upon learning that Faith and I had a rendezvous point in Belle Isle Park, it became an easy thing for Brian to order Oscar and his buddy Damien to follow us there and put a scare into us . . . to give us a good reason to end the relationship. Which I had already planned to do, but of course they weren't aware.

And then everything went sideways. Faith panicked, Crowbar reacted without thinking, and in less than five seconds, Faith was lying dead on the ground.

And now Brian Connelly is even angrier. He sees me as the reason his wife is dead and wants to terrorize me for a while before he strikes. His sister, Angela, shows up at my media interview and asks a provocative question as a way of letting me know my affair with Faith is no secret. Then they put a tracker on my car so they can know where I am at all times. Then they put a note on my car to make me sweat. At the funeral, I noticed Brian never looked at me. Maybe he was sitting there, staring at the floor, and dreaming of the things he wanted to do to me.

As I sat at my desk, the metaphorical clock ticked down. Something was coming, and it wasn't going to be good. Maybe I had seen too many movies, but I felt like it would be something with my car. A bomb. Defective brakes. Maybe someone running me off the road. And I had no doubt that when it happened, Brian Connelly would be sitting in his prison cell, laughing.

As it turned out, it's a good thing Mia didn't call me back because Mary Beth walked in while I was sitting there spinning my little tornado of catastrophic possibilities. It would have been very difficult to explain why I was talking to another woman in the wee hours of the morning on a phone Mary Beth didn't know I had. Thankfully, I managed to slip the prepaid phone off the desk and slide it underneath my thigh when I heard the doorknob turn.

Mary Beth's hair stuck out in every direction, and her eyes were puffy from sleep. She said, "I woke up and you were gone."

"Not gone, just relocated."

"To your office at two o'clock in the morning?"

"I couldn't sleep and didn't want to wake you."

"Why couldn't you sleep?"

I chuckled. "Why do you think?"

She smiled tenderly. "I guess I did drop a bomb on you, didn't I?"

"You did, but it's okay. I wasn't even really thinking about the baby. I was thinking about myself, wondering if I have what it takes to be a good dad."

Just then, the phone underneath my thigh vibrated, giving off a soft hum and causing my heart to flip. Mary Beth heard it and said, "What was that?"

"Probably my phone. It's in my briefcase." The words sounded embarrassingly inadequate as they escaped my lips, but Mary Beth was so locked in on what we'd been talking about that she dismissed them. "I think you'll be an amazing dad," she said.

I was desperate to get out of the office before the phone acted up again. I assumed Mia had just texted me. What if she waited a moment for a response and then decided to call? Taking a huge risk, I stood up, leaving the phone sitting exposed on my chair, and walked around the desk toward Mary Beth. I slipped my arms around her waist and kissed her. "Thank you for believing in me," I said.

Then, I led her out of the room and back to bed.

We snuggled some more and talked about my potential as a father. I'd always felt I would be a good father, mostly because I knew I would be fully committed to the job. Mary Beth, however, interpreted my sleeplessness as a lack of confidence in myself, so I played along and allowed her to build me up. If not for that confounded phone and the mysterious information Mia was trying to get to me, it would have been one of the most beautiful nights Mary Beth and I had ever spent together.

We finally drifted off to sleep. My eyes popped open at 5:30, which is the time that has been programmed into my system by a routine that has been intact all my professional life. It doesn't matter what happens to rob me of sleep throughout the night, I will still wake up at 5:30. At some point, Mary Beth had rolled over and pulled the covers up to her ears, freeing me to make my escape. After a quick pit stop, I returned to my office and saw the phone sitting on my chair. I picked it up and looked at the screen. There was a message from Mia. It contained a link of some kind and then the words:

Read this and call me tomorrow morning.

I tapped the link and was taken to a news article about someone who was shot in the parking lot of a bar in the wee hours of the morning, two days earlier. There were no witnesses, and the victim was declared dead at the scene. The victim's name was Oscar Wells.

- 57 -

Machete—or at least the man I believed was Machete—was dead. Coming out of a bar at 1:00 a.m., he probably weaved drunkenly to his car, and somebody stepped out of the shadows and shot him. His wallet was gone when his body was found, making it easy to assume robbery was the motive.

First Damien Robillard and now Oscar Wells. If I was right that these were the men who confronted Faith and me in Belle Isle Park, it meant three of the four people who were there that night were dead, and I was the only survivor. My mind was struggling to process the possibility and sort out its ramifications. I didn't know if I was suddenly safer with Machete dead, or if being the only person from the murder scene who was still alive meant I was next on somebody's hit list. I was anxious to get Mia's take on the subject, but it wasn't even 6:00 a.m. yet. Even though I'd left Mary Beth asleep in bed, I didn't need her popping her head into my office and catching me on the phone. Or listening outside the door.

Switching my brain to autopilot, I shaved and showered, then kissed my still-sleeping wife goodbye and headed for the school. I was tempted to pull into a Publix parking lot along the way and call Mia, but it was still too early. I decided I would show some restraint for a change and wait until the bell rang for first period. I felt confident I would be able to slip into my office for a few minutes and make the call. As it turned out, a couple of small administrative fires needed to be put out, making it impossible for me to sequester myself and make the call until almost 9:15.

Thankfully, Mia answered on the first ring. I started by once again apologizing for calling her in the middle of the night.

She said, "It's okay. I've resigned myself to never again getting a full night's sleep as long as you're my client." The comment stung a little, but I did detect a note of humor in her tone. I suspected she was used to having clients bug her at all hours and had become philosophical about it. It was probably just one of the hazards of the private investigation business.

She said, "So, did you read the article about Oscar Wells?"

"Yes. I couldn't believe it."

"What was your first thought?"

I didn't hesitate. "That if he was who we think he was, I am now the only person still alive who was in the park that night."

"That was my thought, too."

"So, is that good news or bad news in your opinion?"

"Excellent question. I don't know."

"And another thing . . . I keep thinking his death, in the context of everything that has been going on, is just too much of a coincidence to be a random crime."

"I've been thinking that too. The official police line is that the motive was robbery. But if that's true, then why shoot the guy? He was probably severely alcohol impaired—most people coming out of bars at that hour are—which means waving a gun in his face probably would have been enough to get him to give up his wallet. I can't see any reason for the perp to risk getting charged with murder merely for the contents of a drunk's wallet. And there's another thing that bothers me . . . the timing. Yes, he was attacked late at night, which obviously meant fewer potential witnesses, but if you're looking for money, why rob a guy coming out of a bar in the wee hours? Wouldn't his wallet be lighter *then* than any other time?"

"Criminals are not the sharpest tools in the drawer, or they wouldn't be criminals."

"True, but still, there are things that make me think there's more to Mr. Wells' death than meets the eye."

"So what do we do?"

"I've been thinking. It seems to me we're going to have to speak with Oscar's sister if we're ever going to get to the bottom of what's going on."

"Angela? Why?"

"Because we know she's been involved in what's been happening to you. She showed up at your media interview, impersonating a reporter, which was obviously a scare tactic. And you saw her driving in your neighborhood, which I'm sure makes you a little nervous. It certainly would me. I just think she's the only person who can help us fit all the pieces of this puzzle together. The one thing we need, the one thing that would help us more than anything else, is to know who hired her and her brother to mess with you, assuming her brother was Machete. And then also, we need to know what their ultimate plan is for you, what their endgame is. Does the guy pulling the strings just want to ruin you, or does he want you dead? Maybe now, with her brother dead, sis is no longer interested in following through on the plan. Or maybe she is now more than ever. We know she has a criminal record. Maybe this kind of thing is what she does . . . how she makes her money."

"It has to be Brian Connelly pulling the strings from prison."

"Does it?"

"Who else would it be?"

"I have no clue. But Jason, I've been in this business long enough to know every investigation produces some surprises. I also know that when you do an investigation, you keep an open mind. The worst thing you can do is jump to a conclusion and then go searching for evidence to back you up. You always—*always*—let the facts take you where *they* want to take you, not where you *want* them to take you."

"But why would Angela Wells talk to us?"

"Maybe she won't. But then again, if we tell her what we think we know, and if we're right, it may scare her. She may feel like she has more to gain by helping us than by continuing to do the bidding of her puppet master. And even if she doesn't help us, if she knows we're onto her, she might decide it's in her interest to leave you alone going forward."

"Why would she do that?"

"Think about it. If our theories are right . . . if she knows we've got it all figured out, she would expect us to come up with a plan and set a trap for her. She's already been in trouble a couple of times. She has to believe the next time she messes up, she'll do time."

"And if she answers our questions, and if we're right about everything, then what?"

Mia's voice softened. "Jason, that's your call."

I rubbed my eyes, pressing my thumbs and forefingers into the sockets, feeling the beginnings of a headache coming on strong. "Mia, If I go to the police, I'm exposed and I lose everything I've been trying so hard to protect."

"Maybe not."

"What do you mean?"

"I mean instead of actually going to the police, you could write down everything you know and mail it to them anonymously in a plain brown envelope."

"Would they take something like that seriously?"

"You bet they would. Every year, hundreds of cases are solved using information that's anonymously delivered to the police."

"Really?"

"Yes. Trust me on this. The police get letters with information and packages of evidence delivered to them all the time. And they *love* it. They love anything that helps them crack a case that has them stumped. And why wouldn't they? It saves them a ton of work, and they still get all the glory."

I thought about this for a moment. "But wouldn't it all still lead back to me eventually? I mean, it all started in the park, and I was there."

"But if we're thinking correctly, all three of the eyewitnesses who could testify that it was you who was there with Faith are dead, and you have a fairly solid alibi in the email you sent from your office. Plus, the authorities don't have any evidence to prove you were at the scene of the murder, or trust me, you would be in custody right now. And you told me there was no cybertrail or phone record that incriminated you. What else would there be that could lead them to you?"

"But Brian Connelly obviously knows I was having an affair with his wife."

"Does he? Jason, he can be thoroughly convinced you were fooling around with his wife, but if he can't prove it, he's got nothing. If he makes the accusation and there's no evidence to support it, he comes off looking like a deranged, jealous husband. You were his wife's boss. He wouldn't be the first jealous husband to manufacture a scenario in his head that wasn't true. And the jealous husband persona will be enhanced by his orange jumpsuit and criminal record."

"And would we incriminate Angela? I mean, if she helped us?"

Mia thought for a moment. "The police are going to be sniffing around her anyway. They've probably already talked to her just because of Oscar's murder. Maybe we can use that to our advantage."

"How do you mean?"

"We offer her a deal. If she tells us everything she knows about her brother and who he was working for, we agree not to implicate her. I think that's a deal she'll take because she's already been in trouble twice. She does *not* want to get in trouble again, I'm sure."

Maybe I was so desperate to think things could actually work out I was willing to believe anything, but listening to Mia gave me a smidgeon of hope.

"So you want to talk to her," I said.

"Yes, and I'd say the sooner the better."

"How do you propose to get to her?"

"I have an idea."

- 58 -

The next day, right before lunch, I called Alice into my office and told her I needed to go out for a while. She gave me a suspicious look and said, "Another doctor's appointment?"

I nodded. "Yes."

She sighed and said, "Okay. I'm a woman of my word. I'll run interference for you until you get back."

"Thank you."

Five minutes later I was on my way to Mia's office. Again, I parked in front of the record store and walked. She let me in and led me to the back room where Dr. Watson was stretched out on the floor in his usual spot. I also found Mayford Wing, Mia's blinking techno-genius, sitting in a straight-back chair, both feet on the floor, with his hands folded in his lap.

After exchanging our greetings, we got right down to business.

Mia dropped into her chair and swiveled to face us. Looking at me, she said, "Mayford has hacked into Angela's computer. Fortunately, she's one of those people who keeps her calendar up to date so we know, at least to some extent, where she's going to be over the next few days." When Mia saw me staring at Mayford, she stopped and said, "What is it?"

"You hacked into her computer?"

Mayford blinked. "Is that a problem?"

"Isn't it against the law?"

He grinned, then blinked twice. "I won't tell on you if you won't tell on me."

Mia jumped in: "Jason, people have died. You could be next if we don't find out who's responsible. Not to mention the fact that we're trying to give you back your life and save your marriage. Surely, if we keep those noble goals in mind, we can do what needs to be done without fretting over what are, in the grand scheme of things, minor crimes."

I didn't like her tone. I said, "I didn't know there *were* minor crimes."

Mia sighed and said, "Jason, if Mary Beth was critically injured at your home, would you make sure you drove the speed limit all the way to the hospital, or would you slam the pedal to the metal and get her there as fast as you possibly could?"

I got her point. Shaking my head, I said, "Look, I'm sorry. I guess I wasn't prepared to hear about *any* laws being broken, major or minor."

Mayford spoke up, looking right at me. "If it makes you feel any better, I've broken a lot of laws, but I've never hurt anyone who wasn't a criminal. And I've helped put several criminals behind bars. I've never broken a law for personal gain, unless you would call trying to impress Mia 'personal gain.'" He looked at her and grinned. She looked at the floor and shook her head, but she was smiling. Then, looking back to me, he added, "If you don't feel comfortable with what I do, I can leave and you can carry on without me."

"No, no . . . it's fine. Let's just get on with it."

Mia took a breath and picked up where she left off. "As I was saying, we know Angela's calendar and we've read her recent emails. It appears she is back to being a working girl, which . . . "

"You mean a prostitute?"

"Exactly, though 'call girl' would be the more descriptive term. She appears to work only by appointment at the high-priced resorts and hotels. Instead of walking the streets or hanging out in bars, she is booked through an agency days in advance. Corporate types are always coming into town for conventions, and they want to have their evening entertainment all set up ahead of time. That gives us a great opportunity and lots of leverage. The problem is, when her brother died, she canceled her appointments for the next four days."

I was struggling to follow Mia's train of thought. I said, "Wait a minute. How does her being a call girl give us a great opportunity?"

Mayford said, "Simple" and laid out a plan he and Mia had obviously put together before I arrived. It was at the same time brilliant and frightening. It was like nothing I'd ever been a part of before.

When he finished, I shook my head as if trying to clear out some cobwebs. "You guys are gutsy. And ruthless."

Mia smiled. "Just be glad we're on your side."

Mayford piped up again: "I'm not on your side. I'm on Mia's side and *she's* on your side."

He was indeed a strange little man. I said to Mia, "I had no idea when I hired you that I was getting the freaking CIA."

She cackled. "Oh, I love that! Can I use it in my advertising?"

- 59 -

We talked about other options, such as simply going to Angela's house and confronting her there, but we knew she could simply slam the door in our faces and that would be that. Or she could not open the door at all. Plus, we all agreed the emotional jolt she would get with the plan Mayford laid out would be immensely helpful to our cause. It would leave no doubt in her mind that she needed to take us seriously, even fear us. When she put it all together and realized we were able to do what we did because we had hacked her computer—which Mayford assured us she would never be able to prove—I suspected she would see the wisdom of cooperating with us.

We picked the coming Friday night, which was only two days away, because it was the next night she had an appointment scheduled. Interestingly, her brother's funeral was scheduled for that afternoon, making it abundantly clear she didn't intend to let her grief dam up her income stream. She had appointments scheduled every day of the weekend, all in the same hotel. Mayford checked and confirmed that there was a convention of auto dealers in town.

My number one priority was to come up with a good reason to be out of the house that evening. It wasn't too difficult because Angela's appointment was at nine. It would have been much harder had it been at ten or eleven. I simply told Mary Beth I was going to a movie, which was a common enough thing for me to do. Early on we learned our taste in movies was as different as up is from down. I like thrillers and she likes three-hanky tearjerkers. Not only does she not mind if I go to the movies by myself, she prefers it. And I do too. When I mentioned I might go see the new Bond flick that had just come out, she didn't even bat an eye.

I didn't go to Oscar Wells' funeral for obvious reasons, but Mia did. She told me later that only thirteen people showed up. I wondered if it was because the bulk of his friends were either dead or incarcerated. Or perhaps he just wasn't a nice person, and few people cared about him. Mia said the pastor tried his best to put a positive spin on Oscar's life without coming right out and calling him a good person, which everyone knew he wasn't.

When she told me this, I couldn't help thinking about myself and what some pastor would someday say about me. If everything fell just right over the next few days, maybe my life wouldn't become a pile of wreckage he would have to tiptoe around at my funeral. On the other hand, though almost no one knew it, my life was already a pile of wreckage. By my count, I had broken seven of the Ten Commandments since hiring Faith. What was even more discouraging was that since I had decided to get my life together, I'd gotten caught up in a whirlwind of deceit. It seemed like the more I wanted to repent of my sins and do the right thing, the more I had to lie to protect Mary Beth.

Or maybe I was nothing but a coward trying to protect myself.

I really didn't know anymore.

What I did know was that I was sick of it all and ready for it to be over, for better or worse. If God chose to feed me into the great wood chipper that is his discipline, so be it. I knew I deserved nothing less. On the other hand, if by some miracle of grace, he decided to shepherd me through this nightmare without exposing my sins to the world, I would be eternally grateful and would never make the same mistakes again. The one thing I knew for certain was that I would be the most devoted husband in the world for the rest of my life.

If I got the chance.

Finally, Friday came. All day at school, I was a nervous wreck. I felt like it was the day things would finally start moving toward a conclusion. Mia, Mayford, and I were going to meet at Mia's office at 7:00 p.m. and head over to the Hyatt.

I played out several scenarios in my mind, all of them interesting, all of them plausible, most of them positive because I am, at heart, a positive guy. They were based on all the information we had gathered about all the players on the game board and what we knew of their weaknesses and their current movements. They were based on the brilliant but crazy plan we had all agreed on. If only we had known then what we came to know very quickly . . . that we were wrong about one aspect of the mystery we thought we had figured out. Completely, spectacularly, catastrophically wrong.

- 60 -

The ride from Mia's office to the Hyatt was spent going over assignments. Mine, basically, was to stay out of their way and let them handle things, which was fine with me. Mayford suggested I stay home and wait for them to call me and tell me how it went. I suspected the main reason he wanted me to do this was so he could be alone with Mia all evening. I was glad when Mia vetoed the idea. She said, "Jason's paying the bill. He has every right to be here if he wants." I could tell Mayford was disappointed. The guy really was smitten.

International Drive in Orlando is always busy, but on a Friday night, it's nuts. As I sat in the passenger seat of Mia's car watching the traffic, both foot and vehicular, I envied the people who were simply out enjoying an evening on the town with nothing more important to worry about than where they wanted to eat or what movie they wanted to watch. In the distance, I could see the Orlando Eye, turning ever so slowly, giving its wide-eyed passengers a spectacular view of the city. I made up my mind that, sometime soon, if I could manage to survive the mess I was in, I would bring Mary Beth here and join the happy throngs and laugh the night away. We would cuddle like teenagers while sharing an ice cream sundae, and we'd walk among the cheesy tourist attractions arm in arm. We would . . .

"You okay, Jason?"

I snapped back to reality. "Yeah, why?"

"You looked a little out there."

"I was thinking."

"About something good, I hope."

"Yes. Very good."

"Then I'm sorry I interrupted you. I saw a glazed look in your eyes and thought you might be about to panic and jump out of the car."

I looked at Mia and forced a smile. "Are you kidding? I wouldn't miss this for the world."

A few minutes later, we trooped into the Hyatt separately, Mayford and I looking like beleaguered tourists. I was wearing a polo shirt and shorts and carrying a backpack. Mayford, who was carrying his laptop in a shoulder bag, had on the most hideous tropical shirt I'd ever seen, one with hula dancers and martinis strewn across it in clashing colors. He also wore dark socks with a pair of sandals that were secured with heavy Velcro straps. Mia, because her role was very different from ours, disdained the touristy look and went for casual elegance instead. She wore slacks and sandals with a bright red tank top and a white shoulder bag. She looked stunning.

Our destination was room 429. We knew it thanks to Mayford's hacking skills. He'd accessed Angela's calendar and the hotel computers. Then, I think because he wanted to show off for Mia, he hacked the escort service Angela worked for. It wouldn't take much to convince me the man could hack the government and walk away with the nuclear codes.

I rode to the fifth floor, then exited the elevator and took the stairs back down to the fourth. Mia and Mayford rode on up on separate elevators. Each got off on a different floor and then took the stairs down to join me on four. All of this was for the benefit of the security cameras on the elevator. We didn't want to appear to be together.

We gathered in the stairwell, talked through the plan one more time, and then checked the hallway to make sure it was clear. We figured it would be because of the hour. You don't come to Orlando to sit in your hotel room. Most people are out running around having fun on I-Drive in the evening. The only ones who aren't are either ill or, in the case of our target, waiting for a guest to arrive.

We knew room 429 was rented to Ronald Torbin, a Ford dealer from a small town in Oklahoma. Mayford had spent five minutes on Facebook and learned that Mr. Torbin had a wife and two middle-school-aged children, Sam and Leah. He was also a Little League coach and served on the school board, which served our purposes perfectly. That Mr. Torbin liked to hire prostitutes when he was away from home was nowhere mentioned on his Facebook page.

The three of us made our way down the deserted hallway to room 429. Mayford and I stayed out of sight on each side of the door while Mia stood right in front of the peephole to give Loverboy a good look. She looked at Mayford and then at me and smiled. Then she took a deep breath and knocked.

- 61 -

We heard a television blaring inside, but it went quiet after Mia's knock. About ten seconds later, we heard the door locks being undone. The door swung open, and Ronald Torbin, seller of Fords and buyer of prostitutes, said, "Are you Krissy?" That he didn't use Angela's real name caused no alarm. No one in that line of work uses their real name.

Mia said, "Are you Mr. Torbin?"

"Yes, but you're early." She hadn't actually said she was Krissy; he just wanted her to be so badly he embraced the notion like a mother cuddles her newborn baby.

Mia practically purred: "I know, but I couldn't wait."

I couldn't see Torbin's face from my vantage point, but I imagined him giving Mia the once over and deciding, early or not, there was no way he was turning this gorgeous woman away from his door.

The door swung open, and Ronald Torbin stepped back. "Please, do come in."

This was the key moment. Mayford and I waited until Mia was well into the room—too far in to be pushed back out—then we barged our way in behind her. Mayford went first, and I followed, slamming the door behind me. In about two seconds, the three of us were standing face to face with Mr. Torbin in the cramped space just inside the room. I feel we were lucky he was small (I was at least four or five inches taller) and clearly out of shape. If he'd been a bruiser, he might've started throwing haymakers. As it happened, Mia instantly produced an open wallet with a badge clipped to it and started waving it in his face, calling his bluff with some nonsense about an undercover vice operation being conducted in the hotel. To this day, I don't know what that badge was. I assume it was fake. I never asked. I didn't want to know. What I do know is that the cheerful, giggly Mia was talking tough, barking orders like an army sergeant, and had our would-be Romeo backpedaling toward the bed with a look of sheer terror on his face. He plopped down on the mattress, his eyes darting among the three of us. He was visibly shaking, his eyes wide and finally locking on Mia's because it was clear she was in charge.

Suddenly, she broke character and smiled. She said, "Now that we have your attention, Mr. Torbin, you can relax. We mean you no harm. We do have a little proposition for you, however. If you accept it and do your part, my little friend here won't feel the need to let your wife, Dorothy, know what you had planned for entertainment this evening. He has Krissy's calendar right there on his little laptop, the very one that has a visit to this very room scheduled for, oh, just about forty-five minutes from now. He also has access to the hotel's phone records, which show two calls from this room to a local escort agency Krissy works for. Do I need to go on, or would you like me to cut to the chase and tell you our proposition?"

I had no clue if Mayford actually had all the things Mia claimed. I knew he could get them if he didn't, but I wondered if he had even bothered. Just the mention of Torbin's wife by name was enough to strike terror in the man's heart. I could tell because he looked frightened enough to wet himself. Thankfully, he didn't. Instead, he said in a shaky voice, "Yes, please tell me."

- 62 -

Mia was the picture of confidence. The way she commanded the moment made me wonder if she had done this kind of thing before . . . perhaps many times. She began to stroll back and forth in front of Ronald Torbin as she spoke with all the authority of a tenured college professor.

"Here's the thing, Mr. Torbin . . . we don't care about you. Not even a little bit. If you want to be an idiot and risk wrecking your family and losing the respect of your kids, that's your business. But we do have an interest in the woman you've made an appointment with this evening. You see, she has some information we need. Truth be told, she's been involved in some illegal activities in addition to prostitution. But even that's not our interest. We just want one piece of information she has. Are you following me so far?"

A quivering Ronald Torbin nodded that he was and said, "And you want me to try to get the information?"

Mia threw her head back and laughed. "Oh no, Mr. Torbin. We would never leave such an important assignment to the likes of you. Look at you. You're trembling like a child that's scared of the dark. All we want you to do is leave this room for two hours. Go do anything you want. Have dinner, catch a movie, take a ride on the Eye. We don't care what you do as long as you stay away from here until we have our little talk with Miss Krissy."

"Are you . . . going to kill her? I'll get blamed for it if you do." He clearly didn't believe we were cops.

"Wouldn't that be too bad? But no, we're not going to kill her. We just want to talk to her."

"How do I know that for sure?"

"You don't. But I'll tell you what you *can* know for sure. You can know we have your street address, your email addresses, your wife's cellphone number, and the address of her workplace, which means we can text, email, or snail mail her all the information pertaining to your indulgence in the adult entertainment industry."

Mia looked at Mayford and nodded. He, in turn, started quoting the Torbin family's addresses and numbers from memory, which caused our boy Ronald to turn green.

"Please don't do that," he said. "I'm begging you. I'll do anything you want."

Mia softened her voice, transitioning from bad cop to good cop. "I told you. We couldn't care less about you. We have no interest in wrecking your life. You seem to be doing a good job of that on your own. Unless you insist on making our job here tonight more difficult. Then we might have to reconsider. Mr. Torbin, we only want one piece of information from your Krissy, and then we're gone. You'll never see or hear from us again."

From somewhere deep inside the terrified man the tiniest smidgeon of indignation must have stirred. It apparently occurred to him that he was cowering and needed to man up a little bit. Maybe at some point during his childhood he'd been picked on and swore never to be that person again because, suddenly, he squared up his shoulders and said, "What if I call the police?"

Mia laughed again. It was the laugh of a heavyweight champion being taunted by a kindergartener. "Mr. Torbin, if you would like to call the police, go right ahead. But before you do, keep in mind that we have not committed a crime here tonight, unless you count my friends barging into your room. But then, you would have a pretty hard time proving that, wouldn't you? You, on the other hand, have hired a prostitute, which can be proven through phone and computer records, *and* which is illegal in this state. And, most importantly, all we have to do is tell Krissy you helped us set her up, and I suspect she and her boss will not be very happy with you. Not very happy at all."

"Okay, okay. I won't call the cops."

"Well alrighty then. Sounds like we have ourselves a deal." Mia turned and looked at Mayford and me. "Gentlemen, are you satisfied that we can trust Mr. Torbin?"

We said we were, so Mia turned back to Torbin and invited him to leave, reminding him that he needed to stay away for at least two hours. "We promise not to go through your things or mess up your room while you're gone. My friends and I are fastidious when it comes to cleanliness." I could tell Mia was really enjoying this part of the operation.

We watched as Torbin put on his shoes and grabbed his keys off the dresser. I doubt his hands would have shaken more if his shoes had been wired with explosives. I knew he didn't trust us, but he clearly understood that playing along was the only chance he stood of keeping his marriage and reputation intact. I found myself feeling a little sorry for him because I knew what it felt like to teeter on such a precipice.

He shot us a hard glance but left without a word. After the door closed, Mia looked at Mayford and me and grinned. "I think that went well, don't you? Now all we have to do is wait." Then she flopped down on the bed and said, "Jason, toss me the remote."

- 63 -

Angela Wells, otherwise known as "Krissy," was right on time. Mayford had been designated to answer the door and impersonate Ronald Torbin just long enough to get her into the room. Mia and I were hiding in the bathroom with the door cracked slightly so we could hear. After hearing the locks being undone, we heard Mayford say, "Are you Krissy?"

I could only imagine what she must have thought when she saw such an unattractive man standing before her. Surely, this is something every call girl has nightmares about. To her credit, however, she didn't run down the hall screaming in horror. She actually purred the way she might've if a Hollywood leading man had answered the door, which I guess is a testament to her professionalism. "Why, yes, I am. Are you Ronald?"

"You can call me Ron," Mayford said as he ushered her into the room and closed the door.

Mia and I waited until Angela moved away from the door into the center of the room. Then we opened the bathroom door and stepped out with Mia going first. She said, "Hello, Angela."

Startled by the presence of someone else in the room, Angela flinched and cursed.

And then she saw me.

Her eyes popped wide open as she frantically tried to process what was happening. I doubt any supercomputer in the world worked faster than the one between her ears. Whatever observations and calculations it spat out apparently amounted to the simple fact that she was in trouble and needed to vacate the premises, which compelled her to start for the door.

Mayford, playing his part to perfection, stepped sideways and blocked her path, smiling and blinking like he was trying to send a message in Morse code with his eyes. I could tell he was enjoying himself when he said, "Don't rush off, Ms. Wells. The fun hasn't even started yet."

She whipped her head again toward me but said nothing. I knew she was assessing the situation, trying to decide if she was in physical danger or if we just wanted to talk. And if we wanted to talk, how much of the truth—or how little of it—she should share.

Mia had told me it would be my show from this point forward. She and Mayford would get me face to face with Angela—which they had done—and then it was up to me to ask her whatever I wanted. When I spoke, I said the words I had been rehearsing in my mind, a throwback to the day she crashed my media interview at the school. "Angela, we're going to do another interview, only this time *I'm* going to be the one asking the questions. You want to have a seat?" I gestured toward an upholstered chair in the corner of the room.

She said, "Where's the man I was supposed to meet? Or was this whole thing a set-up?"

"You mean Mr. Torbin?" I said. "Oh, he's very real. We encouraged him to go and enjoy a long dinner or see a movie so we could have a little chat with you. He was reluctant at first, but it's amazing how quickly he came around to seeing things our way." I nodded at Mayford. "All it took was my friend's threat to send his wife back in Oklahoma the records pertaining to your visit to his room this evening."

Angela looked at Mayford.

Mayford blinked and grinned. "Husbands lie, but phone records and computer searches don't."

"Is that how you knew where I would be? From hacking into my stuff?"

Mayford, grinning even bigger and blinking even faster, said, "Hacking is such an ugly word, Ms. Wells. Not to mention that it's illegal."

"But you did it. You hacked me."

He bowed slightly. "Your confidence in my abilities is truly flattering."

Angela seemed to deflate slightly, resigning herself to the fact that we were way ahead of her, that she wasn't going to be able to just walk out of the room and leave. As an alternative, I expected her to simply refuse to answer my questions, putting the pressure on us to up the ante. She had to know we weren't going to waterboard her in the bathroom or pull out her fingernails. She didn't know Mia and Mayford, but she knew I was just a school principal. She probably figured I didn't have it in me to hurt her.

But instead of clamming up, she shrugged, walked over to the chair, and sat down. Giving me a tired look, she said, "What do you want to know?"

- 64 -

I sat on the edge of the bed, elbows on my knees, hands clasped together, not unlike a posture I might have used to pray. I softened my expression and said, "Angela, what do you know about Faith Connelly's murder?"

She smirked. "You mean the woman you were sleeping with?"

The question stung, but I deserved it. "Yes, that's who I mean. Was your brother, Oscar, one of the guys who approached us in the park that night?"

The mention of her brother took a little steam out of her. I knew she'd attended his funeral that very afternoon, but this was no time to get sentimental. I knew the opportunity I had to talk with her right then might be the only one I would ever get. I had to get to the truth.

"Was he?" I asked again.

"He didn't kill her."

"But he was there."

"He was doing a job. They were just supposed to scare you."

"So you're confirming that somebody hired them?"

"Yeah."

"Who?"

"I have no idea."

Anger flared in me. "Come on, Angela. You were a part of it. You came to the school the next day and impersonated a reporter. You even hinted at our affair with your question."

"That was a different deal."

"What do you mean?"

"I mean that was just Oscar doing his own thing. He figured a married school principal who'd been cheating with a woman who'd been murdered would be ripe for a little extortion. He talked me into showing up at your media interview and jerking your chain a little bit to ratchet up your panic so you'd be willing to pay more."

"Did he put the tracker on my car and leave the note on my windshield?"

She looked surprised. "What? No, he didn't do that."

"Tell me the truth, Angela."

"I am! Why would he need to do that? He knew where you live and where you work. Why would he need to put a tracker on your car?"

It was a good question, one that worried me. I decided to go a different direction.

"Did Oscar kill Damien Robillard in the park that night?"

Angela looked at the floor.

"He did, didn't he? Was it because Damien was panicking? He was the one who swung the crowbar and killed Faith, and Oscar was afraid he would freak out and give them both away? Is that right?"

Angela thought for a moment. "I guess it doesn't matter now that Oscar's dead. Yeah, he killed him. Damien was unstable. Oscar said he killed the woman by accident and then started losing it and was going to end up getting them both arrested. My brother did not want to go back to prison."

I scoffed. "So he committed murder? That's how he planned to stay out of prison?"

Angela's voice became heated. "What other choice did he have? He said Damien was talking about going to the police that very night. He was totally freaked out by what had happened. He said they would catch him anyway and he might have a better chance if he confessed and said it was an accident."

"So your brother had to commit murder to keep his secret, but what about extorting me? Did he have to do that too? If he was so interested in keeping his nose clean, why pile one felony on top of the other?"

"I didn't say he was interested in keeping his nose clean. I said he didn't want to go back to prison. He thought extorting you was perfectly safe. What were you going to do? You have a wife and a career. He knew you would pay the money before you would jeopardize those things."

I wondered if Oscar's assessment of me was true, but I couldn't think about it then.

"And you were helping him," I said.

"All I did was impersonate a reporter and drop a hint about the affair. He thought that would scare you and make you more willing to pay."

"You also drove past my house."

The surprised look on her face left no doubt she had. It also told me she hadn't noticed it was me who drove past her that day when I went home to change my shoes. She also didn't know I wasn't totally sure it was her in the BMW, that I was just throwing the accusation at her to see what kind of reaction I'd get. Otherwise, I'm sure she would have bluffed her way through, denying everything. Instead, she suddenly adopted an air of nonchalance.

"Yeah, I forgot about that."

"Why? What were you doing in my neighborhood?"

"That was just me. Oscar had nothing to do with it."

"But why?"

She sighed. "Because I was curious, all right? The night after the incident in the park, he told me he heard you guys talking, that you were there to break up with the woman you were having the affair with, that you were going to recommit to your wife."

"Why did that make you curious?"

"Maybe 'curious' isn't the right word. Let's just say I was having second thoughts about helping him with what he was doing. I had the feeling you were probably a good guy who was trying to do the right thing. One day I drove past your house to see what kind of place you have. I can't really explain it."

I didn't believe her. Other things she was saying made sense, but this didn't ring true. This woman who had a criminal record, who was currently working in an illegal profession backed by organized crime, who was an accessory to extortion, and who was a proficient enough liar to pass herself off as a television reporter was suddenly trying to portray herself as a hooker with a heart of gold who drove past my house for sentimental reasons? I wasn't buying it. But I knew I wouldn't get anything else from her on that subject, so I pressed on:

"Back to my car. I need to know the truth. Did he put a tracker on my car and leave me a note on the windshield?"

"No, I'm sure he didn't. He would have told me if he did. And besides, like I said, he had no need to put a tracker on your car. He knew where you worked and where you lived."

I took a deep breath and rubbed my face with my hands. This conversation was confirming much of what I suspected, but it wasn't answering the one question that mattered most. I leaned forward and spoke as earnestly as I knew how: "Angela, the one thing I really need to know is who hired your brother and Damien Robillard to come to the park that night and scare us. Was it Brian Connelly, the husband of the woman I was seeing? I know he knew Oscar in prison."

"I don't know who it was, but I'm sure it wasn't him."

"Why?"

"Because once my brother got out of that place, he never went back. He never wanted anything more to do with it or the people in there. And besides, he told me that whoever hired him to scare you talked to him face to face and gave him cash."

"How much cash?"

"A couple thousand, he said."

"And you're sure you don't know who it was?"

"I'm sure."

I felt completely frustrated. I had almost the whole story except the identity of the person behind it all. Whoever it was bore a great deal of the responsibility for two deaths, and possibly three, because I was starting to feel more than ever that Oscar Wells' shooting in a deserted parking lot outside a bar was no random crime. If what Angela was saying was true, and I felt in my gut most of it was because it was the only way all the pieces fit, Oscar had been the only person who could identify the mastermind of the whole sordid mess, which meant Oscar needed to die in order to protect the person's identity.

I stood up and walked around in a circle, thinking. I ran my hands through my hair, resisting the temptation to pull it out. I looked at Mia, who was watching me but holding her tongue. Finally, I sat back down, leaned forward, and spoke to Angela: "Has it occurred to you that your brother's death was no random crime . . . that he was taken out by the guy who hired him because he knew too much?"

Angela said, "Yes, that has occurred to me."

"Doesn't it make you angry?"

"Of course it does."

"Then help me find him."

She stared at me for a long moment. It seemed like she was

weighing her response. Then she said something I didn't expect: "How do you know it's a *him*?"

I looked at her. "What's that supposed to mean?"

She stared at me some more.

I said, "What are you thinking?"

She kept staring, waiting for the synapses in my brain to fire.

And then they did.

She saw it in my eyes, a dawning of truth as bright as the rising sun on a crystal-clear morning. She smirked and said, "I can't believe it took you so long."

From behind me, Mia said, "What? What am I missing?"

Angela looked at her and said, "Who has a bigger interest in seeing an affair broken up than the mistreated spouse? Mr. Vincent here has spent this whole time assuming the mastermind behind this whole thing was the *other* mistreated spouse, when it clearly has to be his own."

- 65 -

They say the spouse is always the last to know.

In truth, the spouse is often the first to know.

The proverbial lipstick on the collar gets a lot of play in the movies, but often it's something much less obvious that gives the guilty party away. Like the need to work late more frequently, a sudden desire to buy new clothes, the faint whiff of a scent that seems unfamiliar, a waning interest in lovemaking, an unusual charge on the credit card, or a sheen of sweat on the forehead when the paramour's name is mentioned.

Was I guilty of these things? I thought I was so clever, but did Mary Beth see right through me all along? Did she say nothing, thinking I would come to my senses? And then when I didn't, did she decide to teach Faith and me a lesson we would never forget?

i know what you did

I always pictured Mary Beth at home when I was out with Faith, but could it be she followed me on one or more of those occasions? Did she park just out of my sight and follow me into the park? Did she creep through the trees and see us sitting there on the bench, cuddling and saying sweet things to each other? Did she hear what we said?

The thought made me want to throw up.

I said to Angela, "You said you didn't know who hired your brother."

"I don't, but who else could it be? Who else would care enough about you having an affair?"

I couldn't think of anyone.

Abruptly, I said to Angela, "You can go."

Mia said, "Jason, are you sure?"

"I'm sure. Get out of here."

Angela, seeming pleased, wasted no time heading for the door. Mayford, blinking, let her pass. She put her hand on the door handle and looked back as if she might say something, but then thought better of it and left.

When she was gone, Mia said, "What do you think?"

I moved to the chair Angela had been sitting in so I could face Mia and Mayford. I was suddenly bone weary and my head was starting to pound in earnest. "I don't know. It's almost impossible for me to believe Mary Beth could be behind this, but I have to admit it makes some kind of crazy sense."

Mayford said, "One thing you could do is check and see if two thousand dollars are missing."

I shook my head. "Not that simple. She takes care of the money. I don't even know how to log on and look at the balances. Besides, she keeps cash in the house for emergencies."

Mia said, "Two thousand dollars?"

"At least that."

"Do you know where she keeps it?"

"She has a book that's hollow. She keeps it in there."

"So go home and see if the money's gone."

"It wouldn't prove anything."

"No, it wouldn't. But if it was gone, that would be pretty curious, don't you think?"

Mayford piped up: "Do you want me to hack into your accounts and see if she's made any two-thousand-dollar withdrawals?"

"No," I said firmly. "You stay out of our stuff."

After a few moments of silence, Mia said, "You need to talk to her."

I looked at her.

She said, "You need to tell her everything and get to the bottom of this, once and for all. I know your whole purpose was to keep her from finding out what you did, but this has gone so far and become so dangerous I don't think you have any other alternative. At least not one that'll give you any peace. How are you two going to live in the same house with all of this hanging in the air between you? And besides, what if it wasn't her? What if the person behind this thing is still out there holding a grudge against you? Remember, someone put a tracker on your car and left you a note that wasn't exactly friendly, and they did it *after* Faith died. That could put Mary Beth in danger too. She has a right to know."

I said, "It still could've been Mary Beth who planted the tracker and the note. She could've been trying to provoke me into coming clean with her. She might have been afraid I would never tell her what I'd done."

"Why wouldn't she just confront you? Wouldn't that be a whole lot easier?"

Mia was right, of course. Mary Beth being behind this thing was, at the same time, the most logical and the most illogical of possibilities. When Angela first mentioned it, I was sure she was right. Now, listening to Mia, it seemed to make little sense. But *somebody* was behind it, and until I knew who, I had to continue to keep my head together.

With a sigh, I said, "I think it's time for us all to go home. I really appreciate your help."

Mia said, "We were right about so many things. I feel like we're right on the cusp of the truth. I hate to give up now."

"How about if we all go home and sleep on it and see if we have any bright ideas."

Mayford said, "The evening wasn't a total loss."

Mia said, "How do you figure?"

Mayford blinked and said, "I'm pretty sure we saved the marriage of one Ronald Torbin here tonight. I doubt he's going to be in the mood to dial up a hooker again any time soon."

- 66 -

As I was driving home, my cellphone vibrated in my pocket. I fished it out and looked at the screen. It was a text message from a number I didn't have stored in my phone and didn't recognize. It gave an address and said,

Meet me there now.

I used the voice texting feature to text back:

Who is this?

I got a one word reply:

Now.

I had no idea who was on the other end of the text, but I thought I might know of a way to find out. I saw a shopping plaza coming up on my right, so I pulled into its lot and called Mia. When she answered, I said, "Can you give me Mayford's number?"

"Why? What's going on?"

"I just got a text from a number I don't recognize. I want to see if he can figure out who it belongs to."

"What does it say?"

I told her. She said, "Are you going?"

273

"First things first. I want to know who's summoning me."

She gave me Mayford's number and made me promise I wouldn't go to the meeting alone if I decided to go at all. She offered to come as backup and stay hidden. Not knowing the kind of place I was being summoned to, I didn't even know if such a thing would be possible. I told her I wouldn't do anything without talking to her one more time.

Mayford seemed delighted to hear from me. The guy clearly lived for stuff like this. He told me he'd call me back within five minutes. He did, and when he told me who the number belonged to, everything suddenly made sense.

- 67 -

I called Mia back and told her what I knew. While I had been waiting on Mayford to get back to me, she used Google maps to get a feel for the location I was being summoned to. She explained in detail where I was going and calculated the drive time for both of us to get there. She said, "I'll leave immediately. I'm closer than you are, so I should arrive before you do. But I need you to wait five minutes anyway to allow me to get there first. I'll park far enough away that I won't be seen and make my way to the location on foot."

"Mia, I can't ask you to do this."

"You're not. Remember, don't leave for five minutes. It's important that I get there first."

She ended the call and I sat there in the dark, feeling like I was on the verge of a heart attack. Yet again, my mind drifted back to my unborn child. For the first time, I wondered if I would ever get to see him or her. I had tried so hard to set my life right, to become the kind of man people look up to and who sleep guilt free, but almost from the moment I made the decision, things had spiraled out of control. I felt like I was trapped in a house of mirrors, where no matter which way I turned things became more confusing and hopeless.

When five minutes had passed, I punched the address into the GPS app on my phone and started toward the rendezvous.

- 68 -

Orlando is a town that sprang up in the middle of cattle country. Kissimmee, a small city just to the south of Orlando, even has a high school whose mascot is the Kowboy. Yes, spelled with a K. I guess alliteration was more important than spelling to the school's founding fathers. The only two things more plentiful than theme parks, motels, and T-shirt shops in the Kissimmee area are cattle ranches. It was to one of these ranches I was headed.

My GPS took me a few exits down the Florida Turnpike and dumped me off on Highway 192. From there it was about a ten-minute drive to a blacktop road that took off into the middle of nowhere. According to my phone, I was four miles from my destination.

In the darkness, all I could see were fence rows to my right and left and the branches of towering oaks hanging over the road. I may have passed a driveway or two, but more likely, they were access roads for loading and unloading livestock. I saw no other vehicles, which added to the *no-man's-land* feel of the place. It crossed my mind that you could kill someone and dump the body in these parts without it ever being found. I was glad I'd told Mia where I was going.

I reduced my speed as I approached a gravel road that was

perpendicular to the one I was driving on. It was my final turn, the road that would lead me to the address that had been texted to me. I kept looking for Mia's car but didn't see it. Had she hidden it among the trees? Had she been detained? I felt she would've let me know if something had happened to prevent her from coming. I decided there was nothing to do but press on.

About a quarter of a mile down the gravel road, I came to a small ranch house. There was a light on in the window and a vehicle parked in the driveway. I knew who it belonged to.

I pulled to a stop and got out of my car. I looked around, giving Mia a chance to let me know she was somewhere nearby, but I heard nothing except the chirping of cicadas. Where on earth was she? It occurred to me that I should just drive away, but I felt doing so would only delay the inevitable. At least this way I had the answers, and maybe the resolution of this problem, right in front of me. I preferred that to being stalked and dealt with the way Oscar Wells was.

I walked up onto the weather-worn planks of a porch that ran the entire length of the house. It was clearly a place of good times, a place where weary cowhands sat at the end of a long day, swapping stories and drinking beer. But not tonight. I knew there would be no good times tonight.

I took a deep breath and knocked on the door.

I heard footsteps inside, then a latch being undone.

The door swung open, and I found myself standing face to face with Joe Jackson, Faith's father. He was holding a pistol in his right hand, pointing it at my face.

- 69 -

"I thought you might not come," he said, stepping back so I could walk inside.

As I moved past him, he told me to raise my arms and lock my hands behind my head, which I did. He frisked me, found nothing I could use as a weapon, and shoved me in the back to the center of a small living room, where I turned to face him, lowering my hands to my side. Even from eight feet away, the stench of liquor coming off him was strong.

Again, I wondered where Mia was.

Faith's father stared at me with rage in his eyes, his bottom lip quivering. "You killed my daughter."

"No, sir, I didn't."

"Do not try to defend yourself!" he screamed and extended his arm, gun hand trembling.

Never before had I looked down the barrel of a gun. It seemed almost impossible that a projectile as tiny as one would have to be to travel through that barrel could kill a man. Maybe the thought was my mind's attempt to find a diversion, a way to keep from facing the reality of my situation . . . that I likely had minutes, perhaps seconds, to live.

"I knew she was seeing you," Mr. Jackson said. "At first, I thought it was a passing thing that would end quickly. But then weeks went by, then months. I followed her to the park. I saw the two of you acting like a couple of high school kids. I could tell you were drawing her in deeper and deeper, so I hired those guys to scare you off."

He paused, fighting back tears. I could see his gun hand shaking, his finger on the trigger.

"But those idiots! They killed her all right, but it never would have happened if you hadn't seduced her!"

I didn't intend to die without saying my piece.

"Mr. Jackson, I was wrong to have an affair with your daughter. And I'm sorry for everything that happened. But the night she was killed . . . we had met there in the park to end it. You may not believe me, but it's true. I love my wife, sir. And I know Faith wanted to do the right thing too. We lost our heads for a little while, but we were trying to set things right."

"You lie," he growled.

"No, sir. I'm telling you the truth. Yes, your daughter died that night, but we were this close to setting everything right. What happened was a terrible accident."

Faith's father stepped back and to his left, toward a kitchen table and chairs, while still holding the gun on me. He felt for a chair with his left hand, found it, and sat down heavily. He was sweating profusely, and I wondered if he was having a heart attack. The gun was now pointed more or less at my feet, and Mr. Jackson was taking deep breaths.

I said, "Sir, you're not well. Let me get you to a doctor."

"You don't move!" he shouted, but I could tell he was losing ground.

He said in a faltering voice, "You not only killed my daughter, you killed me. She was the joy of my life. And, if that wasn't enough, you took away a little girl's mama. Little Zoey . . . " He seemed to have more to say, but couldn't get it out.

I said, "Sir, please. You need a doctor."

He said, "Can a doctor fix a broken heart? There's only one way to fix what you have done." He raised the gun and aimed at my chest.

At least ten feet separated us. I knew I'd never be able to lunge at him and grab the gun before he pulled the trigger. Figuring I had only seconds to live, I said a silent prayer for forgiveness and asked God to take care of Mary Beth and our baby.

Then Faith's father put the gun in his mouth and pulled the trigger.

- 70 -

Joe Jackson's head snapped back, and his body fell forward. He landed facedown on the floor with a thud. The bullet must have lodged in his brain because it didn't exit the back of his head.

Seconds later, Mia came crashing through the door with her own gun in the ready position. When she saw Mr. Jackson's body, she lowered her weapon. "You all right?" she asked.

I had so much adrenaline splashing through my system I could barely respond. I bent over and placed my hands on my knees, at once trying to catch my breath and keep from vomiting. Finally, I was able to say, "Yes, I'm okay. Where have you been?"

"I got pulled over. Doing sixty-five in a forty-five. The cop took his sweet time."

Still breathing heavily, I started for a nearby armchair, but Mia said, "Don't sit down."

I froze.

She said, "Have you touched anything?"

"No."

"You're sure?"

"I'm sure. I've been standing right here the whole time."

"Good. I only touched the doorknob, which means I can wipe it down, and we can leave and it'll be like we were never here. It'll look like a simple suicide, a distraught father who'd been drinking."

"Mia, I can't do that. I have to report this."

"No, you do not. Jason, you're about to get everything you ever wanted—the chance to go back to Mary Beth and start over and be the husband and father I know you want to be. If you report this suicide—and that's exactly what it was—you're going to get caught up in the investigation, and everything you've been trying to accomplish is going to be gone forever. And for what? Mr. Jackson is not going to get *his* life back because you decide to be noble and ruin *yours*. If you want to make your life count for something, walk out that door with me and go be the man I know you want to be. You've got a baby coming that needs a father."

I stared at Faith's father's body and the pool of blood that had formed around his head. I knew there was a lot of truth in what Mia was saying, but it felt so . . . disrespectful to walk away and leave what had been a good man lying there. I didn't know if I'd ever be able to live with myself. But if I didn't leave, I was pretty sure I would never be able to live with Mary Beth and our baby.

Mia walked over and took my arm. Looking up into my face, she said, "Come on, Jason. Walk with me."

And I did.

- 71 -

When I got home, Mary Beth was curled up in bed, remote in hand, sound asleep. The TV was tuned to some movie with Julia Roberts, something pretty melodramatic judging from the crying and shouting going on. Before undressing for bed, I stepped into my office and dialed Alice's number. It was a little after eleven and I hoped she would still be up. She sounded chipper when she answered, though she'd told me once she always tried to sound wide awake even when she answered the phone out of a dead sleep. I asked her why, and she said she couldn't explain it—it just seemed important.

"You up?" I said.

"I am now. What couldn't wait until morning?"

"I wanted to tell you I won't be in tomorrow."

"You sick?"

"Nope."

"Got a, quote/unquote, 'doctor's appointment?'"

"Something like that. I plan to spend the day with my wife."

"I think you have an appointment scheduled in the morning. Around ten."

"Cancel it. This is more important."

"I like the sound of that. I'll take care of everything."

I brushed my teeth, undressed, and pulled on a T-shirt and a pair of shorts. I sat on the toilet lid, bowed my head, and prayed. I won't recount the prayer here, but it was full of apologies and promises. I didn't ask God for a thing. I didn't feel worthy. Then I crawled into bed, trying not to disturb Mary Beth.

- 72 -

The next day, I told Mary Beth everything.

And I do mean *everything*.

It came in fits and starts because there were times when we had to stop and cry, or in Mary Beth's case, to cry and scream. I was as patient as I could possibly be, waiting for her tirades to end before continuing. I answered every question she asked with full candor. I made no attempt to sugarcoat anything. I knew I deserved whatever she said and whatever she did.

The conversation started around 8:00 a.m. and wound down just before noon. We'd both cried so much we had no tears left. I didn't ask what Mary Beth wanted me to do; I simply told her I would pack a bag and get a hotel room to give her some space. She didn't argue. When I left, she didn't tell me goodbye or even look at me.

From the hotel, I called Mia and told her what I'd done. She said, "You didn't need to do that, Jason. You could have just recommitted yourself to the marriage and started over in your own heart. Everything that happened could have been left between you and God."

"I know, but I needed to come clean."

"Why?"

"Because . . . if Mary Beth ever tells me she loves me again, I won't have to think she only loves me because she doesn't know the real me. This way, if she ever tells me she loves me again, I'll know it's the best kind of love, the kind that knows everything about you and loves you anyway."

Mia was quiet for a moment. "I hope you get that someday, Jason."

"I do too, Mia. More than anything."

EPILOGUE

The ranch house Faith's father summoned me to belonged to his brother, John, who spent a good part of the year in the Midwest. When he was up north, Mr. Jackson took care of the place. He couldn't have chosen a more secluded spot to execute his endgame.

His death was never questioned. It was recorded as a simple suicide, the final tragic act of a man broken and pushed over the edge by alcohol and grief. To this day, I wonder if he'd intended to kill himself when he sent me the text. Or did my assertion that Faith and I were trying to do the right thing on the night she died persuade him to let me live? Maybe he knew his heart was giving out and didn't want his final act before meeting his maker to be the taking of another's life. I still don't know if he killed Oscar Wells in the parking lot of the bar. I want to believe he didn't, that Oscar's poor life choices finally caught up with him. But the anger I saw in Mr. Jackson's eyes makes me think he probably did.

As for Angela Wells, I felt she was no longer a threat to me. I was willing to leave her to her own life choices and whatever outcome they brought her. I had a feeling the dead-end nature of her career choice would eventually outweigh the favor her extraordinary beauty seemed to win her in these days of her youth.

Through it all, Mia became a friend. We didn't hang out because the last thing I needed was to have someone jumping to conclusions about me and an attractive young woman who is not my wife. But we did stay in touch. I liked her a lot and recommended her to a couple of people I thought could use her skill set. She even charged me far less than what I owed for her services, saying, "It's not every day I get to have that much fun. Charging you full price would seem like stealing." She made me promise I would call her the next time I decided to go out and practically get myself killed.

Dr. Watson still won't give me the time of day.

Mayford Wing was the unsung hero in our little adventure, with his knack for getting us information and getting it quickly and invisibly. I never quite got used to his odd appearance and constant blinking, but I did pay him a visit to shake his hand and thank him for all he did. He seemed pleased and said if I needed any more laws broken I should give him a call. He laughed when he said it, but I knew he was serious.

On the day I confessed everything to Mary Beth, I checked into a low-end local motel. It was the kind that leaves the light on for you, only the light in the lamp on the bedside table was burned out, which seemed fitting. On the third day, Mary Beth asked me to come home, but not because she had decided to welcome me back with open arms. She said, "We can't afford to have you staying in a motel every night. You can have the guestroom." I was encouraged that she felt there was still a "we."

Things were awkward around the house. We were respectful to each other, of course. It's never been our style to bicker. But there were no jokes, no romantic moments, no heartfelt conversations, no playful banter. It was as if we were coworkers running a business. We each had our responsibilities and got them done, then retreated to our separate rooms at night. It was hard, but I was determined not to push. I had confessed everything, apologized, and begged for forgiveness. The rest had to come from her.

One day I walked into the house after school, and she met me with a kiss, the likes of which I'd never had before. I had a crick in my neck for a week because of the way she threw her arms around me and pulled my head down so our lips could meet. The strange thing is, nothing was ever said. No explanation was given for the change in her attitude, and to be honest, I was afraid to ask. I simply chose to ride the wave.

That night we made love, and she held my face in her hands and told me she loved me. It had been thirty-nine days since my confession.

Yes, I was counting.

The next day, I got a text from Mia. She asked me how things were going, which was out of character for her. This made me think maybe she had spoken to Mary Beth, perhaps serving as my advocate and helping to turn Mary Beth's heart back toward me.

Instead of texting Mia back, I called and told her Mary Beth and I were good once again, maybe better than ever. Then I asked her if she had anything to do with Mary Beth coming around so suddenly. Mia said, "Jason, I wouldn't call thirty-nine days 'sudden'" and hung up without saying goodbye, which told me she had indeed talked to Mary Beth. Otherwise, she would have just said no.

Mary Beth's pregnancy was smooth, as pregnancies go, and little Alexa Deen Vincent arrived healthy and with an attitude. (Yes, Deen, as in Paula, one of Mary Beth's Food Network heroes.) It took me a few days to feel comfortable picking her up and holding her, but I really got into the dad thing. One day, Mary Beth said, "Do you mind if I hold her for a while? I'm the mother, you know."

I must say though, I was unprepared for the emotions this little eight-pound beauty has provoked in me. When I sit holding Alexa and looking into her eyes . . . when I feel love for her that is so strong it feels like my heart is going to burst . . . I begin in some small way to appreciate the anxiety Faith's father must have felt when he saw his own daughter going down a dark path. I've heard it said by older parents that their kids are always their babies no matter how old they get. I imagine it's true.

And then there's Faith.

I still think about her occasionally, though not in a longing or lustful way. I just feel sad. She was a good person whose life was cut short by a confluence of poor choices made by a number of people, of which I was one. Despite all the good things in my life, it's that knowledge that keeps me from knowing complete joy. I suppose that's as it should be.

ACKNOWLEDGMENTS

Because I have written mostly nonfiction books, people act surprised when I come out with a novel. They wouldn't be surprised at all if they knew how much I love fiction, how lost I can become in a good story, and how at peace I feel with my feet up and a vintage paperback by Clifton Adams or Cornell Woolrich in my hands.

Someone Knows is an idea that came to me gradually over the years as I counseled various people who had had or were having affairs. It struck me that affairs are easy to get into but hard to get out of. And if one little thing goes wrong, an already hairy situation can grow claws and fangs and become a full-blown nightmare.

An early reader of this manuscript questioned whether a good man with a good wife would really cheat the way my protagonist did. Or if he did cheat, could he really be called a good man? The answer to both questions is yes, he would and he could. In the Bible, King David is said to have been the very best of men, a man after God's own heart. Yet he had an affair with a young woman named Bathsheba that produced catastrophic consequences. The lesson of history is that we're all capable of making horrible choices. Jason Vincent is a fictional character, but very, very real.

I am deeply grateful to Acorn Publishing for taking my humble Word document and turning it into a beautiful book. Holly Kammier, Jessica Therrien, and Lacey Impellizeri-Papenhausen are simply magnificent. Their skill, professionalism, and most of all, their kindness, is unsurpassed. I must also thank Leslie Ferguson, whose editorial expertise makes me seem like a better writer than I am.

As always, I am thankful for my wife, Marilyn. Being married to a writer is not always easy. We tend to daydream a lot and spend hours at a time behind a closed door, pounding out words we are seldom satisfied with. But she takes it all in stride and makes our home an oasis.

Finally, to you, my readers: Thank you. I know money is tight. I know there are lots of other things you could have spent your dollars on. That you chose this book humbles me. I will always do my best to make you feel that what you pay for one of my books is money well-spent.

You can reach me at: markatteberry93@gmail.com. You can also visit my website and check out my other books at markatteberry.net.

www.ingramcontent.com/pod-product-compliance
Lightning Source LLC
Chambersburg PA
CBHW021141310726
48971CB00002B/430